the
heart
break
club

eva woods

sphere

SPHERE

First published in Great Britain in 2021 by Sphere

1 3 5 7 9 10 8 6 4 2

A CIP catalogue record for this book is
available from the British Library.

ISBN 978-0-7515-7586-6

Typeset in Baskerville by M Rules
Printed and bound in Great Britain by Clays Ltd, Elcograf S.p.A.

Papers used by Sphere are from well-managed forests
and other responsible sources.

Sphere
An imprint of
Little, Brown Book Group
Carmelite House
50 Victoria Embankment
London EC4Y 0DZ

An Hachette UK Company
www.hachette.co.uk

www.littlebrown.co.uk

Eva Woods grew up in a small Irish village and now lives in London, where she dodges urban foxes and tuts at tourists on escalators. She ran the UK's first writing course for commercial novels and regularly teaches creative writing. Eva also writes thrillers under her real name of Claire McGowan.

the
heart
break
club

PROLOGUE

To begin with, there were two people, and their names were Niamh and Antony. They didn't know each other, and they never would. But the same life-defining moment came for both of them in turn, within the same short space of time.

For Niamh it was a choice, a half-second's distracted decision to step off the pavement without looking right then left then right again, as she'd been taught in the Tufty Club at primary school. She didn't see the car, a red Vauxhall Astra, driven, it was later determined, two miles under the speed limit. The moment for her was very brief – a flash of red, a snippet of radio playing 'Livin' La Vida Loca', of all the songs in the world, a feeling of being lifted up and falling. For a second the world stretched, the blue sky above, the flap of pigeon wings, the blare of a car horn. That was it.

For Antony – Anto – it was a note, written on lined paper torn from the school exercise book of a child he'd never met and didn't know the name of (Davey Magee, aged seven). It was a rainy day, dripping onto leaves and umbrellas and the windows of the red-brick house. It was the thought he'd carried all morning, a sick, almost-excited terror – *if she offers to go to the shops, I will. If not, then no.* It was writing a name, as neatly as he could, knowing now was the time to be clearly understood, scratching the pen on the paper to make it run. *Caroline . . .*

For everyone, the moment that comes is this – you understand you are going to die. Not just know it – really, we all secretly think it won't happen to us – but understand it, finally. You are going to die.

Caroline

People say mad things to you when your husband has died.

'Ah, sure you're young, there's time for you,' was a classic of the genre, currently being trotted out by some friend of Anto's mother, a woman in a grey trouser-suit ensemble who was shoving a devilled egg into her face. Caroline wanted to scream – *I'm thirty-six! I don't have that much time, you stupid bint!* Even if she had a child right now she'd be considered an elderly mother, and the unfortunate death of her husband had put those plans somewhat on the back burner.

Others chose, 'He's with God now.' Was he, since he was an atheist and had once called the Pope a human-rights abuser? Or, 'He's looking down on us.' Was he, or was he just dead, snuffed out? Likely he had no awareness at all that she was here in his mammy's living room, having struggled through a memorial service for him, followed by tea, drinks and finger food. He wasn't looking down on her, or wanting her to go on with her life or eat a devilled egg or have a gin and tonic, as his drunken uncle Martin kept insisting, though it was 2.30 p.m. on a Monday. He hadn't been taken too soon or given up his fight or any such bullshit. He had chosen to go, and leave her here, stuck with his extended family and neighbours and assorted rubberneckers, and she was just so angry with him she wanted to scream.

Caroline was so deeply, raging mad. Mad at Anto. Mad at these people with their stupid comments, mad that she'd had to take the day off work, because Anto's mother had insisted on holding his memorial service on a Monday for some reason to do with the church being double-booked for a Zumba class. She and Anto would have laughed about that, except for him being dead.

She was also mad that today made it seventy-six calendar days since Anto had been lowered into the ground, in the graveyard nearest their home in Belfast (an issue which Caroline was vaguely aware had caused some ructions within his family, who'd wanted him brought back here to their plot). Almost three months. She barely remembered the funeral, since in Ireland you had to have them within two days or the world would apparently come to an end, and two days after it happened she had still been struggling to breathe, and put one foot in front of the other, adjust to a world that was fundamentally different than it had been, because Anto was no longer in it. Let alone pull together a funeral for two hundred people and field endless questions like *would Anto have wanted flowers? Do you not agree Anto would have wanted live music in church, instead of taped like our Patrick seems to think is acceptable? Would Anto have wanted money behind the bar? A sit-down meal?* How the bloody hell would she know? They'd never discussed their 'wishes', seeing as they were in their thirties. And apparently, she'd known nothing about what Anto wanted anyway. At the very least she had assumed he wanted to be here, with her, but it turned out that was not the case.

'Look at the time,' Caroline mumbled, as Anto's sister Julie elbowed her way across the room towards her, no doubt to discuss whether Anto might have left her annoying kids any money in his will. He didn't even have a will because, of course, he was thirty-eight years old. 'I better shoot.'

'Already?' Anto's mother Mary, the matriarch of the family, looked pointedly at the carriage clock over the mantelpiece. 'You've hardly got here, Caroline.' Never mind the fact that she'd driven all the way down there, missing out on a full day's teaching, so would be playing catch-up all week trying to undo the lax habits of the substitute, who last time had let the kids watch a DVD of *Frozen* instead of learning long division, and Caroline had been paying for it ever since.

'I know, I know, but I have my support group tonight. I need to go every time, sure you know how it is.' Being a sensible sort of person, Caroline had of course got all the help she could find for her situation; grief counsellors, grief support groups, self-help books, even a mad woman called Rosa who 'smudged' the house with sage, making the whole place smell of roast dinners. As she downed her tea, she reflected that the group was also useful as a means to escape from unwanted social situations. So far, it had moved around to be basically every night of the week, depending on what event she wanted to get out of. It actually was on a Monday night, however, so she could say goodbye to Mary without a flicker of guilt, and get back on the Westlink before rush hour kicked in.

Mary hesitated, moving in closer so that Caroline could smell her magnolia hand cream. 'Love. Can we have a wee coffee or something this week? After your work tomorrow, maybe?'

She and Mary did not have coffee together. And why so soon after today? Caroline blinked. 'Well, sure we can. How come?'

Mary was lowering her voice, a rare event in itself. 'We just ... have a few things to talk about, that's all. About what happens now.' The headstone, Anto's assets, that kind of thing, Caroline imagined. Her heart sank further. It was cruel enough losing someone, let alone doing the extra work that all the death admin involved. Deathmin. She hated it.

As she got into her car, she finally let herself think about Anto's grave as she had seen it on her last visit. The fresh wound of the broken earth was healing over already, grass and weeds growing on top of it (Mary had lobbied hard for some 'nice gravel', but Caroline knew he would have wanted something natural. Or thought she knew, anyway. Maybe she hadn't known anything about him at all.) The earth had taken Anto back, time was moving on, and he was still gone. Somehow, that was even worse than when it first happened.

Josh

It was hard to choose the worst thing about your wife being dead. There'd been some bad moments, for sure – identifying her body in the morgue, for one. The image was burned into him. A face the colour of candle wax, her curly fair hair not quite covering the red mark on her forehead. It was Niamh's face and yet not, the life gone out of it.

Then there was breaking the news to her mum and dad, who were in their seventies, and took a long time to get to the phone, because it was him the police had called when it happened. He didn't know what was worse – being the first to know, before anyone else did, or being the last, going on living your life for another few hours thinking everything was fine, when it never would be again.

Then there was planning her funeral with bewildering speed, which they insisted on doing in Ireland for some reason, no one sleeping at all for three days, her brother and three sisters arguing over music and food and flowers, his own mum barely able to make it from London in time.

But this – two months after his wife's funeral – was also a bad moment. He had to clear away her things and throw them out, because she wasn't coming back for them, because she was dead. People had offered to do it, of course. Some strange instinct seemed to kick in in Ireland when a tragedy took place, women cosseting men as if they could do nothing for themselves. He had turned down the help of Niamh's oldest sister Siobhan, who was already a grandma, and her middle one Darragh, and nearest-in-age one Clare, and various aunties and her friends from school and work. 'Mammy' was considered too fragile to do such things, after a brush with breast cancer two years before. Niamh's father, a farmer of seventy-three, had so far said nothing to Josh about her death, except to clap his shoulder and mutter, 'Ah son.' Even the *son* was something, and he'd imagined telling Niamh about it, dissecting this new development for signs that her dad's discomfort with a fella who was not only English but black too had eased, but he couldn't do that of course, because she was dead. Maybe that was the worst bit, in fact. Not being able to tell her anything that was going on and hear her laugh against his neck and say, 'Ah Jesus, I dragged you back to the eighteenth century, so I did.'

He sat back on his heels in what had been their bedroom, having barely made a dent in Niamh's wardrobe, stuffed full of dresses, jeans, scarves, hats, you name it. The woman had never thrown anything away – she still had her First Communion outfit in there. The clock on the bedside table said it was almost six, so that meant he needed to stop and get ready for support group, which was some relief, as he could put the task of clearing out her things off for another day. Caroline would never forgive him if he was late to the group.

Anyway, he reflected, getting up and wincing at the pain in his knees, it wasn't as if her clothes were going anywhere. That was the problem.

*

The support group was held in a shabby community centre not far from the Falls Road. Inside, the corridor was lit up with fluorescent bulbs. There were several events and classes going on at the same time – the local am dram group rehearsing *Hairspray*, the historical society looking at slides of an old workhouse, an AA meeting. Josh still remembered how nervous he'd been on his first night, angry that he even had to be in a place where people were singing songs from a musical (really badly) and there was an honesty box to chip in for loo roll, how ridiculous he felt even trying something so stupid as a support group in the face of his overwhelming loss. He'd been standing in the car park having an argument with himself when a woman walked briskly past in a yellow raincoat, and as she opened the shatterproof door of the community centre, a snatch of song had come out, something about Baltimore. 'Are you coming in?' she'd said to him.

No. It's stupid. 'Um . . .'

She seemed to understand. 'I was the same my first time. Grief support, is it?'

Was it that obvious? 'Um . . . yeah.'

She held the door. 'Come on. I'll walk you in.'

He'd wanted to bolt. Instead, he had mumbled a reply and shuffled forward, into the strip lighting of the centre's corridor, the posters for tae kwan do and Irish dancing and yoga flapping in his wake. And here she was again, several months on, that same woman, walking into the wet car park, in the same yellow coat, with the same air of purpose, and he realised he had been hovering there to wait for her, so they could go in together again.

Caroline smiled at him as she approached, face bright under her hood. 'All right?'

'Ha. No.'

'Me either. Once more into the breach though, anyway?'

'Suppose so. Bloody breach, I hate it.'

'I know. But sure what else can we do?'

They went in.

The room was too large for the small circle of plastic chairs in the middle. Stacked around the edges were yoga mats and blocks, the rubbery smell of them making Josh's nose twitch. There were five people in the room, including himself, the only guy tonight. An older woman in a tunic top and aggressive highlights stood self-importantly by a whiteboard: this was Sinead, the 'group facilitator'. The clock had just ticked past seven.

As Josh and Caroline went in, Sinead took a green marker and wrote *under forties grief support group* on the board. She underlined it firmly, three times. 'You're late,' she said to them, frostily. 'Let's get started, now you're *finally* here.'

The group had been billed as grief support for widows/widowers and/or bereaved partners under the age of forty. It sounded cobbled together, as if someone had complained. Despite the fact that no one was new tonight, Sinead liked to start every session with an introduction. 'Hi, I'm Sinead. For anyone who doesn't know me,' (they all did), 'I'm the group facilitator. I'll share my story with you.'

They had heard this story many times. Caroline whispered to Josh out of the side of her mouth. *'My Terry . . . '*

'My Terry, God rest him, died in 1991. He was a police officer with the RUC – so brave!'

'So brave, such a sacrifice! My job now . . . '

' . . . is to support other young widows and widowers. Oh! And of course, partners of any type are welcome here.' This comment was directed at a rain-soaked woman in exercise gear, who hadn't yet looked up from the floor – Cassie, whose wife Lisa had died from ovarian cancer four months earlier, at the age of forty-one.

'We're here to help . . . '

'We're here to help each other through the shocking and unexpected blow of losing your partner young. Now. Whose turn is it to share tonight?'

A while later, they sat there listening as Cassie talked to a fixed point on the floor. 'I gave up my family to be with her,' she said flatly. It was as if she'd spoken these words many times before. 'They're fundies. Religious, like. I'd never told them I was . . . like this, but when I met Lisa, I had to. I wanted to bring her to weddings and birthdays and christenings and that. But they – Mum cried. Dad threw me out of the house, said they'd pray the sin left me. They didn't even come to our wedding. Lisa . . . her parents were good, they tried, but they're old.' She twisted a wedding ring on her cold, white finger. She'd told them she was training for a marathon, and she ran to and from each group meeting from her house all the way across town. Josh wanted to wrap her in a blanket and tell her not to go out in the fierce Belfast night, black sheets of rain whipping off the Lough. To go straight home instead and stay in, watching mindless telly and drinking tea, find comfort where she could.

Sinead's eyes rested on Josh, as Cassie finished her monologue and slumped back into her chair to a smattering of applause. Her grief was like a leaden thing, weighing them all down. *Not me not me not*, begged Josh silently. The gaze moved on. 'Ruma? Do you – please feel free to say something if you like.' Ruma, a headscarfed woman with a gentle smile and sad eyes, had been coming to the group for weeks, but she never said a word, just shrugged and nodded. They didn't even know anything about her bereavement – maybe she wasn't ready to talk. Ruma, once again, didn't say anything, just smiled in slight confusion, so Sinead's beady gaze moved on. 'Caroline?'

Caroline gave an easy smile. 'Ah, sure I think everyone knows my story, Sinead.'

Sinead tutted. '*Yes*, but how are you this week? What's changed?'

'Nothing's changed, he's still dead.' Sinead scowled. Caroline relented. 'We had Cemetery Sunday at his ma's parish today. Not actually on a Sunday, and he's not buried there anyway, which was a bone of some contention if you remember.'

Sinead uncapped her marker with an aggressive pop. 'And did that help you find any healing, Caroline? The power of the ceremony?'

Caroline shrugged. 'Not really. They had some really nice jam tarts though. Marks and Sparks, I think they were.'

Josh stifled a laugh and Sinead pounced on him. 'And what about you, Joshua? What have you done this week to promote your healing journey?'

'Um, well, I made a start on clearing out her—'

'You must say her name! It's important!'

'Right, OK, on ... Niamh's things.'

'Good! That's very good! Did you get far?'

'Um ... not really.' He'd not actually moved a single thing so far. It was all still there, her clothes and shoes and bags and books and toiletries. The clutter of a life well lived.

Sinead sighed. Her thoughts were clear to read – why was she stuck running this group with people who couldn't even *grieve* properly? '*Right.* No Matt this week?'

Matt was another guy who came to the group sometimes, in his late thirties. He had three kids and his wife had unaccountably dropped dead two days after having the youngest, leaving Matt shell-shocked, trying to support a five-year-old, three-year-old and a baby through the loss of their mother. 'Couldn't get childcare,' said Caroline, who kept in touch with everyone via a vast network of WhatsApp messages. 'His mammy fractured her wrist putting the bins out.'

Another sigh. '*Fine*. Well I suppose we better get on to tonight's topic – gravestones and memorials. Any views on headstone engraving, anyone?'

'I think Sinead hates me.' Caroline and Josh fell into step with each other as the small group straggled out into the cold night.

'She hates us all! Mostly because our grief is so fresh and juicy' – Josh wiggled his eyebrows – 'and my Terry . . .'

'*My Terry*,' mimicked Caroline.

'He's been dead for years. And he wasn't killed on the job like she makes it sound, he got run over taking a piss on the motorway while he was hammered. The *Chronicle* reported on it. Sinead's been widowed for years, and here she is sucking up our fresh new grief.'

'Oooh, give me your juicy tears, slurp slurp!' Caroline pretended to lick Josh's cheek, then they quickly straightened their faces as Sinead came out past them, jangling the keys to the room, hands rammed into her gilet.

'Do try *not* to be late next week, you two. It's *very* disrespectful, both to myself and the rest of the group.'

'Sorry, Sinead,' they muttered. Cassie had already left, running off into the night, and Ruma had gone for the bus with her usual silent waves and smiles. Soon, Caroline and Josh were left alone in the car park. Over time, they had developed a ritual for this part of the evening.

'Pub?'

'Pub.'

They moved off down the street. Josh again remembered the first time he'd come to the group, when Caroline had grabbed him afterwards. 'Thank God, an actual normal person. Do you want to go for a drink, because I think I'm going to kill Sinead if I don't vent at someone?'

Josh had been newly widowed then, sunk and stunned by his grief. He hadn't been to the pub, or anywhere in fact, since Niamh's death, had turned down every social invitation that came his way, barely left the house in weeks, but all the same he found himself saying yes to the woman with the blonde bob and raincoat. 'OK.'

'Great. There's one round the corner.'

As they'd walked there, he'd asked, 'So ... how does it work with this group? Is it like prison, and you're not meant to say why you're here?'

Caroline had laughed, and he'd marvelled she was able to do that still. 'You can say. My husband Anto, he died.'

Imagine being able to say it so matter-of-factly. 'I'm sorry.'

Caroline waved a hand. 'You can forget all that sorry stuff, we're in the same boat here. I'll save you wondering if it's rude to ask what happened. He killed himself. *Took his life*, or *ended his life by his own hand* seem to be the PC terms, but feck it, I'm the one who found him – he killed himself.'

'Jesus.' He didn't know what to say. Condolences, platitudes, would clearly not be right here. 'Well. My wife—'

'Niamh – you must say her name!' said Caroline, mimicking Sinead's sharp tones.

'Sorry, yes, *Niamh*.' He was copying Caroline's droll style, but he winced on the long syllable of the name all the same. 'She was hit by a car crossing the road – nice old fella out to buy the *Irish News* and boom, she runs into the road and he hits her.'

'I'm so . . . ' Caroline stopped herself. 'I'm doing it now and all. That's awful, Josh.'

'Ah well.' He shrugged. 'What can you do? A very useful Irish phrase, that. I've learned a lot of those since I got here. *Ah now*, as well.'

'That's a grand one,' said Caroline. 'You can say it at least six different ways with different meanings. Good for getting rid of ageing cousins at wakes. Now, let's get the drinks in.'

Josh had hesitated at the door of the pub, suddenly afraid. 'If you don't mind . . . I'm not sure I'm ready to talk about it more tonight. Her. Is that all right?'

Caroline had clapped a light hand to his shoulder. 'Everything's all right in the heartbreak club, kid.'

'Is that what we are?'

'Sure.' Caroline had pulled off her yellow coat as they headed into the warmth. Underneath she wore a soft jumper of some sparkly silver wool. 'The first rule of heartbreak club is – get your heart broken. That's all really.'

'OK, then. Thank you.' And that was how it began.

Caroline

Caroline still wasn't used to coming home alone. As she dropped her keys into the little lumpy dish by the door, made by a young Anto in Year Five, her muscle memory still expected it, his sing-song *Hello, baby*, bounding up to greet her like an eager puppy.

You're here! Grabbing hold of her – *I've got your arm! You're mine now!* On bad days, she used to know things were wrong because of his silence. Because he didn't run to the door to see her, talking a mile a minute about his day, pulling her bag from her shoulder and flinging it down on the couch. Like that day. The worst day. It had been the silence, hadn't it, that made the hairs rise up on her neck?

This was a different silence. Not of someone there, breathing, mired in pain. Of nothing. No breath, no disturbance of the air. No one there at all. It was a strange kind of pain – she loved this house because she had lived here with Anto, but it was haunted too, because this was where she'd lost him.

'I don't know how you still live there,' her friend Jenny had confessed, half-cut on whiskey at the wake. 'Stay with me a while, will you not?'

But she couldn't. Even though every time she came home she lived it again. That day. Unlocking the door, balancing her re-usable cloth bag of shopping, feeling slightly martyred in a pleasant way that she'd been the one to get up and go to the shops on a rainy Sunday. He owed her one – maybe he could cook something later. She'd expected to find him sprawled in front of Sunday sport, or to hear the gush of the shower, but the house was silent. 'Hello? You didn't go back to bed, you lazy article?' She put the shopping away first, and when she thought about it now her hands curled into fists of frustration. *Leave it, you eejit! Go to him! Now!*

But she hadn't, because she was sensible. She'd put the juice and bacon in the fridge, rolled the cloth bag up in the drawer. Then called again: 'Anto?' Up the stairs. One step. Two. Perhaps the base of her spine was already zinging with some kind of lizard warning. It was too quiet. The wrong kind of quiet.

She'd stepped into their room – the bed made, the curtains pulled. Where was he? Must be in the bathroom. She stopped short. Something was attached to the door. A sheet of lined paper, fixed up with Sellotape that he must have taken from her school supplies in the office. She could imagine him rummaging, trying to find it, like when you had to wrap a last-minute gift. She walked a few steps to read it. Her feet creaked on the landing but there was nothing else, no sound of throat-clearing or flushing or toothbrushing.

The note said: *Caroline. Please don't go in. Call police first.*

And that was all.

Now, Caroline pushed away her memories of after – the long moment, that might have gone on for hours, of understanding what had happened and trying to take it in – and went into the kitchen to put away her few groceries, just as she had that day. She'd planned to make a late dinner after support group, but had ended up getting chips on the way home from the pub, as well as buying an enormous bag of Cool Original Doritos that she was now going to eat all by herself.

She did everything as she had before, opened the cupboards, put things into them, tidied away the tote bag. It was the same bag, in fact. She still used the bathroom, too. Where else would she go? Anto's ghost was there, a silent presence, greeting her at the door like he used to. *Babeeee.* If he was here she'd tell him about the group. She'd say how Josh was doing, that his skin looked grey and his eyes bloodshot, how in the pub they'd laughed till their cackles turned into howls. How angry Sinead was, despite 'her Terry' being dead for decades. How despairing Cassie was, how silent Ruma. How Matt hadn't even turned up, struggling to bail out the lifeboat he and his kids were sinking in. It had been fun, though, the pub, doing impressions of Sinead and all the ridiculous things she told them to do to try to manage their grief. Tonight it had been rubbing essential oils on their pulse points. In the pub, Josh had waved around a bottle of malt vinegar, shouting, 'Car! Give me your wrist, I shall anoint you!' Until the landlord took it off him and told them to quieten down, it was a Monday night and they were disturbing the other punters.

They'd stayed in the pub for hours before Caroline had stumbled home, and she was now going to slump in front of the TV, eating crisps and watching old *Friends* reruns, which were funny, but in a way that hurt because she'd watched them all with Anto, who'd initially dismissed it as sappy American pap, then one day she'd caught him alone, remote in hand, chuckling along to 'The One Where No One's Ready'. She wondered would anything ever be enjoyable again, not tinged with sadness at the memory of doing it with Anto. Perhaps that was why she liked Josh, because the friendship was brand new, something belonging to the afterlife she found herself living in now.

Not long after this revelation, Caroline passed out on the sofa, surrounded by bits of crisps, where she woke up four hours later, freezing and stiff. Without Anto, she felt untethered. There was no one to tut and shake their head if she stayed up too long, or to make her tea and toast when she came in drunk – not that she'd ever really done that when Anto was alive, too happy to stay home with him. Caroline held out her forearm in the cold living-room air. 'Baby?' she whispered. 'Are you there?' Wanting to feel a slight breeze, a raising of hairs. But there was nothing.

She stood up to go to bed, wobbly-legged, and shook out the crisps that had lodged in her bra. As she brushed her teeth, her eyes kept drifting to the bath. It was morbid, she knew, but she couldn't help it. What was she supposed to do? Move out, never set foot again in her own lovely home? 'I miss you,' she said, to the still, empty air. Anto's ghost said nothing back.

Josh

Josh was also not used to the empty flat. Right before he met Niamh, back in London, he'd finally managed to afford his own place, a half-studio in Peckham, and was only delighted with himself, as she would say. *Would have said.* No more finding dirty dishes in the sink or hairs in the soap. It was small but cosy, and he'd arranged his records on some reclaimed-wood shelves, and even bought a cushion. When girls came over, as they did comfortably often, he had candles and vases and more than one towel, and it depressed him that they found this impressive, that the bar for straight men was set so low.

Now he lived alone again, in a newbuild flat in Belfast, and when he turned his key in the lock, the silence was overwhelming. No dishes in the sink or coffee mugs on the table, no bras drying over radiators or shoes kicked off in the hall. Niamh's untidiness had been an irritant, the source of numerous complaints. *Babe, please can you,* and *Babe, I'm going to lose my mind if you don't stop ...*

He'd got what he wanted in a terrible way. A sterile, tidy, unchanging home. Niamh's friends and sisters had offered to help him with the cleaning as well as with her clothes, and he'd tried to explain why he was laughing; that Niamh, the youngest of five, barely knew how to use a washing machine, that he'd had to ban her from going near his jumpers because she always shrank them. He'd always liked cleaning, finding it brought order to his mind, but now with every dust and hoover session, he knew he was wiping her away, her hairs and skin cells and her very breath from the air.

Not for the first time, a kind of helpless annoyance settled over him, another imaginary conversation with her. *Why'd you have to walk into the street, you daft cow? Could you not have looked before you ran out? Because all this, your death and funeral and the sheer bloody pain of living without you, is so very inconvenient.* He'd had things to do, a career to build. He didn't have *time* to be a grieving widower, at thirty-four. But here he was.

Over the fireplace was a framed shot of their wedding. Josh had insisted he could pull off a loud suit, petrol blue, and Niamh was in hippy princess mode, braids and lace and flowers all over her, beaming despite the freezing and lashing Irish rain. He'd felt dazed that day, to have something as grown-up as a wife. And yet now he'd leapfrogged to an even later stage, and been widowed. It was gas, as Niamh would say. *Would have said.* Ah, tenses were a bitch.

Josh moved the picture a little, straightening it. He was slightly drunk from the pub with Caroline, a warm glow that he felt leaking away now he was back in this flat, so empty without Niamh. He'd never set much store by such things, had only tried the support group because he was literally going out of his mind, but he had to admit it helped. Caroline had been his rock this past while. She radiated a sort of warm understanding of the madder moments of grief, and having lost her husband a month before he lost Niamh, was a kind of pathfinder for him in the early days, when he was totally shell-shocked, an animal just trying to stay alive.

He looked at Niamh's picture over the fire, smiling for ever, never to be any older than thirty-two. 'I'll keep going,' he promised, speaking out loud, because he was a little drunk. 'I know you would want me to try, at least.'

Caroline

Rather than enjoying the following evening doing what she'd planned, watching more of *Friends* and eating a whole Prosecco and raspberry cheesecake by herself, Caroline instead had to drive out of town in the rush hour and gird herself for the latest grief-obstacle – coffee with her mother-in-law. Was Mary even still that, if Anto was gone? She wondered what it was about, this coffee. By tacit agreement, they had not discussed anything about the future all through the funeral and initial grieving shock and the intervening three months and memorial service, but now she supposed it was time.

She hit traffic on the way out of Belfast and arrived at M&S at Sprucefield ten minutes late. As she ran in, she reflected with annoyance that Mary always wanted to meet here, as if a cup of weak tea among the pants and bras was the height of sophistication. She wouldn't come into the city because she had a phobia about parking, specifically about paying for it. *Eight pounds, Caroline!*

'Sorry,' Caroline said breathlessly, flopping onto an inexplicably high stool at the raised counter. She didn't embrace her mother-in-law. They'd never really done that. Irish families didn't; usually they saw each other so often it wasn't needed.

Mary had ordered a tea, which she liked as it came in a little metal pot, though she always complained one bag wasn't enough. Caroline asked for a latte, and didn't miss the slight lift of Mary's eyebrow at her pretentious notions. Her mother-in-law, or former mother-in-law, or whatever she was now, was dressed in white loose pedal pushers and a voluminous patterned blouse. Her hair was 'set' in the manner of a granny from the 1950s, and her lipstick was smudged over the cup.

'How's everyone?' Caroline offered.

Mary sighed. 'Ah sure everyone's just in pieces, aren't they?'

Anto had been the second child of four, their father dead years ago of a heart attack, and they all lived within an hour of their mammy. When Caroline and Anto first got together, she'd shouldered the burden of Christmas and birthdays for his many nieces and nephews with a resigned sigh. They were his family, and of course she didn't have to, but it wouldn't be done otherwise and she'd get the blame.

Mary was just telling a story about Grainne, the granddaughter who was an Irish dancing champion, all bouncing curls and eye-wateringly loud dresses, when she stopped suddenly and said: 'Caroline, I brought you out so we can have a wee talk. About Anto's wishes.'

'You mean the headstone? I told you, I'll sort—'

'No, not that.' Her fingers were shaking, laden with heavy gold rings, her pink varnish chipped around the edges. The woman who'd borne the man Caroline had loved, and lost. 'It's about his . . . er. His stuff. The wee lads.'

Caroline didn't understand for a second, then she realised what was going on here. Mary couldn't bring herself to say the word 'sperm'. She was talking about the frozen semen sample they still had, which had been stored in a Belfast fertility clinic before Anto got sick again and they'd had to leave their IVF plans literally on ice. 'Oh?'

She imagined Mary would urge her to use it, get pregnant immediately and give her another grandchild to boast about, a

20

part of Anto to live on after him. Caroline had barely thought about it, so engulfed in grief had she been, but the idea was there in the back of her mind, that maybe she could still use it, once she could think about such things again, which might be a while still. Not that she had a while, that was the annoying thing. Time was not on her side.

But that wasn't what Mary said at all.

An hour later, she slammed in the door of the house, shaking, no, *vibrating* with rage. *It wasn't true. There was no way! It was none of her bloody—*

Where was it? It had to be here somewhere. Caroline rooted through the 'random bits' drawer in the kitchen, scattering items to the ground in her anger – string, tissues, light bulbs, allergy meds. She found a crumpled Post-it with a number on it, which at one stage she had been calling almost every day, hoping for a better answer than the ones she was getting.

'Hello, Belfast Fertil—'

'Hello, it's Caroline Hooper.' Her voice shook. 'I've just seen my husband's, er, that is . . . ' What did she call him now he was gone? Ex-husband wasn't right. 'Antony Carville,' she said finally. 'I've seen his mother and she said . . . '

'Is this about the consent form?' On the other end, the woman's voice was strong and cool, finding order in Caroline stammered nonsense. 'Mrs Carville has already spoken with us about that, yes.'

'Yes. It's not true. Is it? She's making it up – it can't be true.'

A sound of rustling papers. A throat clear. 'I'm sorry, Mrs—'

'*Ms.*' Caroline bridled.

'Of course. Ms Hooper, did your husband not discuss his instructions with you?'

'Um, well, no.' Obviously not, since she was so angry her nails were digging into the old-fashioned Bakelite phone Anto had found in a junk shop. 'It can't be true. It's so stupid.' This was about her and Anto. Mary had nothing to do with it. It couldn't be true that Anto had ticked the box on the consent form to say Caroline wasn't allowed to use his frozen sample in the event of his death. Or that he'd told Mary this and not her. It just couldn't. Mary must have the wrong end of the stick.

'I'm sorry, but the information I have is that he ticked the box to have the material destroyed in the event of his death, which we understand, regrettably, is the case now. My condolences, by the way.'

'You mean . . . you'll just get rid of it?' Caroline still couldn't believe it. And why did Mary want the sample destroyed? Her own potential grandchild. Caroline didn't understand. Because with Anto gone, Mary wouldn't have the same influence she did over the other grandkids, tentacles creeping into every aspect of their lives? Or because she was religious – she thought IVF, post-death IVF, was meddling in what God wanted or something mad like that? Caroline had been too angry to ask her the reasons. She hadn't even paid for her latte before storming out of the lingerie department, getting her bag tangled up in a size-twenty bustier, and took some grim satisfaction in the thought of Mary having to stump up for it. What was she going to do? Her last hope of a child – Anto's child – was frozen in that clinic.

Since Anto had gone, one-sided conversations with him were a major part of Caroline's life. She'd just had so much more to say to him when he'd gone that day. Like the fact that the green jumper he'd bought didn't go with the brown cords. Like she didn't much enjoy superhero films, so could he go with his mates instead? Like was it OK if, given he was planning to die, he'd leave her the sample she'd pinned all her hopes on?

She stood in her kitchen now, heart hammering with rage and confusion, and tried to think back to that day, signing the forms for fertility treatment. The tastefully appointed waiting room with the Nespresso machine in the corner, both of them nervous but hopeful, filling in consent forms on separate clipboards. The box to tick to say what happened if one of them died. It had seemed just a formality, another thing to fill in. They hadn't ever discussed it, she'd been so eager to get in there to start the process. And why would they die, sure weren't they young and healthy? Despite Anto's . . . issues, the ones that had mostly caused the fertility trouble in the first place.

Some days it felt like everyone else had a baby, appearing casually in the world, squashy little bundles with wide eyes, while Caroline just carried on as normal, her stomach swelling only when she'd eaten too much pasta. All those years being absolutely shit-scared of getting pregnant (blame the nuns) and it turned out it was like trying to hit a moving target in the dark. IVF had been her light in that dark, and even when Anto asked if they could take a break, let him get his head straight, she'd been sure it was just a small setback to her plans. On hold, on ice. Not cancelled for ever. But Anto knew he was leaving her! He knew she couldn't just rush out and find some other man to knock her up, and even if she could, she didn't have the time to date and get to know someone for a few years. She was thirty-six years old. Anto knew that! He could count! But all the same, he'd ticked the box to say that the only thing she had left of him – those little guys in the freezer – should be destroyed after his death.

Caroline was literally pacing, like a caged animal. There had to be something she could do. Through all these months of searing grief, the only thing that had kept her going was knowing that a bit of Anto remained, that she could maybe still have his child one day in the future when she could breathe and walk and eat without having to remind herself to do it. And now she might have lost even that.

For a second she thought of calling Josh and pouring it all out to him, but quickly squashed that idea. She didn't want him to see her like this, in all the rawness of her grief. She'd always tried to stay positive for him, give him some hope that he could get past his loss. Josh probably thought she was coping just fine with bereavement.

Josh

At that very moment, Josh was also having a dark moment. He was standing at the side of the road, freezing in the sweeping wind and non-stop drizzle of Belfast, eyes fixed on a nondescript spot. Nothing at all to look at. A bit of tarmac where a smaller street opened onto a larger one, with a few shops and takeaways nearby. Not even a blind spot or concealed bend. No reason for Josh to have come here every day for the last month. Nothing to suggest why this was the patch of earth where Niamh had died, on a cold sunny morning two months before.

There was more to the mystery than that. What had brought Niamh to a place like this in the first place? It was a part of Belfast she'd never mentioned, not near any of her friends – Josh had actually plotted this out on a map, during one of his madder moments – and weirder than that, she'd died in the middle of the working day. What was she doing out of the office? Had there

24

been some appointment or errand she'd told him about and he'd forgotten, or which (more likely) had slipped her mind to mention? Josh had scoured her messages from that day looking for clues, mundane texts turned to precious jewels by the fact she would never contact him again.

We're out of milk.

Upstairs tap dripping again. Urgh.

When you back.

Usual time.

Where you at today?

That was the last message he'd ever sent her. Not checking up on her; they weren't that kind of couple, and he was often out and about reporting on stories. But she wasn't, she worked in an office, which was miles away from this place, at a desk-based job. She shouldn't have been here at all, that was the fact. There was nothing nearby to explain it – a narrow street of terraced houses, a Nisa shop on the corner, down the road a big Tesco. He took out his phone and checked her messages again, stopped for ever at 11.27 a.m. on 5 February. She'd seen his question, but not replied. Because she was busy, or because she couldn't tell him the truth? Which was it?

He was jolted out of his reverie by a lorry zooming past, so close it ruffled his hair. Bloody crazy drivers. If only they had more speed cameras, bumps on the road, anything to slow people down. OK, so the old man who'd hit Niamh wasn't speeding, but if he'd been going even slower, might she be alive still? Josh had to put the thought away. He'd learned that you could go mad that way, tangled up in *if onlys*. Besides, he was meant to be working right now himself. Maggie, his boss at the paper, had him on some incredibly boring story about whether members of the City Council were fiddling their expenses. Josh was trying to track down an assistant at City Hall who might know the truth, but ultimately he didn't really care if someone had falsely claimed a lunch at Abrakebabra or not. Not when Niamh was dead.

He headed back to his car, face lowered from a stinging shower of rain that had just decided to pepper him. He had to keep going, find out what Niamh was doing here that day. He didn't even know where to start, was the trouble. Ask her workmates, her friends, maybe even her family if he could find a way to do it subtly. Go through her things yet again, looking for a clue he'd missed. He would try whatever it took. He wasn't going to tell Caroline though – she was far too sensible ever to do something like this.

Caroline

At the next support group meeting, someone new came. Sinead had just finished writing *Welcome* on the whiteboard, in big spiky green letters (not very welcoming in fact), when the door creaked open. Standing there was a little old lady, shuffling inside a cocoon of scarves, drapes, hats, jewellery and what looked like a genuine fox fur.

'Can I *help* you?' Sinead should be friendlier, Caroline thought, wincing at her hostile tone. The poor lady was probably lost. Could she be here for the musicals group, or AA? It didn't seem likely, but you never knew.

When the older woman spoke, it was in a wavery, sweet voice. 'Oh, hello. Is this the widows' support group?'

'It's the *young* widows' group,' said Sinead, harshly. 'And widowers-slash-partners, of course.' She nodded to Cassie, who didn't nod back.

'Oh. Well, I'm eighty, so I don't know if that counts as young.'

Sinead frowned. 'It's *specifically* for people under forty who've lost a partner, so I'm afraid—'

'She can stay.' Caroline couldn't help butting in. Sinead glared at her and she quailed. 'Can't she? I mean, she came all this way.' Not that she knew how far it was to the lady's home. But she did know what a gargantuan effort it was, to get up and leave the house and walk in here to a room full of strangers, a tea urn bubbling in the corner. It wasn't fair to turn someone away, not when they'd managed that much.

'Of course,' Josh chimed in, leaping to his feet and grabbing a spare chair. 'Come and sit down, Mrs . . . ?'

'Just Sylvia, dear, thank you.' The lady's hands emerged from the layers of clothes, brooches glinting among them. Caroline saw that her glasses had green rims. 'It's just that the other widow groups aren't quite right – I was never actually married, and they only want to talk about pensions and wills. If I could stay for tonight, I would so appreciate it. I'll be as quiet as a mouse.' Even Sinead could not enforce the rules in the face of such honesty. Could she?

Sinead sniffed. 'Just once. We do have to stick to the remit.'

Josh rolled his eyes at Caroline. She rolled hers back. *Urgh, Sinead.*

Once she'd settled herself in a chair, Sylvia's eyes swept the room. 'Oh dear – do you mean to say you've all lost people? At your ages?'

'Well, *yes,* that's the point of an under-forty group,' said Sinead, a tad huffily. 'We should do introductions. My Terry—'

Nope, Caroline couldn't listen to the story another time. She cut in. 'I'm Caroline. My husband, Anto, he died a few months ago. Suicide.' Caroline marvelled at how she could say it now, after months of practice, like it was any other word – *door* or *envelope* or *peanut*.

Next, Josh said his name and that his wife, Niamh, had been killed in an accident. Cassie explained, staring at the floor again, that her partner had died of cancer – she didn't say Lisa's name, Sinead would be raging – and Ruma just smiled and nodded, as always.

Matt, who had actually turned up tonight, ran his hands over his face, which was as rumpled as his unironed shirt. He was thirty-eight, a tall cool guy who rode a Brompton and drank flat whites, and the month before had suddenly found himself a widower with three small children to care for. 'Um. I'm Matt. Um, my wife, Patricia, she died having our youngest. It still happens! I didn't know that. Did you know that? Um. Yeah. So it's me and the kids – the baby, Maddie, she's five, and Peadar, he's three. It's. Well.' He threw up his hands. 'We're barely coping.'

Matt's wife had been younger than Caroline and she was already dead. A terrible thing. But she'd had three kids by then. Caroline had no kids. The sense of opportunity running out gripped her again, and she tried to force it down. Mary's news was still churning around inside her, while she tried to figure out what to do.

Sylvia was biting her lip. 'Oh, how awful. Those poor children. And so recent. I must confess – I lost my love some time ago now, two years.'

'So why did you . . . ?' Caroline trailed off, feeling rude at what she'd just blurted out.

'Why did I come here? To be honest, dear, I thought I might be able to help.' She looked around them, the young faces hewn with loss. Her eyes were bright and sharp. 'You see, when it comes to grief, I have quite literally been there and written the book.'

'I'm really all right,' said Sylvia, tottering out of the community-centre car park on her walking stick. Caroline saw that it had a gold top, in the shape of a wolf's head. So cool. She'd get one of those when she hit sixty, now that her husband was dead and she was going to be a mad lonely widow for decades. She'd wave it at children if they kicked their balls into her garden. 'There's no need to come with me, dears.' Despite what she'd said about staying quiet, Sylvia had been an active participant in the meeting, even contradicting Sinead a few times, which made Caroline and Josh hide smiles in their hands, and Sinead look even more boot-faced. Now it was time to go home, and they were reluctant to let her struggle off into the night alone.

'Ah no, please, we'd love to,' said Caroline, itching to take the woman's arm. 'You said your house isn't far?'

'Just a few streets away. You are kind. Thank you.' She stumbled on, the two of them forming a protective guard around her. 'It was good of you to let me join your group. I just never quite fit with the old widows. I felt a fraud.'

'I think everyone does,' said Josh. 'Like, there's always someone with a worse story.'

'Like Matt,' sighed Caroline. 'Poor Matt.'

'That was the man with the little ones? So terribly sad.'

'Yeah. It's just awful, I don't know how he's coping.' Caroline resolved to try and help more. Perhaps she could babysit, let Matt get out now and again. His mother was doing what she could, but she was in her seventies and now she had the broken wrist as well. Josh was right, there was always someone worse off.

After what seemed like an agonising amount of time inching

down the streets near the community centre, matching their pace to Sylvia's, they were at the front door of a red-brick terrace, slightly crumbling but lovely, spring flowers struggling out in colourful pots along the tiled front path.

'Thank you, my dears.' Sylvia was out of breath even from the snail's pace they'd walked at. 'You will come in? I have sherry, liqueurs, gin!'

They exchanged glances, and Caroline knew exactly what Josh was thinking. It was a work night, and already late, and she'd been looking forward to their usual debrief, but on the other hand, neither of them had anyone to go home to.

'Of course,' said Caroline stoutly.

Josh gave a small nod of agreement. 'We'd love to.'

Inside the house was a fascinating cave, and Caroline felt like a small child who wanted to run amok, scan all the titles of the overstuffed bookshelves, spin the antique globe, riffle her fingers over the strings of glinting beads hung from pegs on the wall, the pictures, the glass decanter. A proper grown-up home, filled with the treasures of a life well lived.

'This place is amazing!' she gasped, and Sylvia smiled at her.

'Thank you, dear. It was Iris who had the taste. We had some wonderful trips – you can do that, of course, when you don't have children.'

'Iris?' said Josh politely, just as Caroline was figuring it out.

'My beloved. I lost her two years ago now.'

Over the fireplace was a picture of a young Sylvia, arm in arm in front of the Taj Mahal with a striking dark-haired woman wrapped in an Indian-print scarf.

'Oh,' said Josh, twigging.

'So you see, I'm not actually a widow. Wasn't possible in those days and when it was – well, we'd lived our whole lives as just good friends to the world, so it seemed too late to change.' Sylvia moved the picture a millimetre, aligning it. 'Now! Drinks. What would you like – sherry, whiskey, gin?'

'I'll help.' Josh moved forward – he had lovely manners, of course – while Caroline sat on an old sofa draped in rugs and cushions, which exhaled dust as she sank down.

Sylvia showed Josh to an adorable drop-front drinks cabinet, which Caroline immediately coveted, filled with dusty, half-drunk bottles and sparking glasses. Anto, with his passion for the vintage (and for alcohol, of course), would have loved that.

Once they had their drinks, sticky-sweet in tiny cut glasses which Anto would also have loved (though he'd have thought them too small), Sylvia sat down, spreading her skirts around her.

'Now. Iris, my love, died two years ago, as I said. For you, I gather, the loss is rather more … raw.' Caroline and Josh exchanged glances, nodded. 'Right then. My dears, I want to pass something on to you, if you will accept it. When I went through this, there was no map. No manual for heartbreak, for how to live without the centre of your world. So – I wrote one.'

A short silence.

'You wrote one?' said Josh politely.

'Let me see.' Sylvia got up, tangling her skirts and beads, and hopped precariously onto some library steps to rummage in her bookcase, dislodging paperbacks as she did. Caroline's fists clenched with the urge to help her. What Sylvia pulled out was a loose-leaved binder, like Caroline had used at school, punching holes through pages and reinforcing them with little white circles if needed. A simpler time. Sylvia carried it over, legs unsteady. 'This is everything I know about how to survive the next period of your lives. I call it *How to Be a Widow* – although, of course, I wasn't one.' She nodded to Josh. 'Widow is just a word. It applies to all who have lost. Would you like it?'

Silence. Caroline swilled the liquid in her glass, watching light filter through its facets. *What am I doing here?* she thought. She was thirty-six years old. She should have been out at a bar or on a date or at spinning class, or curled around Anto on the sofa like baby animals squished into a den, watching Netflix, hands dipping alternately into a family-sized box of Heroes. Not here in this dusty old house, grief and loss leaching out of the walls, with an old lady who was sweet but possibly a bit batty.

Josh spoke first. 'It's really kind of you, Sylvia. But are you sure? That looks like the only copy.' Some of the sheets appeared typewritten, like with an actual typewriter, and others were handwritten, scrawled in tiny scribbles.

'It is, but there's no sense in it mouldering away here. I want it out in the world, helping people. That's why I came to the group. It's time to share what I've learned. Otherwise what was the point? Of going through two years of crushing pain?'

It was a good question. Another quick glance between the two.

This time it was Caroline who spoke. What else could she say? 'Thank you, Sylvia. We'd love to have it. After all, we need to do *something*. I don't know about you, Josh, but living like this pretty much sucks ass. Oh, sorry – but it does. I've tried everything else, so why not this?'

Josh

Josh wasn't sure about this whole book thing. The old lady was sweet, but everything in her house was furred with dust and cobwebs, and as they walked in he couldn't help wondering if she was all right, or if she needed people to take care of her. He might not have gone in at all if not for Caroline – after all, Sylvia was a stranger. He could hear Niamh's voice in his head: *Oh go on with yourself, it's Belfast not London, she isn't going to stab you with her letter-opener.* Niamh had always trusted everyone implicitly, and he remembered her wide-eyed bewilderment when their land-lord held the deposit back because of mould in the bathroom, or a colleague took credit for her ideas. Poor, credulous Niamh. Had that led to her death somehow, her trust in people? The question roamed around his head, like a hamster in a wheel. He still hadn't thought of a good place to start investigating.

After leaving Sylvia's, Josh and Caroline had, without discussing it, gone for another drink. The traditional hard-drinking old men you found in every Irish pub looked up as they came in, nodded, stared back into their pints. Josh still expected someone to have a problem with him in situations like this. Again, Niamh would have burst out laughing, saying, *It's not Mississippi Burning, love, it's the Lisburn Road, you're grand.* Once they were seated – gin, pint, two shots of whiskey to chase – Josh said, 'That was a bit weird.'

'She's just lonely,' said Caroline, putting the blue folder on the table. 'You understand that, don't you? You feel you need to do something, like, or you'll go clean mad. This was her project.'

'But you can't, like, game it. Grief. What would help, anyway? You have to just wait, don't you? Until it stops hurting so much.' Though currently he couldn't imagine a time when that would be the case.

'Why don't we see what it says?' said Caroline. 'Maybe she found the magic solution. Apart from booze, I mean.' She tipped her gin at him ironically and, with her other hand, turned the cover of the binder. It was a collection of pages hole-punched and clipped in, some typed, some handwritten in neat block capitals, a little wavy in places, and here or there were splodges of what looked like coffee. It appeared to be a twelve-step programme for overcoming grief, each step outlined in detail, with instructions and anecdotes. Page one read – *How to Be a Widow*.

'Sorry, Josh,' said Caroline, glancing up. 'Though widow's just a technical term, isn't it, like she said.'

Yeah, for someone lost, grieving, adrift in the world. It was maybe worse for the widowers, Josh thought. You were almost expected to shrug off the death of your wife, find another. The old ball and chain. Her indoors. Widows were meant to be helpless, the recipients of charity and endowments. Whereas he was, what, just supposed to get on with it? Marry again?

'What does it say?' His voice was too loud, so he took a gup of beer. Maybe he was afraid to try this book. To try and have it, like everything else so far, not work.

He watched Caroline across the table, the way her bobbed blonde hair fell over her face. They hadn't ever talked about it, but these pub trips had become the highlight of his week. He didn't know how he felt about that. It was just so comfortable, the booze and chatter and warmth and the bag of chips after, and Caroline's kind and undemanding company, that it reminded him of . . .

Well. It reminded him of being with Niamh. The level of comfort they'd achieved after three years. The ability to communicate in shorthand and grunts. But he had to remember that this wasn't Niamh. It was a different woman, with a complex pain and loss she hid almost too well. And Niamh had not been as uncomplicated as he'd thought, had she? For a start, she'd gone to a place she'd no business being, which she hadn't told him about.

'Will we try it then?' said Caroline, looking at him enquiringly. 'I could copy it at work. So we each have one, like. Then we try the different suggestions one by one. What do you think?'

Josh sighed. She was right, it was better than nothing. Better than this endless cycle of questions, never to be answered. 'OK then.' Nothing else had worked, so why not this? It could hardly be worse than where they were now.

And that was how they ended up following Sylvia's plan for what to do when you've lost the love of your life.

1. REACH OUT TO PEOPLE

Caroline

'Baby! You were so long! Where've you been!'

As soon as she'd walked in the door, Anto was nuzzling up to her like a friendly dog.

She struggled past him, wanting to take off her shoes and sink onto the sofa. 'I'm always home at this time. I went to the shops.' Something Anto would never think of, that milk and cereal and loo roll didn't replenish themselves, but had to be bought.

'It seemed like ages. Listen, I've got an idea.' At this point, a year into their relationship, that phrase had already led to so many crazy adventures – kayaking in Belfast Lough, line-dancing classes, abseiling down the Europa hotel – but also a few disasters. Running out of petrol in the middle of Donegal because Anto felt they had to go for a drive in the middle of the night. Throwing a dinner party only to find, two hours into it, that he was already drunk and had forgotten to defrost the chicken.

'Oh?' she said, cautiously. She started to take off her coat, but Anto stopped her.

'Keep it on. I'm taking you somewhere.'

Her heart sank. She was so tired. One of the kids in her class had tried to attack another with scissors today, and although it was impossible to hurt someone with the safety ones they had in class, unless perhaps you very slowly battered them into submission, it still meant a lot of paperwork for Caroline, not to mention some serious heart-to-hearts with the parents.

'Babe, it's just . . . '

'No! Don't do that.'

'*Do what?*'

'*Rain on my parade. Give in to* I'm tired *or* it's a work night *or* I want to watch Love *bloody* Island. *That's how your life slips through your fingers, Car. I don't want that for us.*'

He cupped her face in his huge hands. She wondered fleetingly if he'd done any work that day (Anto was a photographer, and there was always invoicing and retouching and editing to be done). He seemed manic, quivering with excitement.

'*All right.*'

She let him do her coat back up, and lead her to the car. It was a beautiful summer evening; it would be bright until almost eleven, sun burning high on the hills over Belfast, and she felt a matching excitement stir. He was right. They'd always remember this evening, whereas otherwise it would just have gone by in mindless TV and eating Minstrels.

*Anto drove them down towards the Lough, to a pebbled beach where the grey water lapped, turned pewter in the sun. '*Stay here,*' he instructed, switching off the engine. '*Come down in five minutes.*'*

'*Wha— OK.*' *She waited, watching the car clock click around, then got out and tottered down the steps to the beach, wishing she'd thought to change her shoes.*

*Anto was a small figure further down the beach, where wet firm sand lay. He waved and called. '*Stay there! Look!*'*

At his feet were pebbles spelling something out. Caroline squinted – she needed her eyes tested – was that – did it really – oh God.

The stones at Anto's feet spelled out Marry Me? *She wondered had it been too much work to add the* Will You, *as she walked towards him in a daze. It was happening. The moment she'd idly dreamed of so many times. It was now.*

He was practically hopping up and down. From the pocket of his old tweed jacket he took a ring box, crushed green velvet, and popped it open to show her an antique ring, white gold, sapphires, a 1930s style. It was

*perfect. Exactly what she'd have chosen for herself. Lots of thoughts whizzed
through Caroline's head, at the speed of light. This was so romantic, so
moving. She loved him so much. But he was sick, no doubt about that, and
would never truly get better. He was not reliable. He drank too much. But
she was reliable, and he was full of fun, and joy, and life. Maybe, together,
it would work.*

*'Well?' Anto was trembling with nerves, his eyes fixed on her. A deep
and aching love hit Caroline in the stomach. She would do this. She would
take care of this extraordinary man and they would be happy. They would
have an amazing life.*

'Yes,' she said. 'All right then.'

'I can't believe it,' said Jenny.

They'd met for a coffee after work the next day, in line with
Sylvia's advice to reach out to people. Meeting Sylvia and getting
her book had somehow galvanised Caroline into taking some
action, instead of brooding about the bombshell Mary had
dropped on her, having one-sided conversations with Anto in
her head, crying at random times, and snapping at the kids in
her class, as she'd been doing all the week before.

Jenny was drinking a green tea and looking longingly at
Caroline's latte. 'What did you tick?'

'That he could use whatever he wanted, of course. Though
he'd have had a struggle.' She tried to imagine a world where
Anto was still alive and she was dead, where she'd left him alone
with this decision to make. She couldn't. 'I don't know what he
was thinking. I guess ... maybe he wasn't feeling the best.' He
was already going a bit funny, she meant. He must have been.
You didn't suddenly decide to kill yourself out of the blue. Anto
must have been slipping away for months and she hadn't noticed,
so wrapped up in the pain of not conceiving. Even when they'd

had to stop the IVF because he wasn't quite himself, because his meds needed to be increased, she'd told herself it was all right. They'd had his sample frozen because the meds affected sperm quality, and knowing it was there had made her feel a little better. They'd get past this storm, as they had others. Anto was always going to be ill. It was just something they coped with – or so she'd thought. 'Maybe he thought I couldn't manage alone,' she wondered aloud.

'Car, you're the most capable woman in Belfast, of course you could manage. Can I lick the foam off your spoon?'

'What? OK. But why don't you get your own?'

'Eleven stone four on the scales this morning,' said Jenny gloomily.

She'd been dieting ever since Caroline had met her at the age of eleven, on their first day at Our Lady Immaculata School for Girls. Fasting, 5:2, no carb, the Cambridge diet, Slimming World – you name it, Jenny had tried it, and yet she always weighed exactly the same. She lived in a little terraced house with her cats Hermione and Ron, worked as an accountant, went on cruises with her sister, did Pilates. She was happy, wasn't she? Caroline tried to imagine herself going on like this, single, childless. She didn't even like cats that much. Once Anto had come home with a kitten, a little scrap of silver-grey fur and huge eyes that he'd bought for a tenner off a man in the pub. She'd made him take it to a shelter.

She sighed. 'God, this is so shit. The one bit of hope I had left and now this.'

'I'm so sorry, Car. Maybe he ticked the wrong box or he just didn't think about it or ... I don't know. What did his ma say?'

'Just that this was his wish, and she'd do everything she could to respect it. It's OK for her, every other kid popping out babies right left and centre.'

Other people got pregnant, just one month of trying then – whoops, a pink line. They got pregnant when they didn't mean to, they weren't ready, they were on the Pill. Caroline and Anto had been trying for two years, and now the last ray of hope was snuffed out. She couldn't use Anto's frozen sample. He hadn't wanted her to.

'Can you appeal it?' Jenny was scraping out Caroline's cup with a spoon, dropping the foam into her mouth, eyes half-closed in bliss. 'You know, there was that woman in England who went to court to get her husband's lads?'

Caroline came out of the damp, cold fog she'd sunk into. 'Hmm?'

'I think her husband died or something, he'd frozen some sperm 'cause he had cancer, something like that? Anyway, Anto probably didn't read the form right, you know what he was like. He'd have wanted you to have a baby, wouldn't he?'

That was what she couldn't understand. He'd said a hundred times that she'd be an amazing mother. As a teacher she spent her days with kids, and she already knew First Aid, how to make origami seals out of a single sheet of paper, and how to diffuse a tantrum in ten seconds flat. 'I thought so.'

'Then probably it was just a mistake – you can fight it,' said Jenny, absent-mindedly pouring sugar into the remnants of milk and coffee and mixing it into a paste.

'But his mum knew what box he ticked! She seemed sure he meant to.'

'Well, who knows, maybe she got the wrong end of the stick, or he just wasn't in his right mind that day. You know how he was.' She did know. 'Don't give up, Car. That's not like you.'

And she was right. It wasn't.

Josh

Reach out to people. That was the first bit of advice in Sylvia's book. Josh was thinking about it as he got home the next day, having stayed in the office as long as possible to avoid the empty flat (ever-efficient, Caroline had already had it photocopied and sent over to him). Sylvia had written:

> Your friends will surprise you, in ways both good and bad. The people you most trust will let you down, and people you barely thought of will come through for you. Afterwards, it will be like an earthquake upturned your world, and the buildings left standing will not necessarily be the ones you expected. You have a different life now.

In the kitchen, Josh switched on the kettle with a bit more force than was needed. He hadn't *wanted* a new life, was the problem. He hadn't wanted to go to grief support groups, or get whiskey-drunk on rainy Monday nights, or take advice from strange old ladies. He'd been perfectly happy with his life the way it was. Yes, his family and best friends were in London, but after two years he'd settled in here, enjoyed his job, played five-a-side, been embraced by Niamh's friends and made some of his own.

Sylvia was right, all the same. People had surprised him, in ways both good and bad. Billy from the football team, a gruff maniac on the field whom he barely knew, had asked him to dinner at least once a week since it happened. Josh made excuses every time. Meanwhile, Sam, his own brother, hadn't even messaged since the funeral. He knew people didn't know what to say – it was what a lot of them told him when they met:

Josh mate, I don't know what to say – but try, people. At least bloody try, you know?

He picked up his phone, the one connection between him and the world when he closed the door of the silent flat, once filled with Niamh's terrible music – Westlife, for God's sake! - and tuneless singing, banging of doors, cursing as she dropped things. There was a string of messages from his mother, various gifs and inspirational memes. He usually dodged her calls, since she would only cry down the line to him. He'd made the mistake once of admitting how lost he really was, how he was drifting through his life here, and she'd told him right away to come home, come back to London. Which he couldn't do because ... he wasn't sure why. Because Niamh had been here and so he had to be as well. Because he needed to find out what she'd been doing that day, before he could even think about moving on with his life.

On his phone was another message from Billy. *All right mate? Kickabout sometime?*

Instead of ignoring it as usual, Josh made himself reply – *Sure thing, fella. At a loose end right now.*

Billy wrote right back – *Come to ours for a wee bite sure,* then some food emojis. Josh's heart felt hollow. He barely knew this guy. Did he really want to spend a night with him, pretending everything was all right? He forced himself to type back – *sounds good* – and added a thumbs-up.

Next, he clicked on the message stream from Niamh's family, which had grown quiet since he never replied. He knew they had another thread, an endless parade of jokes and arguments about who was bringing what to their Saturday-night family dinners, and he'd had to opt out because it was too painful to think about, her family going on without her, nephews and nieces growing up and her numerous sisters and sister-in-law getting pregnant, when Niamh never would, when the 'lovely brown babies' they'd joked about, making fun of something her great-aunt had said at their wedding, would never materialise.

With a heavy heart, Josh readied himself type out a message to the Donnellys. He didn't want to. *Damn you, Sylvia, and your stupid advice.* But on the other hand, he couldn't go on like this, alone in this flat, a glass wall between him and the world, as if he'd tried to follow Niamh wherever she'd gone and got stuck, not dead but not alive, either. Plus, there was always the chance her family might know something, anything, that could shed some light on what the hell Niamh had been doing that day. It was a place to start, at least.

Hi guys. Was thinking I might come out to see you at the weekend, if that's all right.

Seconds later, his phone buzzed, and buzzed and buzzed. *Ah Josh pet we'd love to see you.* More emojis. Had this entire country just discovered them? Thumbs up. Smiley faces. Two social engagements planned – he could hardly believe it.

Finally, he opened Facebook, which after months of neglect was like a grown-over garden, red notifications clustering like a rash. He had so many comments and messages, *Are you OK dude? So sorry, Totally shocked.* He could hardly bear to read the posts on Niamh's page, which was stopped for ever as it had been on her last day on earth. Her last update was an observation about how she couldn't wait for the Eurovision Song Contest (her favourite night of the year, including Christmas and her birthday). How strange that any mundane post or thought could be your last. So many comments on her page, too. People who'd barely spoken to her when she was alive, pouring out their grief and shock, heart emojis, sad faces, even though she would never see them.

He hated it so much. Without really thinking about it, he started a new post.

> Sorry I haven't answered your messages. The truth is I don't know what to say, either, so it's not helpful to hear that you don't. It's not helpful to hear how much you miss her too, especially if I know you hadn't talked to her in months. It's definitely not helpful to hear I'll meet someone else and I'll move on soon or that she's waiting for me in some afterlife I don't believe in. But if you'd like to meet up and just treat me normally, I'd love that. Thanks. Sorry. Tbh I am not coping all that well, but I'm trying.

God, that was going to alarm his mum. He didn't know where it came from – some spurt of anger like a pocket of lava. His finger hesitated over the delete button, but something made him leave it. Sylvia's advice, perhaps; the realisation that things had to change if he was ever to re-join the world of the living.

Are you happy? He turned to Niamh's framed photo over the fire. *Is that what you'd want me to do, make an effort? See your family? Go out?* As usual, trapped in amber, she did not reply.

Caroline

The more she googled, the more excited she became, until her hand was sweaty on the mouse and her eyeballs dry. She hadn't even taken her coat off since coming home. She and Jenny had swiftly moved from coffee to wine and she was definitely a little bit drunk for the second night in a week – in the old days she'd have been in bed already with a pint of water and pre-emptive

Solpadeine. But it didn't matter, because what she'd found out was very encouraging. There was a case in England where a woman had successfully taken the Human Fertility and Embryology Association, or HFEA, the body which decided these things, to court so she could use her husband's sperm, frozen before he'd died of cancer, and she had a baby now. It could happen! There was hope again, for that child Caroline had dreamed of, with Anto's wild energy and dark hair, tempered hopefully by her own common sense. A child both dynamic and with cop-on, who could do anything. Who could rule the world.

Yes, the cases were a little different, given that the other man had signed his permission on the form to begin with, it just hadn't been renewed in time and the law set limits on how long the material could be stored, but how different were they really? Anto had clearly wanted to have a child with her – he'd frozen his semen in the first place, for goodness' sake. No one would go through that if they were on the fence about kids. Would they? He'd just ticked the wrong box on the form, as Jenny had suggested. She could almost feel the phrase revolving in her head, as if she were going slightly mad. *He ticked the wrong box he ticked the wrong box the wrong box*. And Mary? Well, she'd probably misunderstood. She still thought she had to tell Facebook not to use her photographs.

In the past, Caroline had never been the type to panic about babies. She wasn't like the girls at school, determined to be married by twenty-five. She'd enjoyed her twenties, living in Ecuador for six months, backpacking with Jenny, building her career up to be deputy head of a primary school that never fell below 'outstanding' in its Ofsted rating. Then, on a night out with work, she'd met Anto at the Limelight club. He was so tall. Caroline was five eight, a 'great big heap of a girl' as her grandfather had once put it, so when she saw him towering over the crowd at the bar, she was determined to speak to him. He'd seen her too and nodded over people's heads, as if to say, *Oh yes, it's you,* and she felt an intense connection and familiarity she'd never had before. When he came over, she saw he had the pale, sculpted face and floppy hair of a poet. He hated places like the Limelight, it turned out, had gone there only because it was his sister Mary Anne's birthday. It was as if it was meant to be, although Caroline, being sensible, of course didn't believe in such notions.

Sometimes Caroline thought about that night, how she almost didn't go because she had an inspection approaching, and a tough week with a nits outbreak in Primary Four, and she'd forgotten her makeup bag so had to go shiny-faced from school, and she also felt she was too old for clubs at thirty-two. If she'd never met him, what would her life be now? Would she be married to some other man, perhaps with a couple of kids? Would she not be a widow at thirty-six, a childless woman pinning all her hopes on some vials of frozen semen in a clinic across town?

They'd married two years after meeting, her thirty-four, him thirty-six. Anto was not bothered about marriage, but he cared what his mammy thought, and Caroline was secretly pleased, after so long, to have the white dress and top table and cake, to have bridesmaids and a hen do of her own rather than always organising other people's (Caroline had a reputation for running an amazing hen do, options for all tastes, conflicts defused with tact and Prosecco, the bride put to bed before she made a holy show of herself). They'd started trying for a baby on their honeymoon in Cancun, and although they told

49

each other it would take ages, sure there was no rush, part of her believed it would happen that first month, as it had for so many of her friends.

It didn't. Six months went by, with a slight sinking of her heart each time, until it was somewhere about her knees and she hadn't even realised. A year. Eighteen months. By then she was past the mythical thirty-five cut-off, and that was when they tentatively began to discuss getting help.

Caroline was a sensible person; it was what she most prided herself on. But all the same, she couldn't help herself opening up one of the websites, the forbidden ones she wasn't supposed to go on. But oh, how perfect. Little T-shirts in duckling-yellow and sky-blue. Tiny shoes for feet that couldn't even walk yet. Babygros with patterns of dinosaurs and trucks and stars. She'd dress her baby gender-neutral of course. Her mother would have to be restrained from buying everything in pink.

She caught herself on. Of course, there'd be a legal challenge to mount first. And they cost money. But the thing she wanted above all else was in her grasp again. Think positive, that's what Anto would have said. He was always the optimistic one, sure that they could redo the kitchen for half of what it would really cost, or drive double the distance in a day that was possible in their clapped-out Micra. Caroline had been the sensible one, saying, *It'll cost too much; It's too far; We can't do it*. Raining on his parade, as he put it. This time she would try to be more like Anto. Upbeat, hopeful, dynamic. Anto on his good days, that was.

Jenny was right. It wasn't like her to give up at the first hurdle – that Year Four nit outbreak would still be continuing unabated had Caroline not stepped in – and she wasn't going to do it this time. Anto had just ticked the wrong box, whatever his mother seemed to think. If Mary wanted a fight, then a fight she would get.

Josh

He looked at his watch, a stylish vintage one he'd bought with his first pay packet, and then at his phone, just in case it showed a different time. It didn't. The headhunter was late.

Josh had been working at a local south London paper for two years by then, the kind that clung on with tooth and fang, reporting crime and corruption, both of which there was plenty in his borough. It survived mostly on ad revenue, and they were never sure if each year would be their last or not. He liked what he did – crime fascinated him, the small details of lives blown apart, the search for justice – but he was ready for more. More money, more stability, more visibility. Hence meeting this woman about a job on a major broadsheet.

But she was late. He'd almost finished his oat-milk latte and still no sign of her. He was just skimming through his phone, wondering if he had the wrong coffee shop, when a woman ran in, carrying a large handbag pressed to her chest like a child. As she scanned the café, the bag began to slip from her grasp and items fell out, clattering to the floor, a notebook, several pens, a makeup compact and a small toy car.

'Niamh?' He'd looked up how to pronounce the name, which made no sense to him, but then people often struggled with his own surname. 'I'm Josh.'

'Hi, hi! Just a sec!' She made her way towards him, picking up her trail of destruction and dropping more things as she bent over, bumping into chairs and tables. 'Oh God, sorry, sorry, I'm so sorry, Josh, I had no idea it would take me this long to get here. I've only been in London two weeks so I have, and Jesus, it's massive, isn't it?'

'It is, yeah.' He looked at her properly. Despite her chaotic entrance she was very pretty, curly blonde hair around a heart-shaped face, wearing a tea dress printed with cherries. It turned out she was new in the job, had moved over from Belfast for it, and was adjusting quite badly to London life.

'Please don't tell my boss! I'll get the sack for sure.'

'I won't,' he said, amused. He had been nervous about this interview, but now he felt completely at ease. He bent down to pick up a tube of lip balm, strawberry-flavoured, that was rolling round his feet. 'I think this is yours.'

She burst out laughing. 'Well, now that I've shown you exactly how to not be brilliant in a job interview, will I tell you about this role?'

In the end, Josh didn't get the job, since the post was being cut for financial reasons even as he and Niamh spoke, and the paper would go under soon, but all the same, he already knew, as he went to order them more coffees, that this encounter had tilted his life on its axis.

Niamh had worked in HR, which suited her personality – kind, sympathetic and overwhelmingly nosy. She wasn't supposed to tell him anything about it, obviously, but she couldn't always help herself, and her attempts at code names were so poor and the office so small that he'd worked out quite easily who it was who'd had the affair and gone to England for the abortion, who'd been caught weeing in the office kettle, who'd embezzled the funds for the Christmas party and so on. 'So, eh, Simon – er, I mean, Mr X, we caught him red-handed in the kitchen, or should that be red-willied, trousers round his ankles this time . . . '

It was strange to go there now, knowing she wouldn't be behind the darkened glass of the city centre building. He'd never been entirely sure what it was the company did – insurance of some kind, or financial services, maybe. The company had a huge turnover of students working in their customer-service department, and Niamh had been the one to whip them into shape and lend a shoulder to cry on when they failed their exams or got dumped by their terrible boyfriends. He'd arranged to meet her 'work wife', Brida. Niamh had joined the company with her when she and Josh moved over two years ago, when her mother got sick and London became too hard for the mammy's-girl country lover she was, and Josh, too much in love to make sensible choices, had followed her here, lured by promises of cheap housing and mighty craic. His own mother had wept, sure he was going to be blown up, until he'd pointed out that these days he was far more likely to be stabbed in Peckham than shot in Belfast. Brida had sent him a message after seeing his Facebook post – so had a lot of people – and Josh realised that here was an opportunity to find out a bit about Niamh's movements that day.

Brida was a few years older than Niamh, run ragged by a toddler called Jack, about whom Josh knew more than he'd ever expected to know about a child who was not a blood relative, let alone one he had yet to meet. 'Ah you'll never guess what Jack said last night,' Niamh would regale him with most days, often with photographic or video evidence supplied, showing a gnome-like small child giggling over the contents of a potty or spouting some cute nonsense. Now, this unwanted knowledge came in handy. 'How's Jack? Still obsessed with Peppa Pig?'

'Ah Josh, love.' Brida's dark eyes filled with tears, and she produced a tissue from the sleeve of her M&S cardy and wiped her nose. 'Sure he's in bits, we're all in bits. I can't believe it, so I can't. I still expect her to come into the office with her lovely bright smile and singing her Taylor Swift songs.' Niamh had been a morning person, a point of contention between him and her, because he didn't like to talk to anyone before ten, let alone become involved the debates about whether anyone had ever been killed by a narwhal or how bears peed while in hibernation, questions the like of which Niamh would often wake him with.

'Yeah. Brida, I hope you don't mind, but I'm looking into the accident. You know, the police are so swamped.' He made a shrugging gesture, banking on the habitual distrust of Northern Irish people for the police.

Her eyes narrowed. 'Sure they'd hardly stir themselves, that lot. Have you found anything out?'

'Well, they know who the driver was; it wasn't his fault. The question is why did she run into the road. Really, what I'm wondering is why she was there at all.'

Was it his imagination or did Brida's eyes shift away? They were walking through the third floor now, and he had on a little pin badge with *Visitor* on it. 'Will you take a wee cup of tea, Josh? Or coffee?'

'Ah, no thanks.' He still remembered the kettle-weeing stories.

She led him to the HR HQ, as Niamh used to call it, a set of four desks with cubicle walls between, all tacked over in cards and photos and amusing photocopies. The HR Harem (another nickname) were all female. As well as Brida there was Susan, a fifty-something chain smoker with a poodle perm and raspy voice, and Clee, a twenty-something in smart glasses and asymmetric hair, whom Niamh had been sure had designs on Brida's job, despite her claims to be only saving up to go to South America.

And then there was an empty desk – which had been Niamh's, which had not been filled yet. Josh hadn't thought that part through. And the loss hit him in the gut all over again, like a kick from a cow, as Niamh maintained had once happened to her daddy on the farm.

'You're sure you won't have tea now?'

Josh's secret shame was that he didn't even like tea. You couldn't say that in Ireland though – they'd run you out of the place with pitchforks. He didn't really like hot drinks of any kind, but in this country they were used as a sort of essential social lubricant, to fill awkward moments or sad ones or happy ones. A hot day? Make some tea. Raining? Make some tea. Your wife just died? Kettle's boiling.

'No thanks, I'm fine.' Was Brida trying to put him off? 'I wanted to check Niamh's work diary, if you still have access to it. See what she was doing that day.'

'Oh. Well, I do, actually, we've a shared team one.'

'So anything she was up to that day, it would be in there? If she was out of the office?'

'It should have been.' Clee's efficient voice floated over the partition. 'Otherwise we don't know who's where.'

'Great. So, you can check for me?'

Brida hesitated. Was it loyalty, respecting the privacy of her dead friend?

'Of course,' said Clee again. 'I can check, if you want, Brida?'

A slight eye-roll from Brida. 'No, you're grand, I'll do it.'

Josh understood now why Niamh had always said the younger woman was gunning for their jobs. Brida wheeled herself to her desk and began tapping away.

Josh looked around him. The office was a depressing space,

despite the photos and funny signs, and it made him sad that Niamh had spent so much of her life between these walls, instead of out in the sun, not that there was much sun in Belfast. 'It just says private appointment,' said Brida, showing him the screen. In among the meetings and reminders, a portion of Niamh's day on 5 February was blocked out in pink. Even looking at the date made Josh feel sick. Nothing remarkable when it started, just an ordinary work day, but by the end it was the date on Niamh's death certificate. On her headstone. The last day of her life.

'You've no idea what that meant? She didn't tell you where she was going?'

'I was off that day,' said Brida sadly. 'Jack had a cold. Maybe Clee . . . '

'I wouldn't have asked,' came Clee's voice from round the corner. 'It's very violating, and as HR professionals, we owe a duty of care. She just said she was having the morning off, and I didn't ask why.' Brida rolled her eyes at Josh.

'Susan?' Josh called.

'Eh?' The older woman wheeled herself round, panting at even that small effort.

'Do you know where Niamh was that morning, you know, when she . . . ?'

'I don't, pet, sorry. I thought maybe a hospital thing, but I don't know for sure.'

Josh was wondering how Niamh, so sunny and open, could have managed to keep her plans from her three professionally nosy colleagues, as well as from him. They'd shared everything. Hadn't they? Frustratingly, her own personal diary was on her phone, and he'd so far not been able to get into it. He'd thought he knew her password, at least roughly, from seeing her key it in a thousand times, but he'd never actually asked her what it was. He'd trusted her. The code he'd had in his head didn't work, anyway, and he'd given up trying, afraid to lock it for ever.

There was nothing more to learn here. 'OK. Thank you. Sorry for interrupting your work.'

Susan and Brida exchanged a look. Hesitantly, Susan said, 'Josh, pet . . . since you're here . . . No one ever came to pick up her stuff. You know, from her desk. We had to . . . they made us clear it out. We're meant to be getting someone new but you know what they're like, it'll be months yet no doubt, and in the meantime, we're covering it all with no overtime . . . '

As Susan was babbling, Brida fished a box out from under her desk. It had once contained printer paper, now it held Niamh's things – the items she had left in her desk, because she'd presumably expected to come back from her mysterious appointment safe and sound, with no one any the wiser.

He almost couldn't look at them for a moment. A bobble-head of Mother Theresa, a joke Christmas present from her brother Liam which had scandalised their mother, who'd made them all say a decade of the rosary in penance. A framed picture of Josh posing at some cliffs in Kerry, smiling when really he'd been utterly terrified that the high winds would buffet him over the edge. Niamh had made fun of him for being a 'city boy'. Various snacks and chocolate bars, elastic hairbands, worn-out pens, tampons, and what looked like a loose photograph. Why would she have it in a drawer and not pinned up with the others?

Josh didn't want to take the photo out in front of the women, so he forced a smile. 'Thank you. It's nice to have these things. Like a little piece of her.'

Susan was softening into tears. 'Ah pet, we loved her, so we did. We're lost without her.'

Brida was already sniffling, rooting through her desk for a tissue.

'The workload's been challenging,' admitted Clee, a disembodied voice. 'Niamh was . . . everybody liked her. That went a long way to smoothing things over. Even if she was, you know, a bit . . . ' She silenced herself before she said more, and Josh was glad, because he couldn't handle a scene right now.

Brida made one last-ditch attempt to force tea on him – 'You're sure now, I'm making one anyway?' – and he escaped, carrying the box with her few possessions in it. He walked back to the car, the items rattling with each step, and got inside the warm, cushioned exterior. The box rested beside him on the passenger seat, where Niamh would once have been. What it made him think of was grave goods, the Egyptian princess in the Ulster Museum, mummified with things she'd need in the afterlife. Would Niamh need a Country Harvest granola bar, which he kept telling her had more sugar than a KitKat, or a bobble-head of a dead missionary, or a pack of fluorescent-yellow Post-its? She didn't need anything now. That was another shock of death, that someone who left as long a trail as she did – hair elastics, crumbs, shoes – could suddenly minimalise so effectively. Nothing left of her but memories. Memories and questions, which he was still no closer to answering. And he was going to be late for work. Maggie, his boss, was understanding, but he had started to take the piss a bit, and he knew it.

But he couldn't leave it, all the same. Josh lifted out the photograph. It was of a young man, a teenager really, dressed in a tux, smiling. A handsome kid with a curtains haircut, no one Josh recognised. Too tall and fair to be her brother Liam. He couldn't tell exactly when the picture had been taken, but it looked old, from the 1980s, perhaps.

Why would Niamh have a picture of a stranger in her desk?

2. CHANGE YOUR ROUTINE

Caroline

One of the suggestions in Sylvia's book was something Caroline found personally offensive – *change your routine*. She didn't need a new routine – hers was already perfect, thanks very much, worked out over many years of fine-tuning.

Every day she woke up at six, drank tea in bed while meditating with an app called *Calmerama*, a soothing-voiced woman telling her to imagine she was in a forest glade, which to be honest didn't sound all that relaxing to Caroline – what if you stepped in squirrel poo, or got pine needles on yourself? Then she showered, body-brushed, flossed, these days doing her best to think of nothing while she was in the bathroom. It was just a room, that was all. She was practical, she wasn't going to dwell on things. Then she put on ironed clothes left out the night before. Ate porridge and flaxseed while catching up on the news. Filled her travel mug with coffee to save paying a fortune in a café (gougers, they were), picked up her coat and keys which were always left by the door ready to go, and went to work, where she wrangled small children all day. After work she went to the gym, cooked a healthy meal, watched highbrow TV, often with subtitles. She also had routines for the week – cleaning, phone calls to parents and friends, sheet changing – and month – car wash, social life, pedicure, Facetiming her nieces in Australia. But she had to admit, the absence of Anto had left gaping holes in her day. It was him who used to bring the morning tea and cook dinner half the time, and prop up against her on the sofa in front of something engrossing. *'Breaking Bad?'* *'Aye.'* Sipping tea and sometimes eating the one biscuit Caroline allowed herself a day. Then, a single pound of extra fat was not allowed to accumulate on her body – she could feel it, and would adjust accordingly. Alone, she had started to eat more, pick up a bag of Haribo with the shopping, or a chocolate cake. There was no Anto now to hoover up the majority and gain no weight, so she filled the long evenings with sugar. It was better than booze, she told herself, as she held her breath to squeeze into her jeans. Although she was drinking more as well. She'd never liked to drink alone, but now, when she was out, in the pub with Josh, or having lunch with Jenny, she gave in more easily to the 'ah go on, sure what's the harm?' self-indulgence she'd never allowed herself in the past – another gin, a Prosecco, a mimosa. She could see it in her face when she cleansed – sagging cheeks, bloodshot eyes. *Anto, your girl is letting herself go.* That was the scary thing about being alone. There was no one to stop you as you rattled around the house, like a pea in zero gravity. Too much freedom. She realised that what she needed was to fill up her time. So maybe Sylvia had a point.

The next night, she leafed through the binder while waiting for her sad-pizza-for-one to cook through. In the section on routine, Sylvia listed all the things she had tried in order to overcome grief – reiki, flower arranging, martial arts even. Caroline raised her eyebrows and considering texting Josh a round-mouth emoji at that. Art appreciation, Saga holidays, jewellery making, volunteering, support groups, cooking. Anything to stave off the horror of a silent, empty house, that one particular person was never coming home to, not ever.

Caroline had a familiar feeling, the one that was like an elevator sinking down and down. Maybe things weren't going to get better. Maybe this was her life now, for ever. She already had hobbies – yoga with Jenny, singing in a choir, gouging haphazardly at her flowerbeds – and none of it helped. None of it would bring Anto back. How would changing her carefully calibrated routine make a difference? All the same, she resolved to try it, and thought, resentfully, that she knew enough of her own conscientiousness to realise she'd actually do it.

Sure enough, the next morning her alarm went off even earlier than usual. Caroline wished she was the type to ignore it, lie in bed, ring in sick even. But she wasn't, and it was too late now to change her goody-goody, arse-licky ways. So she got up, showered, dressed. So far the same routine. Then she made herself leave the house without her usual warming bowl of porridge, eaten plain as befitted a weekday morning (Caroline had inherited from her mother a suspicion of coddling oneself too much). The air was brisk and chilly, and she pulled her blue scarf around her neck. Anto's sister Julie, mother of Irish-dancing Grainne, had given it to her for Christmas, and Anto had expressed disbelief that she could have any use for 'another bloody scarf'. This from a man who'd owned only two pairs of shoes when she met him. The memory took a familiar form. Warmth, laughter creasing the edges of her mouth, then a slamming down of iron doors. Anto was dead. This store of memories of him was finite now, and soon would be worn thin and insubstantial, like potpourri with its scent all gone.

She increased her pace. No sense in dwelling on it. Keep moving, that's what she had to do. There was a café between the school and home that she passed every day, looking in with disapproval and jealousy at all the adults who had the time to loiter over lattes and pancakes on a workday. What did they do, with their Macs and headphones? They couldn't all be students, surely. Today, she pushed the door open, feeling the warm coffee-scented air of the place envelop her, the noise surround her. She took a seat and picked up the menu, printed in a fake-typewriter retro-y font, on a wooden clipboard. Stupid. She'd no idea what half the things were. Avocado toast. Dukkah, whatever that was. Belfast was so trendy these days. When the waitress came over she made herself smile and ask for pancakes. Her husband was dead. There was no reason to try and stay slim.

'D'you want a wee bit of bacon with that?' The girl had tattoos up and down her arms, and Caroline wanted to ask had they hurt, but was too polite. Cassie had a tattoo of Lisa's name on her wrist, and the thought intrigued Caroline, but she could only imagine her mother's reaction. *Have you joined a biker gang or something, Caroline, is that it?*

'Sure, why not.'

She waited for her food. She was warm, the place was bustling and smelled nice, she had plenty of time before work. Maybe old Sylvia was onto something. Caroline knew from her diligent self-help reading that getting out of your routine could actually rewire your brain, force you to pay attention to your surroundings. Up to now, she hadn't wanted that, since her surroundings were usually the place Anto had died. But this café was a place they'd never been to together – he was more of a pub kind of guy, which in retrospect had been part of the problem. Caroline was smiling around her, feeling vaguely benevolent towards the world, when her gaze swept over to the corner and she froze.

Babies. So many babies. Crying ones, plump happy ones,

ones with shocks of hair, ones in Babygros and ones big enough to stand on unsteady feet. A toddler group. A world she had never been part of, the daytime meet-ups, the singalongs, the hours at home with a tiny helpless being. Caroline switched chairs, turning her back to the group, and when the waitress came with the latte she looked puzzled. Caroline forced a smile. 'That's lovely, thank you.'

Although her back was turned, she was painfully aware of the babies behind her, the crying and gurgling and *there there, eat your organic raspberries pet, don't spit them onto Mummy's top.* She'd always known she would be a good mother – she was firm but kind, and she understood kids and wasn't afraid to get her hands dirty. But she had to face the facts. If she couldn't get Anto's sample from the clinic, there was a good chance she wouldn't meet someone else in time, and that meant she would never be one. She'd be childless.

As Caroline's mouth filled with bitter coffee, she resolved to get on and find a lawyer, as quick as she could.

Josh

Sometimes, when he was half-asleep just before his alarm went off, Josh would find himself in a kind of loop reliving that last morning. You never know it's the last morning, of course, with accidents and suicide and heart attacks. He never thought he'd be jealous of people who had to watch their loved ones slip slowly away in an agony of cancer, but he was. At least they knew it was coming. At least they could say goodbye.

The truth was he barely remembered that morning – there'd been nothing remarkable about it at all. Niamh had seemed normal as far as he recalled, taking too long in the shower, singing 'One Day More' from *Les Misérables*, a musical Josh hated with the fire of a thousand suns, leaving toast crumbs all over the kitchen. Pressing a jammy mouth onto his. His last words to her were, 'Could you not leave the place in a total state like yesterday?' Not: *I love you.* Not: *Please be careful crossing the road.* Not: *Where the hell are you going today?* Just a moan about toast crumbs. He'd relived that moment every day since.

Then his alarm would go off and he'd find himself living through a version of the same day again. Shower, dress, breakfast. Except now everything in the house was as clean as he'd left it the night before. No blonde hairs plastered in the soap, no steamed-up mirror with smiley faces drawn on it. No socks strewn in the general area of, but not inside, the laundry basket. The worst thing was he thought he'd wanted this. And now here he was, alone in his clean house with his heart breaking.

Then he'd drive to work, as he had that day. It had been an adjustment when he moved here, losing his Tube reading time, but he'd switched to true-crime podcasts and enjoyed shouting along to political panel shows on the radio as he fought the Belfast traffic. Work was at a paper called the *Belfast Chronicle*. His boss, Maggie, was a tough, chain-smoking reporter who'd been shot at more times than he'd had hot dinners, as she liked to tell him. She'd lost part of a finger when the Jeep she'd been riding in hit a pipe bomb, back in 1987. Josh was more than a little intimidated by Maggie.

He'd arrive at the office, in a depressing block surrounded by a windswept car park. Then he'd pop on his lanyard, pick up his KeepCup of coffee, lock the car, go into work. It was the same every day. Then it was just a matter of sitting at his desk waiting, pretending to work, as the clock ticked around to the time Niamh had died. Thinking – *I didn't know by now. I didn't know. I was happy at this point. I got a Twix from the vending machine. Oisin gave me a flyer for his ska band. I said maybe I'd come but I didn't mean it. Maggie asked me to work a story about expenses at the City Council. I said,* Sure thing boss, *even though I'd hoped for something a bit meatier. I didn't know. I didn't know. Then – the phone rang.*

And then I did know. And I'll never be the same.

That was one of the hardest things, he thought. The implacable linear nature of time. That he could never go back to that morning before, the minute before, even, when Niamh was already dead on the street and he didn't know, and he was half-heartedly googling red-faced councillors who believed the world was only five thousand years old, and thinking about eating the second bar of his Twix. They didn't tell him over the phone what had happened. It was policy, maybe. It was a nurse calling, an unfamiliar country accent, asking was this Mr Mkumbe, and she actually knew how to pronounce it which was impressive, and she said was his wife Niamh Donnelly. Niamh hadn't taken his name and Josh was fine with that – her family were so much a part of her. He'd said yes, not even alarmed yet, and then she said where she was calling from and he knew.

Then he'd got up and run out of the office, and he didn't think he'd even told Maggie he was leaving, and he still remembered her blinking at him as he ran past, her half-finger tapping against her coffee cup.

He didn't remember much of the drive to the hospital, and realised later he should have taken a cab, because finding a parking spot and paying for it lost him valuable time, and anyway he was half-deranged with fear. But it wouldn't have mattered anyway, those few minutes. Niamh had died seconds after the car hit her, from a catastrophic head injury. That was how the doctor described it when she met Josh at the reception of A&E – *I'm sorry but your wife has suffered a catastrophic head injury* – and he knew from the way she said his name that it was bad, but all the same he clung to hope until she actually said the word that ended it all. First she'd said, *I'm so sorry but Niamh did not recover consciousness.* He didn't know what that meant, his brain wouldn't process it, so he said, *Will she be OK?* The pity on the doctor's face, seared into his memory for ever, the freckle on her nose and the gold wedding ring on her thin hand. *Do you understand, Josh? Niamh is dead. She has died.*

That time, before being told for sure, was much worse than the time before the phone rang, but much better than after he was told, because he still had hope.

Then he was taken to a small quiet room with a cross on the wall. 'I'm sorry,' said the doctor. 'She just ran out. The driver had no chance. The police are here but – it's clear it wasn't his fault. I'm sorry.'

I'm sorry, I'm sorry. So many people would say that to him afterwards, but it was no one's fault except her own. Oh Niamh. Sitting at his desk, he ran through his questions again. What was she up to that day? Why did she have that photograph of a boy he didn't recognise? Was it something innocent, or somehow linked to what happened to her? Why was she in that place, at that time? Why had she run? He had no idea.

'City Boy.'

Now, Josh looked up; Maggie was standing over him.

'Oh, hi, sorry. Just thinking.' He wondered if Maggie knew he couldn't do any work now until after 11.35 a.m., which was when the phone had rung that day. It was as if his body knew to the second when he'd lost her.

'How's that expenses story coming?'

'Oh. Yeah. Well, they're all fiddling. They don't even try to hide it. Can't prove it, though.'

Josh had tracked down a possible source, a recently fired assistant at City Hall called Davina, but she wasn't answering his messages and no one else would talk. Part of him knew he'd work harder on the story if he weren't so deranged by loss. It had been months already and he'd not written a word.

Maggie inclined her head. She was old school, still smoked out her office window, and her nails were short and yellowed. She had been very beautiful back in the day, a fierce and fearless young journalist who'd jump over grenades, plunge into riots, down a bottle of whiskey with the lads. 'Josh. Have you ever thought about writing something a bit more ... personal?'

'Hm?'

She sighed. 'It sounds like complete bollocks to me, but you know our online readership isn't exactly setting the world on fire.' Older people bought the *Chronicle* for the funeral information, the crossword, the classifieds, but younger people didn't do any of those things, and they hadn't migrated online, either. No wonder, since the website was a clunky monstrosity filled with late 1990s-era Clip Art. 'The owners think we could pep things up with some personal *essays*.' She said the word viciously. 'Imagine. This place, Belfast, it used to be a non-stop news machine. Shootings. Bombings. Scandals every day of the week. Now we're just like everywhere else.' She sighed, apparently nostalgic for the cut and thrust of living in a war zone. 'So what do you say? Want to write a personal piece?'

'What about?'

Maggie's eyes flashed to the photo of Niamh on his desk. One of his favourites, it showed her posing on a beach by a rubbish sandcastle she'd built. Her legs in shorts were turning blue; it was Ireland after all. But she'd insisted. *We have to enjoy the weather!* 'I saw your wee Facebook rant. Got a lot of responses, didn't it?'

'Oh. Yeah, I just got a bit . . . fed up. People mean well, but they say some stupid things.'

'I agree. And I've never read much about being a widower. Everyone assumes the husbands'll go first. So you'll write something?'

'You mean . . . about Niamh?' Josh frowned.

'Yeah. What it's like to lose your wife at whatever age you are, twenty-three.' She knew he was thirty-four.

Josh weighed it up. On the one hand, he despised that trajectory of journalism, mining your heart and soul for clicks, baring your worst secrets in the hope of stirring up a Twitter controversy. On the other hand, it would be easier than following overfed councillors around or reporting on the latest non-doings of the Assembly, which had been suspended for three whole years, and he didn't understand why that wasn't a national scandal. And maybe, just maybe, someone would see it who knew why Niamh had been there that day, and they'd get in touch. It was a long shot, but so was everything else he could think of. 'OK,' he said. 'I'll try.'

'Great. Two thousand words. Due next week.'

As Maggie stomped off, pausing to berate the layout manager about some wonky margins, his eyes flicked to the clock: 11.42 a.m. A weary sadness washed over him. He'd got through it for another day. *Now I'm driving to the hospital. I don't know it, but she's already dead. She's already gone.* And he realised Sylvia was right. There was no point in carrying on his usual routine, spending every morning paralysed as he waited for the clock to tick around. He had to try something else instead.

3. HAVE A CLEAR-OUT

Caroline

One thing no one told you about being a widow was the sheer bloody admin involved. Caroline and Anto had never got around to setting up a joint bank account, and in any case she hadn't wanted him to see exactly how much she spent getting her hair done (Anto had been known to cut his own hair with nail scissors). She'd paid for some things – the window cleaner, the mortgage – and he'd paid for others – Netflix, the milkman, the house insurance. Now he'd gone, without leaving so much as a list of passwords, and she had to wade through the baffling tangle by herself. Who knew you had to get a death certificate when someone died? Caroline hadn't. The only people who'd ever died on her had been her grandparents – apart from Granny Mary, who was still alive, going strong at eighty-four, doing t'ai chi once a week at the village hall – and all she'd had to do then was hand around ham sandwiches at the wake, made in a kind of grim assembly line in the kitchen by her Auntie Theresa and Auntie Connie.

Now here she was, still with a living grandmother, and she was a widow. Her husband, only thirty-eight years old, was dead. Sometimes she turned the figures over in her head, thinking how crazy it was, that the numbers looked about-face. Eighty-three, that was an age you'd die at, though nowadays maybe not even then. And you didn't just need one death certificate, you needed a whole clatter of them, because places wouldn't accept a photocopy or even just showing it off your phone, and if you didn't know to ask for multiple copies you'd be traipsing back there to the records office week after week. It was 2019, for God's sake. Why did paper still hold so much sway? You had to go down there, in the grip of your grief and madness, and report your husband dead and ask for multiple copies of the bloody thing, then take that to the bank and the phone company and the mortgage people, and she didn't know the account numbers because everything was in Anto's email inbox, which she couldn't get into since he didn't have it on his phone, an old-school model he'd insisted worked just fine.

Caroline was on her knees in the spare room, rooting through a pile of papers in search of something, anything from the fertility clinic that might prove Anto hadn't meant to tick the stupid box. *God Anto, why were you such a slob?* The state of his paperwork, stuffed into an old box that had once held a limited-edition *Star Wars* figurine. He'd queued for four hours to get it, and when Caroline called him an eejit he reminded her she'd once camped out in the rain to get Garth Brooks tickets (zero regrets, one of the best nights of her life). How she wished he had carried on loving *Star Wars* or any other stupid old thing, instead of gradually loving nothing. Not even her. Not enough to stay alive, anyway.

She put the thought aside and kept rooting. So much endless rubbish, the dandruff of a life. A wristband for a concert in 2009. Electricity bills from the house he'd been living in when they met, him and four other boys who drove up from the country every Sunday night with vast Tupperware cake-boxes full of sandwiches their mammies had made. Had they come to the funeral, the 'boys' (all in their late thirties now)? She didn't know. Caroline wished almost every day she could remember the funeral more. All those people there for Anto, loving him, saying nice things about him, and she'd been out of her head with grief (plus the mysterious yellow pill her Auntie Connie had slipped to her before the ceremony, saying, *Don't tell your mammy now, pet*), and she could hardly remember a moment. *I wasn't ready, Anto. If you'd died at a normal age I'd have made sure to be awake and not high for your funeral. Or, you know, if you'd thought to give me a bit of notice you were going to die.*

Caroline sighed. Suddenly it all felt overwhelming, the pile of paperwork, the mountain of admin she still had to clear. Anto's clothes in the wardrobe, his toothbrush still in the bathroom where he'd died. Sylvia's book suggested having a clear-out, but it wasn't so easy. Josh had admitted he'd not got very far with clearing Niamh's things either, and she understood that. It was hard to make your brain understand they really weren't coming back for their belongings, their shirt or wallet or the old razor still clogged with their hairs.

As she was scooping papers out of the box – she would have to sort them sometime, though most of them could just be shredded, all these documents that had once been vital, even Anto's passport and degree certificate, because he was gone, and that nullified everything, a lifetime of bureaucracy in an instant becoming landfill – she saw something. A glossy leaflet had slipped to the floor. She bent to pick it up. *Consent for DNA storage*, it said. *What you need to know.*

It could have been innocuous – Anto had been an inveterate picker-upper of clutter - but something told her it wasn't. Standing in the cramped office, the empty house silent around her, Anto's guitar unplayed in the corner (could she bear to charity shop it? Maybe one of his nephews would want it?), the remnants of her husband's life in a box – she knew suddenly where she had seen this leaflet before. In the waiting room of the IVF clinic, warm and wood-panelled, Anto clicking and clicking his pen as he filled the form in, restless, she'd thought because of the upcoming plastic-cup scenario.

But had something else been on his mind back then? Had he already known this day would come, that even as he was about to give his sample, he was planning ways to prevent her using it? It didn't make any sense, and for the thousandth time she wished she could talk to him, just for five minutes, to ask where the lid of the juicer was and what was the password for Netflix, oh and did he actually not want to have a child with her? Had he never wanted that? Because maybe he could have mentioned it, if so?

Oh Anto. I can't believe you did this. You absolute bastard. Caroline kicked his guitar as she went out, the discordant twang following her down the stairs into her clean, perfect, lifeless living room.

Josh

That stupid book of Sylvia's. He found himself resenting it, the very idea that a collection of scribbled pages might make any difference to the well of grief he found himself in. All the same, he was doing it. At least it took his mind off his other quest, his attempt to find out what had happened to his wife. The next item in Sylvia's book was *have a clear-out*.

> It's tempting to hang onto your loved one's things for ever, but this is just delaying the process of moving on. Think of all the happy customers at the charity shop who can benefit from their possessions.

He felt vaguely bad about Sylvia, how dusty the house was, how lonely she seemed in that old place by herself. He'd go to visit her again. He knew Caroline would anyway, but he shouldn't leave it all up to her. Emotional labour, Niamh had started calling it, after reading a book entitled *Woman's Work*. All the same, he wasn't sure he was up to helping another person. Like on a plane, he needed to fit his own oxygen mask before helping others, and he was choking, suffocating in grief and mystery and confusion.

He didn't know who would be keen to buy Niamh's clothes, which reminded him of a scene in *The Sound of Music* about the poor not wanting Maria's worst dress, a film which Niamh had made him watch at least once a month whenever she had a hangover or PMT or just felt sad. She had been a bargain-hunter, a Primark girl, Zara at a push, and her collection of cheap polyester work trousers and blouses, plus holey jeans on the weekend, wouldn't bring a glint to the eye of the Oxfam store manager.

He'd been putting this off since it happened, fighting off the advances of her various sisters and friends, who seemed to feel he should immediately empty the house of everything she'd owned. Because that was what you had to do, when someone wasn't coming back. Maybe it was the same urge that made Irish people rush a body into the ground in two days of manic activity and drinking. Get it done. Then take stock. Rip the plaster off, but take the leg with it. Josh wasn't sure what had happened to the things she'd been wearing that day – they were ruined, no doubt. Blood everywhere, torn from the impact on the tarmac. Her handbag, which had been thrown clear of the accident, had been returned to him, and he'd gone through it several times but found nothing of interest, just a lot of fluffy mints, and yet more tissues.

Now he stood at the doorway of their room, which still contained so much of her. The book she had been reading when she died, *Harry Potter* for the seventeenth time. Her winter coat hanging on the door, which she hadn't taken to work with her that day, since it had been quite mild (Niamh had an Irish person's over-optimism about the weather, and could be found turning blue from March onwards with bare legs and arms).

God, there was a lot of it. Niamh was a pack-rat who'd never had to clean up after herself– it was a wonder they didn't have mice. A pen leaked all over his hand, and he went to the bathroom sink, scrubbing it irritably. All her handbags would have to go in the bin, he concluded. Her coats were equally bad, the pockets full of lint and even more tissues. The woman had never been near a dry-cleaner until Josh, taking one of his suits in, had asked if she had anything to go too. She'd frowned. 'What kind of things do you dry-clean? Is it not just like duvets and tents and that?'

Tents. Tents! It had been a joke between them, the idea of dry-cleaning a tent. *Well, how else do you clean them*, said Niamh, laughing. The memory hurt, a thin blade between his ribs.

He made a pile. Skirts, jeans, bally socks, pants with holes in, bras with the underwire poking out. She hadn't seduced him with her lingerie, that was for sure. She couldn't even say the word without putting on a seedy, deep-breathing voice. *It's your birthday, big boy. Maybe I'll wear some … lingerie.* And then she'd burst out laughing. Jumpers her mammy had knitted when she was a teenager, full of dropped stitches and dog hairs from the family pets. Her books, dog-eared and swollen from being dropped in the bath. Her jewellery, such as it was, cheap and tarnished and tangled. The hospital had given him back her wedding and engagement rings, taken from her dead hand.

They were in a Ziploc bag in his chest of drawers. He couldn't bear to look at them, remember the day he'd given the diamond to her, on a blustery walk in the Botanical gardens, her glasses fogging up in the steam of the palm house, the splash of terrapins in the water. Niamh had loved it there, and when she turned around to ask something about whether terrapins were the same as turtles and saw him holding the ring she had screamed, right out loud, and for a moment he hadn't known if she was scared or just surprised.

There was nothing unusual in her clothes, not in her pockets or slipped inside a book or hidden at the bottom of a drawer. Just rubbish. He looked up at the box of junk she'd collected from her childhood and refused to throw out, gathering dust on top of the wardrobe. Josh, growing up in a series of tiny London homes, then moving countries, was much less attached to things. Now Niamh was gone, he wished even more that he'd known her as a child, the funny little precocious thing her family described, with blonde curls and a sing-song voice, doing her party piece at adult gatherings and demanding sweets. He'd had so little of her, and now she had run out. There would be no more Niamh in the world. But maybe there was some clue in there? Inside the box were drawings, stiff with old paint, flaking off and leaving a mess on the floor. Josh sighed; he'd have to get the hoover out. One appeared to be some kind of Confirmation preparation project. Niamh had been delighted when she found out Josh's family were Catholic too, even though his were Catholic by way of Nigeria, the faith exported there by people like her ancestors, now sent back in the form of African priests.

Ten-year-old Niamh had dutifully filled in the questions about the gifts of the Holy Spirit and so on. She had written and crossed out many options for her confirmation name – *Charlene.*

Holly. Miranda – before settling on the rather prosaic 'Catherine'. Since there wasn't a Saint Charlene, it was probably for the best. He leafed through, idly, smiling at the ten-year-old she'd been, the dreams she'd had. What do you want to be when you grow up? *A nurse. Or else a pop singer.* Who is your best friend? *Karen Cole.* This was then viciously crossed out, some kind of pre-teen argument, probably. They were still friends, Niamh and Karen, so they must have made up. She'd been at the funeral, had pressed his hands with her cold red ones, as so many did. *Ah Josh, I'm so sorry.* One question in the booklet said: Will you have children when you grow up? Niamh had written: *Yes I will have five children.*

His smile faded. She never would now.

The night stretched ahead of him, work then just a stir-fry and a round of Xbox, surrounded by the discarded, worn possessions of his untidy wife, which he had still not finished going through. Her essence everywhere, coating it like a fine dust. Piled on the bed were her handbags, five or six imitation-leather jobs with grease or ink stains on them. He picked up one of them, brown leatherette with two handles, and feeling deeply dispirited, rooted around inside. He'd actually planned to get Niamh a real Marc Jacobs for her Christmas, but she'd found out and told him he was an eejit, the one from the market was just as good and only fifteen quid. That was her all over. Cheap and cheerful, and irreplaceable.

He was just about to throw it out when something made him check inside one more time, for anything other than junk, and there it was. A scrap of paper his roaming fingers had almost missed. He drew it out. On it was scribbled an address, an unfamiliar one, but which he knew from looking was near where she'd been killed.

Caroline

'I'm sorry,' said the fertility doctor, but in a sort of bland, professional way, gazing over Caroline's shoulder. It made her blood boil. *You're not sorry! You don't care at all, you'll be onto the next patient in five minutes.* 'If your husband ticked the box to not preserve the material . . .'

Caroline gritted her teeth. She'd had to fight hard to even get the doctor to see her, since she wasn't a current patient, and was painfully aware of her allotted slot ticking away.

'Material?' She couldn't help interrupting, though she knew her mother would have dropped dead on the spot at the thought of contradicting a medical professional. *Yes, doctor. Of course, doctor. May I kiss your feet, doctor?* 'Is that what you call it?'

He had the grace to look momentarily ashamed. 'The . . . sample. I'm afraid either of you had the right to prohibit the procedure from going ahead, and he did. So there we are.'

'But . . . what if he ticked the wrong box on the form?'

The doctor frowned. 'You think he'd have wanted you to use it?'

'Why wouldn't he? It took so much to get this far.' Frustration made her clench her teeth. If only she could ask him.

'Only you can answer that, Mrs Hooper,' he said smoothly. A glance at the clock.

'It's *Ms*. So it'll just be destroyed.'

The doctor put his pen down. 'Caroline. I know you must be devastated by your husband's death . . .'

No, she wanted to correct him, *I'm coping very well, everyone says so*. Instead she just tutted.

'The thought that you can't have his child – I'm so sorry, I really am. But that's why we have the forms, so we can respect people's wishes when they're gone.'

'But I don't think this *was* his wish. I think he was, I don't know, he didn't read the form properly or he wasn't in his right mind. I mean he killed himself, of course he wasn't in his right mind.' She felt despair rise up in her chest. 'There must be something I can do? Wasn't there some court case, where a woman wanted her dead husband's sperm but they wouldn't let her?'

The doctor sighed, clearly thinking, *God spare me from mad women*. 'In that case the deceased had signed a form to give consent for the material's use, but it had expired. The widow went to court to change the laws on expiration dates.'

'But she won, yes?'

'Yes.'

'So I could do the same? Go to court?'

She had a feeling he was choosing his words very carefully. 'This clinic is bound by current HFEA guidelines. But if you were to challenge those guidelines in court, we would of course follow the revised ones. In the meantime, as a goodwill gesture, we'll maintain the sample free of charge.' This was said nonchalantly, as if to cover up what a huge, huge thing it was he was telling her. What he was saying was this: there was hope.

Josh

'Thanks, Darragh, thanks Clare, I'm fine, honestly I am. I just ... need to make a phone call.' Josh shut the door behind him, breathing in the cold night air of the Donnelly family's back garden. A swing-set built in the 1980s, a whirligig washing line, garden gnomes dotted here and there, watching him accusingly. They were lovely, really they were, Niamh's family. When he came to the door that night, they'd all hugged him,

86

and even taciturn Daddy patted his shoulder extra hard, and before long Josh was embroiled in one of their loud and shouty conversations about whether Mammy and Daddy should subscribe to Netflix, sure they could just use Siobhan's password, why waste your money, but then Daddy gets confused about all that rubbish Siobhan's weans do be watching, superhero this and monster that, and he just wants a nice documentary about Hitler, and Liam, the brother, was losing his patience trying to explain about profiles, *what in the name of God is a profile?* And Josh just had to get out for a minute. Which was easier said than done. He was tempted to invent a smoking habit, just as an excuse to be alone.

What was he doing here? This wasn't his world, semi-rural Ireland with intense opinions about potatoes and local politicians he'd never heard of, decades-long grievances against the neighbours about the status of something called the Big Hedge. He thought of his mother's words in her last message: *Come home, baby. Come home where you belong.*

But no. He couldn't do that until he knew what had happened to Niamh. She had gone to a street she shouldn't have gone to, and she had a strange picture in her desk, and an address in her bag, but he didn't know how these things were connected. Her friends seemed not to know, either, so his options were limited. He'd hoped the family might reveal something, but of course they never talked about real things. He would have to ask if he wanted to know, and he didn't even know how to form the question. It was so hard.

He heard the door open beside him and someone stepped out. It was Niamh's oldest sister, Siobhan. Without speaking, she took something from the pocket of her long cardigan, and he saw the flare of a match as she lit a cigarette. 'Want one?'

Josh was a little shocked, which was ridiculous, because she was a grown woman. 'Oh – no. I didn't know you smoked.'

She took a deep drag. 'Now and again. Don't tell Mammy.' Siobhan was almost fifty, and her eldest daughter Lucy had a toddler herself already, but that was how things worked in Ireland. You never escaped the wrath of your mammy, even when you were a grandma yourself. 'How are you, Josh? I saw your wee Facebook post. Sorry it's been rough. People don't know what they're saying half the time.'

The Facebook post had got a lot of responses, from crying-faced emojis to heartfelt comments urging him to reach out, that various people were there for him. He still felt totally alone. He shrugged now, which Siobhan probably couldn't see in the dark. He'd never been sure if Siobhan liked him or not. She'd been in her teens when Niamh was born, and he'd always had the impression she held as much sway in the family as the parents. She was the one to win over, even more than placid Mammy and silent Daddy. 'You know how it is. One day at a time.'

'It's like the heart of us got cut out,' she said, quietly. 'But what can you do? Life goes on. Lucy's pregnant again, sure. I'll be a granny twice over. Can't believe it.'

That was the hardest part, almost, another baby in the family, one who would never even know Niamh. Great-auntie Niamh! And he'd be a great-uncle again, if that counted now his wife was dead. He thought of the collage of pictures on Niamh's cubicle wall in the office. Her family had meant everything to her. It was her mother's breast cancer that had sent Niamh rushing back across the Irish Sea, away from her fun life and good job and burgeoning relationship in London, and he still remembered how she'd broken the news to him, gulping and sobbing like a child when she turned up at the door of his little flat in Peckham Rye.

They'd been going out for less than a year then. It had taken him a while to get out of her that Pat was not terminal, it was stage two and hopefully treatable. 'I have to go back,' Niamh had wept. 'I have to be with them. I can't be here.' And Josh had weighed it all up, their relationship of just ten months, his job in London, his flat, his friends, his own family, all of that against Niamh, her blonde curls and green-framed glasses and sudden, bubbling laugh, and known with a sinking feeling that, yes, he was going to move to Belfast to be with this woman.

Now, he looked at her sister from the corner of his eye, her face half-lit by the glow of her cigarette. Probably she knew nothing, either. But he had to try.

'Siobhan . . . one thing that's really been bothering me. When Niamh – the day of the accident, I never understood why she was there. In that part of town, I mean. I even asked her work friends, and they didn't know. She'd booked out time from the office but they'd no idea what for. Was she – do you know if she was sick or something? It's near the hospital, kind of.' There had been an autopsy, which happened when there'd been a violent or sudden death. Josh didn't like to think about that – cutting into the body he'd loved so much – but he knew they'd found nothing. She had been perfectly healthy except for the injury to her head. He thought about showing Siobhan the photograph, or the address, but something stopped him. Maybe he didn't entirely trust her – and if Niamh had been keeping secrets, was it Josh's business to tell her family about them? He'd already scoured the photo albums Niamh had in the flat, not to mention gone over and over her Facebook pictures until he could have drawn them all from memory, and found no trace of the boy from the desk shot.

Siobhan took another drag. Then she said, 'I'd hardly be the one to know if she was.'

'What?'

But Niamh told Siobhan everything. She messaged her every day, checked every decision with her, secretly and not-so-secretly made it clear all the time that this was her favourite sister. Didn't she? *Hadn't* she, rather. Niamh would never message anyone again, and he imagined everyone who'd met her reading the last text or email they'd ever had from her, however banal it had been. Knowing it was the last time.

Siobhan was quiet for a moment. 'You didn't notice? The last few months?'

Josh didn't know what she meant, and then suddenly he did. It was true, they hadn't seen the Donnelly clan as much as usual before she died. Had Niamh stopped relying on her sister as much? Was she finally cutting the apron strings, as he'd often wished? He remembered the barbecue they'd been planning for Niamh's birthday at Easter (over-optimistic on the weather front again). 'We'll invite Siobhan, will we?' he'd said.

A cold: 'No. No family this time.'

He couldn't remember if he'd thought anything of it at the time, or had been relieved that they wouldn't have to suffer an onslaught of Donnellys every day for the rest of their lives. But yes, now that Siobhan mentioned it, there had been a cooling between Niamh and her family in the last few months. 'She fell out with everyone?'

'Only me.' Another drag. 'I wondered if you knew why. I hardly heard from her for months before . . . before.'

'Jesus, no, I didn't even notice until you said.' He felt ashamed. So much for knowing everything about his wife. 'You've no idea why?'

Was she hesitating? Again, smoking was useful for covering up your emotions, giving yourself a moment to think. Shame about the whole killing-yourself thing. She exhaled. 'No. I've no idea. Maybe it was nothing. She was just busy, could be.'

A bleakness rolled over Josh, the fact that he'd never be able to ask Niamh what had been wrong, that he'd never ask her anything again. That all their conversations were stopped dead, for ever. 'I'm sorry.'

Siobhan sighed. 'We're all sorry, Josh.' Without offering any words of comfort, she ground out her cigarette on the wall and went back inside, leaving him alone.

Caroline

Anto was there. In her work. Not something she'd ever seen before, this massive man among the tiny shelves and coat hooks the kids used.

'Er ... are you supposed to be here?' She came up behind him in the corridor, resisting the urge to run her hands up under his massive holey jumper. With his beard and his wild appearance, she was amazed he'd got past Gwen, the school secretary, who would have made an excellent MI5 operative, so reluctant was she to give out any kind of useful information.

He turned, and a huge smile broke out. Wolfish, she'd always thought. That hint of danger that thrilled her down to her neatly trimmed toenails. 'Baby. I just couldn't wait.'

'Oh?' A nervous shudder. Maybe he wanted to have her right now in the staff loos. She'd have to explain why that was a sackable offence, but maybe she could meet him somewhere en route from work.

'I've bought us a house.'

'What?' They had discussed buying somewhere, of course, but were only in stage two of Caroline's strategy – research and consolidation. She hadn't

even decided if she wanted old or newbuild, house or flat, brick or concrete, parking space or terrace. 'How is that possible?' He approached and picked her up off her feet. 'Anto! The kids!'

'What, they can't see that their teacher is the most wonderful woman in the world?'

'Put me down, love. Explain what you mean.' Use your words, she would have said to the kids, and sometimes being with Anto felt uncomfortably close to that.

He began to pace around the corridor. He could never stand still for long, always jiggling on his feet or whistling or throwing his keys up and down. 'I saw this amazing house, you see. I was just walking past and it called to me. It's so beautiful. A teal door, the same exact shade of duck feathers. Red brick, wisteria growing over it . . . '

Wisteria was pretty, but eventually it'd punch a hole in your brickwork. 'And . . . number of bedrooms? Bathrooms?'

He waved a hand. 'Does it matter?'

'Er, yes? Is there parking? I absolutely need a parking space, I'll lose my mind if I have to trawl around for one every day.'

He groaned. 'There's an apple tree in the garden. With a swing on it!'

'Does it need much work? Structural or cosmetic?'

Anto just stared at her, his face full of exasperated love. 'Baby. Where's your sense of poetry? This place, it's magical.'

'Not much poetry in leaking pipes or dry rot. What do you mean, anyway, you bought it?' He couldn't have. Not in one day.

'I put an offer in.' He sounded sulkier now.

'Ach, Anto. Without me even seeing it?' Even after knowing Anto for years she was incredulous.

'I thought it would be romantic! I wanted to carry you over the threshold. Tread softly, because you tread on my dreams . . . '

A twist of alarm went in Caroline's stomach. Quoting Yeats was something Anto did when he was on the verge of an episode. She stepped forward, *heedless of the children watching from every classroom door, and took his face in her hands.*

'It is romantic. Thank you. But . . . let me see it first?'

'All right.' He was practically pouting.

'And we'll get a full survey. For dry rot and rising damp and that.'

He sighed. 'You'll love it, honestly.'

'I'm sure I will. But I'll love it more if it doesn't have dry rot. Someone has to be practical. Text me the address, I'll meet you there after work.'

'Can't we go now?'

'Now I have to wrangle thirty eight-year-olds into thinking long division is fun.'

She looked about her – no obvious eyes on them. She planted a kiss on his lips. He tasted of whiskey, and she wondered fleetingly if the house decision had been made under the influence. He wasn't supposed to drink with the meds. Maybe she needed to take him back to the doctor, but the problem was, when an episode had taken root he wouldn't go.

These were all things Sensible Caroline thought. But the thing about Anto was he could chase Sensible Caroline away, let Fun Caroline come out. He was just excited. Maybe the house really was amazing. 'Meet me at four? Text me the address.'

'OK.' Mollified, he moved off down the corridor. Before turning out of sight, he whirled about and shouted, arms wide: 'I love Ms Hooper! I love her!'

'You eejit.' Caroline laughed. A large part of her thought it was charming, romantic, wild. Another part – a growing part – wondered if she needed to call his mother and ask her what to do.

Jenny was holding a glass of wine, peering out of the stained-glass window into Caroline's back garden. 'I don't know, love. It seems a shame, after all the work you put in.'

'You were the one said you didn't know how I could stay here!'

Caroline opened a bag of Kettle Chips and set them on the coffee table. She noticed how Jenny kept darting little glances upstairs, to where the bathroom was.

'I'm sorry. It was just – I was worried. But you love this place.'

'I know. But I'll need money.'

Caroline looked about her at the house Anto had found for them. As he'd said, it was beautiful – old red brickwork, stained glass above the door, roses in the back garden, the promised apple tree. As she'd worried, it had needed a ton of work, an overhaul of the electrics and plumbing, a new boiler, the partition wall knocked down between the poky living room and tacked-on kitchen. But she'd gone along with it, because it made him happy. Because she was doing her very best to not control everything, to let go, embrace life. And now she was maybe going to do a very Anto-like thing: put the house on the market, and use the money for her legal fees. She was seeing a lawyer soon and even that was expensive – it would mount up fast. If she failed, she may as well have heaped the cash up and set fire to it.

Caroline stood up. 'Well, I think I'll put it on, test the waters. I don't have to go through with the sale if I don't want to in the end, right?'

'I suppose.' Jenny still looked unsure. Caroline suppressed a dart of irritation. When Anto first died, everyone had assumed she'd sell the place, given what had happened there. What was different about selling it now?

'Can you check on the roast? I'll just finish this off.'

'Sure thing. I'm starving so I am – three weeks on the 5:2 and I could eat a scabby donkey.'

As Jenny trotted off to the kitchen, Caroline pulled her laptop over. She was glad Jenny was here, despite everything. Sundays were the worst day now she was alone. Too much space. The sense of other people out at brunch or on bracing walks, eating roast dinners in warm pubs. And of course this was the right thing to do. She could have everything she wanted – she just needed cash. If she'd learned anything from Anto's wild abandon, it was that sometimes money was worth spending. That it was just a symbol of what you could get with it. It was there to make you happy, and there was no point having it otherwise. And if that meant selling the house, their lovely house they'd worked on so hard, well, that was just what it took.

She bent over the computer once more, pushing aside the memory of her friend's doubtful face. She'd always thought of herself as steady, an anchor to her parents and brother and Anto and Jenny and everyone else she knew, with their problems and crises. Caroline did not have crises. She stood firm. But now Anto was gone and she was ricocheting around her life like a coin through a drinks machine. She'd have to go and visit her parents, too, and tell them her plan before they found out from someone else (country parents had eyes everywhere, even in the city). But despite all this, perhaps it was time to be selfish. Just a little bit. Just to get what she wanted most of all. She wondered if Anto would be ashamed of her, if he could see what a mess she was. Or if he'd realise it was his fault for leaving her. She couldn't sink under the weight of this. She had to keep going, hold her head above water.

As she clicked out of the estate agent's website, having firmly ticked the box for *I have a house to sell*, she silently spoke to Anto again. *Are you happy, babe? I finally learned to take a risk.*

4. TRY TO EAT WELL

Josh

People had been kind to Josh since he was widowed, there was no doubt about that. Niamh's family and friends, work colleagues, his own friends in England, they'd all done their best. People here followed the old ways – Mass cards in the post; food left at your door; strict mourning schedule, visiting the graveyard in rotation, a 'month's mind' for when you might be feeling adrift, and after a year had passed there'd be an anniversary mass, and then another, presumably on and on until no one who remembered Niamh was left. Since his Facebook post, the messages had been pouring in, more genuine this time. He felt vaguely guilty about his rant. People did care. It wasn't their fault Niamh was dead. It wasn't even the driver's fault – it was no one's fault but her own, running out into the road.

It helped, maybe, the rituals of grief. He didn't know. He'd never tried losing a wife without all this. So yeah, he had people, invitations to the cinema, to parties, to dinner, to play football or go round the Titanic museum (never would he understand the obsession with that place, or why they were so proud to begin with of building a ship that had famously sunk on its maiden voyage). Plenty of people to do things with. Trouble was, he didn't *want* to do things most of the time. It was a full-time job, grieving, reminding your exhausted brain and lonely arms that she wasn't there and wasn't coming back, not ever, yes really! Not ever.

But are you sure? What about next week? his brain would go.

I'm sure. Never.

Oh. Next year, maybe? Your birthday? She wouldn't miss your birthday, she loves them. Loved. Tenses were hard. A large part of his brain simply didn't accept that he would never see Niamh again. Sometimes it seemed as if it spoke with her voice, her teasing wonder at the world and his own London ways, playing up her homespun Irishness. *Go away with you! You never had to fast on Good Friday? Or even go to the Stations! Sure you don't know you're born, do you?*

There were people to do things with, yes, but no one just to *be* with. Slump on the sofa, mindlessly eating from the same jumbo bag of Doritos, hands red with crisp dust like some kind of terrible skin disease, laughing in a kind of wheezing symphony at episodes of *Parks and Recreation* they'd seen a hundred times. That was what he missed. Niamh's feet on the coffee table, her uncut toenails poking through one of her prized selection of animal-print socks. His hoody from university football, stained with bleach from cleaning the kitchen floor, something Niamh hadn't even realised you were supposed to do on the regular when he'd met her. Just . . . being. Perhaps you could have looked at them and said the magic was gone, hoofing pizza into their mouths and squabbling over the tub of garlic dip as they were, but he'd never seen it like that. Now those nights together seemed like precious gold, because there was no one to do nothing with. Now he was always alone, and the rest of the time he was acting, forcing a smile, aware of people watching to see if he was all right, ready to report back to girlfriends or husbands or parents, *Ah God love him, can you imagine? He must be in bits.* Then locking the door, snuggling down with their own partner in just-being, whoever it was. Ever since Niamh had died Josh felt he was on the outside looking in, an urchin with a face pressed to a bright window. He hated that.

It was Sunday night, and he had dragged himself through the week. He'd tried Sylvia's advice to make new friends, reach out to people, but he felt no different. He had tried changing his routine, too, going into work earlier the last few days. All that happened was he ended up doing more work for no extra money, and having to field some mad calls from readers annoyed about things in the previous edition of the paper. He'd finally done some decluttering, only to find something that had sent him into even more of a tail-spin. Now there was both a photograph and an address to make sense of, add to the growing pile of clues about Niamh's last moments, if they were even connected. He'd even tried asking Siobhan, and ended up only with more questions. If Niamh had fallen out with her sister, surely she would have told him – wouldn't she? On Friday night he'd gone to the pub on his way home, but had felt stupid, standing there with his pint among the other lonely men, the old ones staring into their beer, the younger ones in suits and frazzled expressions, turning wedding rings around on their fingers and blankly watching sport on the big screens, as if they didn't want to go home to their wives. Josh didn't want to be one of those men, because he'd have loved nothing else but to go home to his, but he would never be able to. It was fine going to the pub with Caroline, to laugh and talk and share a packet of crisps, but not on his own.

So he was at home. There was nothing on TV, just some local politics show that was incomprehensible to him, people arguing over flags and marches and battles from four hundred years ago, ridiculous if it wasn't the kind of thing that could get you shot. A pizza in a greasy box beside him, with the little white plastic thing from the middle – a yoke, Niamh would have called it, and a spasm went through him at the word, because he'd never heard anyone use it before he met her, and she used it for everything from the remote control to her credit card, *ah sure I'll put it on the yoke*. And it was such a perfect word.

Josh sighed. He was so tired of being alone. It was so hard, so boring, going through all this. Couldn't Niamh just come back now, and he'd agree to treasure her for ever and never criticise her holey socks or tell her to cut her toenails when they scraped him in bed? But there'd been things she was keeping from him, it seemed. She even used to tell him when she had a smear test, had made him come with her once so he could understand 'the female experience'. This strange secrecy was not like her. Or so he'd thought. If only he could ask her, what were you doing that day, and who is this teenage boy in the picture? And she would likely have given him some totally innocent answer, laughed at the way he was tying himself in knots over nothing.

His phone beeped – a sound that both cheered him, because it meant people, and ruined him, because it would never be Niamh again. Caroline had sent him a picture. Her own pizza, with only two slices gone, her feet propped up in socks which, he saw, had a fish pattern on them. *Saddo Sunday night for one*, she'd typed. *Isn't it shite? So much for the 'eat well' bit of Sylvia's book, eh?*

Shite, he agreed. *Did you only have two bits??*

It repeats on me, she wrote back. *I'm not cut out for carb bingeing. I've moved onto the Dairy Milk.*

What are you watching?

That thing with your man from Game of Thrones.

Your man. Another of Niamh's sayings, meaning *that man there*, or just 'a man'.

On impulse, Josh typed: *What would you call that thing in your pizza? The little white thing that keeps the lid off it?*

The yoke? said Caroline. *I just call it the pizza yoke. Why?*

Josh smiled to himself. Caroline and Niamh, they would have

102

really liked each other. He wished Niamh could have known that somehow, that he had a friend who was a woman, who'd have sided with her, shot her knowing looks across the table as they complained about Josh's selfish pizza-eating, his nerdiness about *Star Trek*, his insistence on listening to albums all the way through in order.

If you want, he found himself typing, *you can come over here and be sad with me.*

After he sent it, a strange moment of worry. Was it too much? Were they just support-group buddies? She wouldn't think something else, would she?

But she wrote back – *RU just after the rest of my pizza?*

He laughed out loud. *Busted.*

Fair enough. I'll come so. Your man is pure shite in this thing.

Caroline's leftover pizza turned out to have goat's cheese on it, which he hated but she seemed to love. 'It would never work between us,' she joked, as he turned up his nose at her offer of a slice, and something shifted in his stomach. Fear? Nerves? *It's just pizza, for feck's sake*, is what Niamh would have said.

They squabbled good-naturedly over what to put on TV, realised they both loved horror films but had never been able to watch them with their partners – Niamh was a total scaredy-cat, who couldn't even sit through *Stranger Things* without shrieking when the wind blew a branch against the window, and Anto's meds had given him horrible night-mares – then settled down with *Zombie Outbreak Four*. It was fun. Uncomplicated. Caroline had driven over in pyjama bottoms and a giant hoody that was clearly Anto's. Josh took his shoes off and put his feet on the sofa, and they barely talked, just posted pizza into their mouths and stared at the screen, and it was exactly what he needed.

Caroline

She had pictured the law office as a buzzing, warm haven, where people ran on coffee and justice (she'd been watching a lot of *The Good Wife* since Anto died). Instead, it was in a down-at-heel building near the docks, and the smoked-glass windows rattled with winds off the Lough. The kind of building that was full of faceless companies, their names just acronyms. As she went up in the lift, seeing her face in the smudged metal doors, she felt nerves coil in her stomach. There was nothing warm or fuzzy about this place, nothing that made her think of soft baby heads and brushed-cotton Babygros and stuffed plush penguins. It was hard to imagine this place could help her fulfil her dreams, the ones about plump little wrists and starfish hands and gurgling laughs.

She was seeing a family law specialist, one that Jenny's sister-in-law's cousin had used for her divorce. She gave her name to the receptionist and sat by the water cooler, which dripped steadily and had run out of plastic cups. The receptionist was playing Solitaire, and had adopted that hunched, PTSD posture of someone who really doesn't want to be asked to do anything.

Caroline sat, her mind too restless to flip through one of the out-of-date magazines on the coffee table. She was also once again slightly hungover, which was becoming a near-permanent state for her. But it had been nice with Josh, the night before. She'd approved of his very tidy flat, and his taste in films, and it was the first evening for a long time when staying in hadn't made her feel so lonely she worried she might lose her mind. Maybe it could become a regular thing. Two friends, eating pizza, drinking red wine, watching bad films. All the same she hadn't told him about what she was doing, that she hoped to have Anto's baby. She wasn't sure why, she'd told him everything else about her loss. But this was the most personal thing, and anyway, she was used to putting on a brave face for Josh, who'd been such a mess when she walked into the rainy car park outside the community centre and saw him there, clearly about to bolt. She had to protect him.

After a while the sullen receptionist looked up, reluctantly. 'Caroline Hooper?'

'Present,' she answered, absently, then kicked herself. What was that, some weird school flashback? She was Ms Hooper, scourge of Year Four. She was in charge, fearsome yet sympathetic. She was in control. And yet when she stood up, she knocked her bag off the chair, spilling pens and makeup all over the place. A tampon came to rest at the foot of an elderly man, who jerked away from it as if it was a mouse. Scooping up her things with as much dignity as she could muster, she went down the corridor, which could have used a hoover, and into a small office heaped with files. The woman behind the desk was blowing her nose loudly, and gestured to Caroline to sit down. She did, taking in the dying pot plants and calendar that was still on February. Did these people have a grip? Could they help her?

After a long, long final blow, the lawyer – Jane Adams was her name, frizzy hair in a halo round her head, a suit that Caroline could tell was from Dunnes – held out a hand, which Caroline shook after a momentary longing for Purell. 'Oh God, sorry, I've a terrible cold. So, Ms Hooper.'

At least she'd got the Ms part right. 'Caroline's fine, please.'

'Right, right.' Jane was hunting through folders. 'Now remind me, it was . . .'

'My husband died. I want to use the semen sample he gave for IVF. It's frozen in the fertility clinic.'

Jane blinked at the bluntness, but really, they were on the clock, and Caroline wasn't paying her to blow her nose and faff around with files.

'I see. And you want to . . .'

'He ticked the box to say I couldn't use it if he died. I think he wasn't in his right mind, or he read it wrong or something.'

'Do you have any grounds to think that?' Jane was scrabbling for a notebook.

Caroline had one in her bag, a pen already clipped into it, so she wouldn't have to hunt for one. She had been on time, looking up the route the day before. Caroline was organised. Why on earth couldn't the rest of the world be? Most of all Anto, who had obviously planned to leave her, but not done anything to prepare her for life with him gone. 'Because,' she said, feeling the weariness of the last few months hit her all at once. 'He killed himself in the bathroom of our house when I was out at Sainsbury's. I think that's a fairly strong indicator, don't you?'

An expensive hour later, Caroline exited the building, rushing to get to support group on time. It was raining again, and she took out the fold-up cag in a bag she always carried. Anto had teased her about it, but what was teasing compared to having dry, non-frizzy hair? Jane Adams could take a leaf out of her book.

The lawyer had snapped into action after what Caroline told her. 'It would be a landmark case,' she said with some excitement, her cold fogging up her consonants. 'It's been done in England but not here. And with the more conservative climate, it could be very interesting indeed.'

'So you'll try for me?'

'We'll try. We'd go for a judge's ruling first, save the cost of a full trial. Subject of course to terms and conditions, and the understanding of . . . ' She had droned on for another few minutes here, in lawyer speak, always so dry and careful, and Caroline had stopped listening. The gist of it was, someone was going to help her.

There was just one more thing to ask. 'How much will it cost, if it goes to full trial?' Again, she was blunt. No sense in running up the bill even more.

Jane had mentioned a sum that made Caroline's stomach turn over, in that casual way lawyers have of saying things like *thousands* and *life in prison*. Caroline had made herself nod. This was the most important thing in her life, it wasn't a time to skimp. She would find the money one way or another.

'All right,' she'd said, lifting her chin. 'Let's do it.'

Although it might make her late, and Sinead was sure to give her the evils, Caroline couldn't resist running into the office loos to freshen up before she left. Pizza with Josh had been fun, but afterwards she'd felt uneasy somehow. Maybe because she'd worn what was essentially pyjamas to go over to his. Mind you, he'd been in his oldest, grossest, bleach-stained tracksuit bottoms, so it was definitely just a friends thing. All the same, she felt like dressing up a little for tonight, brushing her hair, putting on a bit of makeup. It didn't do to let standards slide entirely.

Josh

Where did you look for evidence of your wife's secrets? Josh knew he should forget about it for now – he'd spent all of Sunday and Monday brooding over it, trying to fathom out what Siobhan had told him. He was due at support group, and was going to be late if he stood here in their bedroom much longer.

But he couldn't help it. All his thoughts were on the address from Niamh's bag, as he once again stood looking at her things piled all over the bedroom. He had googled the address over and over, but found nothing at all.

Frustrated, Josh touched the small rectangle of Niamh's phone, feeling its weight in his pocket. He liked to carry it with him for some reason he didn't quite understand. It was long out of battery, and he could sort that – her charger was still plugged in beside the bed where she'd left it – but without the code it was useless.

Of course, there was always her laptop. Josh hadn't thought about it before because Niamh didn't use it much – she rarely worked from home, preferring to leave things at the office, and it was a clunky netbook that took for ever to boot up. But he might have more luck guessing the password for it. After hunting about a bit, Josh located the computer underneath the sofa, coated in dust and with the inevitable crumbs in the keys. It made him sad, thinking that Niamh had probably kicked it under there, bored of work, imagining she'd come back to it soon. But she never would. It was out of battery, so he then had to search for the charger, which he eventually found in a cupboard in the kitchen (why? God, she'd been so untidy!) Eventually it had enough charge to turn on, and the password screen greeted him. What would it have been? His own name? Niamh was not the type to have a rigorous system with numbers and special characters. He tried: *password* (he wouldn't have put it past her). Nothing. He tried *IloveJosh*, imagining her laughing at him. *Someone's got notions about themselves, haven't they.* Then he thought of something, and raced back into the kitchen, almost dropping the laptop in his haste. There it was, a piece of paper tacked to the noticeboard, among the reminders about bin collection days and takeaway flyers. Something else Josh had to sort when he got a moment. In Niamh's loopy handwriting, a phrase was scrawled on the edge of a letter from the council about recycling. *September16*. The month and year they had met. Oh, Niamh. How like her to choose something romantic as a password. How also like her to write it down in a place it could very easily be found. Never thinking about the consequences.

Back in the living room, he keyed it in, and watched as the old laptop struggled slowly to life. Then, heart hammering, he called up her Google search history. Some of it was to be expected – *do camels have one or two humps*. That made him laugh out loud for a moment, then gasp at the pain of it, the essence of her left behind in this hunk of plastic and metal. Barbecue recipes. *Hotels Galway*. *Pictures of Harry Styles* (she'd a crush on him that he liked to tease her about). Then – *how to get a DNA test*. Eh? He racked his brains trying to remember if they'd ever had a conversation about that. Or seen something on a TV show. He couldn't think of anything. There was also a Google Maps search. It was for the address he'd found. It was done the day before Niamh had gone there, and died in the street.

What did it mean? God, it was so frustrating, piecing together these confusing clues, tiny breadcrumbs left behind her.

He needed some advice about what to do next. From someone sensible. Caroline, of course. Maybe it was time to tell her what he'd found. He'd wanted to, when she was there the night before. That had been so nice. When she went to the bathroom she'd said, 'God that does my heart good, a sink as shiny as that, so it does,' and he'd felt absurdly pleased. Maybe just having someone in the flat, to notice that he'd cleaned, that he was still trying, breathing, living. But in the end he hadn't told her any of it, finding the picture in Niamh's desk, or the address, or Siobhan. Why not? Maybe because it would sound too crazy to say out loud, and he was ashamed to admit how often he drove down to the site of her death, just to stare at a patch of tarmac. He checked the clock – if he left now, he'd see her at support group in twenty minutes. Josh grabbed his jacket and ran out.

Caroline

Having driven over in a mad panic at being late, Caroline was irritated to find herself at support group so early she surprised Sinead, who was lining up the cups in a precise mathematical formation. Even when she tried she couldn't manage to be late for things. 'Oh! Caroline.' No one else was even there yet.

'Hi.' Caroline really didn't want to make small talk with Sinead, and thought about pretending she needed the loo. Then lingering in there long enough for bowel problems to be suspected. But what if Josh or someone came in and Sinead mentioned Caroline had been in the loo for ages and he thought she had stomach troubles? God, she was really keyed up, she didn't normally overthink things so much. It was only Josh.

'How are you finding the group, Caroline?' Sinead used eye contact as a weapon.

She hated it when people overused her name. 'It's great, thank you. Makes a difference to find people in the same boat.'

Sinead narrowed her eyes. 'Yes, I see you're very pally-pally with Josh.'

Caroline felt obscurely angry. 'We're just friends.'

'Mm. Just remember it's not about making *friends*. It's about acknowledging your grief, head on.'

'I am doing that.'

'Hmm. Yes. I'm sure you're *trying*.' Sinead uncapped a marker, checking it.

Caroline was annoyed. What, she wasn't doing grief right? She'd made too many friends? She couldn't wait to tell Josh about this, which perhaps proved Sinead's point. Then she remembered Sinead was a volunteer and felt guilty. 'Thank you for . . . you know, for hosting.'

Sinead sniffed. 'I don't *host*, Caroline. I do much more than that.'

'Sure, sure . . . excuse me, I just . . . I need the loo.'

On her way out she spotted Josh coming in, a red scarf wrapped round his neck. She hissed, 'Thank God you're here. I got a drive-by Sineading.'

'Oh, poor you. Any sign of Sylvia? I was hoping she might come along tonight.'

'I doubt she'll be back, after the welcome she got last time. Maybe we can persuade her to try the older widows group again.'

'Yeah. Maybe.'

'You OK?' Josh looked tired and drawn, as if he wasn't sleeping.

'Oh. Yeah, just . . . got a lot on my mind.'

Caroline sighed. 'Me too, mate. You reckon it'll ever get easier?'

Josh just shrugged, and Caroline knew that neither of them wanted to think about the possibility they never would.

Just then the door opened, and it was Sylvia, a purple hat on her shining white hair, a sparkling brooch on her coat lapel, a smile on her face. 'Hello, my dears! I hope you don't mind that I came back? You were all so welcoming last time.'

*

111

Cassie was sharing again. Sinead had asked Ruma first, but of course she just smiled and nodded, and after an awkward moment Sinead moved round the circle. Her eyes lingered on Sylvia, who was leaning eagerly on her cane, then passed on, eyes narrowed. Matt was there, but had arrived late, and kept looking at his phone. His T-shirt was on back to front and he looked like he hadn't slept in days.

'Matt, we do have a no-phones rule,' said Sinead, glaring at him.

'Sorry. Sorry. I have a new babysitter with the kids, not sure she can cope. My mum's gone down with the flu so she can't mind them, it's a nightmare.'

Caroline noticed that he had what looked like dried porridge on his jeans. She should do more to help him.

'Yes well, rules are rules. Cassandra, your turn, please.'

Cassie was, once again, soaking wet. It wasn't even raining that night, so Caroline wondered if it was sweat, or if she had deliberately washed her hair before coming and then gone out in the cold. A way of punishing herself for something, maybe. For being alive. Cassie stared at her feet, talking in her usual monotone. 'This week's been hard. It's all hard, to be honest. Lisa was everything to me. My family, they don't ... I can't reach out to them. Her family, they're nice but ... I feel like they sort of want to own the grief. Like it's theirs not mine, because they knew her longer.'

Caroline shifted in her seat, recognising this feeling. She felt guilty hearing Cassie's tale of rejection and loneliness, the conversion therapy her parents had sent her to, the way her mother had cried when she told them she was in love with a woman. Caroline had nothing like that to contend with, and yet she'd isolated herself from her parents all the same. She hadn't told them yet about the legal challenge, or Anto and the form. Perhaps because it was too hard to explain what she was doing and why, to see in their faces that they thought she was mad, how much they worried for her. It was easier to be alone, and yet she could see from Cassie what a burden this was, dragging your grief through every day like a millstone. She should go and see them.

Cassie said, 'I don't know. I can't see it getting any easier. Ever.' Her voice was small, but it dropped into the room like a stone.

Caroline saw Josh was staring very hard at his hands. What if it never *did* get easier? What if all this, the group, Sylvia's book, it was just ... a distraction? And when it all ran out, all the tasks and quests and projects, would they still be alone with what had happened?

'Are you sure you can't reach out to your family, Cassie?' Sinead said bossily. 'You know, a death can be a good time to heal old wounds. It puts it into perspective. Why bear a grudge when life is so short?'

Cassie blinked, and Caroline wanted to shout at Sinead that it wasn't a grudge, it was your parents refusing to accept who you were, the person you had loved and now lost. And she might have, might have braved her fear of Sinead if Sylvia hadn't spoken up instead.

'The thing is, Sinead, dear, you're asking her to forgive people who couldn't accept her right to love. The woman she chose. And who haven't even asked for forgiveness, I believe, Cassie sweetheart?' Cassie shook her head. 'There. She's already going through enough, without having to do all the work of forgiving the very people who should be there for her and aren't. Tell me, dear, do they even know Lisa passed?' When she said the name, this woman who had never met Lisa, a shudder went over

Cassie's face, and Caroline realised Sinead was right when she made them say the names out loud, whatever else she was wrong about. It mattered.

'I don't know. It was in the paper, they probably saw. Or someone will have told them. But I haven't heard a thing from them.'

Sylvia reached over and patted Cassie's cold white hand. 'I'm so sorry. This country – hate is so often allowed to triumph. It was the same when my Iris and I fell in love.'

Caroline watched the understanding dawn on Cassie's face, and the shock on Sinead's. She caught Josh's eye, stifled a smile. The corners of his mouth lifted briefly then fell again – something was up with him tonight. That was, even more so than usual.

'Yes ... well ... I think we better go back to tonight's topic – alternative therapies and their uses.'

When Sinead turned around to write 'reiki' on the whiteboard, Caroline leaned over and tentatively touched the damp edge of Cassie's running top. 'Come for a drink with us after?' she whispered.

Cassie looked startled. She opened her mouth as if to say something, then just nodded. Caroline thought back to the first suggestion in Sylvia's book. *Reach out to people.* There, she'd done it. She'd tried. She had changed her routine and cleared things out and she was trying to take care of herself and move forward. *Now can it get easier, please?*

'Is this OK?' she hissed to Josh as they walked out, Cassie up ahead with Sylvia. Her hand was pressed on the older woman's arm as they talked intently, and there were tears in her eyes. Josh and Caroline had never invited anyone else to join the post-group pub session. 'Sorry, I just ... she looked so sad.'

'Of course. I tried to ask Ruma too, but I don't think she knew what I was saying. Do you think she, like, understands us?'

Matt had already rushed off to relieve his incompetent babysitter, muttering something about Peadar having emptied the laundry basket into the bath.

'I don't know. I wonder why she comes to the group, Ruma.'

'God knows. I feel bad I know nothing about her.'

'We can only do what we can,' recited Caroline. A quote from Sylvia.

Josh glanced at her. 'You're doing it, then? The book?'

'I'm ... trying. I did a clear-out, and reached out to a few people, changed my routine. But it feels pointless sometimes. Like pasting on a smile, taking up crochet or whatever, when inside I want to ... burn everything to the ground.'

'I know what you mean. I've tried too but – things are still the same.' He sighed. 'Car, can I tell you something?'

'Sure you can ... oh, wait, is Sylvia leaving?' The older woman had turned around at the end of her street, and was waving to them. Cassie had already gone into the pub. 'You'll join us for a drink, Sylvia?'

'Thank you, my dears, but it's very late for me. I don't hear too well in noisy places. But perhaps you'll come and see me soon?'

'Of course we will. Won't we, Josh?'

'Uh, sure.'

Sylvia looked keenly between Josh and Caroline. 'Did you try it then? The book?'

'Oh! Well, we did, yeah,' said Caroline. 'I went to a café before work, and I started clearing out some house stuff, I saw my friend, and ...' She glanced at Josh, and it seemed to flash between them: *Don't tell her we had pizza.* Why? Sylvia might get the wrong idea, maybe. Think it was more than just friends.

115

Josh cleared his throat. 'Yeah, me too. I cleared out some of Niamh's stuff, and messaged some people, went to see her family . . . yeah, I think I did a fair bit.'

'Oh, I'm so pleased! It was helpful then?'

Was it? Too soon to tell, really. How could these small things help with everything that was going on, Anto and the legal case and maybe selling her house? 'Of course,' said Caroline. 'Now, I'll come to visit next week sometime, will I? Actually, I have my end of term concert Wednesday – would you like to come to that? It's in the evening, six o'clock.'

A smile melted Sylvia's face. 'Oh, if you're sure! I would love that!'

'Of course, I'll send you the details. I mean, don't get your hopes up, it's not exactly *X Factor.*'

Sylvia looked at Josh. 'What about you, dear, will you come?'

'Me?' Josh looked surprised. 'Um – maybe. I can see.'

Caroline would never have thought to ask Josh to the concert – he was far too cool to want to watch a load of under-rehearsed children dressed as sunflowers and angels – but she let herself consider the idea. It might be nice to have him there. Anto had always come to watch them, at least when he wasn't in one of his spirals.

Once they'd made plans, then gone in and helped Cassie defend a table in the packed pub (Caroline was very good at getting tables, with a firm yet cheery manner that could clear a spot in five minutes) and ordered their drinks, she'd completely forgotten Josh had been about to tell her something.

Her idea to invite Cassie out for a drink turned out well in the end. Cassie maintained her monotone and floor-gazing only until they persuaded her to have a glass of wine. It was like a magic charm. Within minutes she was in full flow about how patronising Sinead was, how interfering Lisa's parents were about the grave headstone, and how her work hadn't given her compassionate leave because she was married to a woman, which was probably against the law, and did they think maybe she could sue them. Caroline, who after her earlier trip to the lawyer felt like she was starring in an episode of *The Good Wife*, urged her to do it, topping up Cassie's glass with Merlot until it sloshed.

'Maybe you should talk to your family, you know,' Josh had said, surprising Caroline, as usually he didn't do advice. 'I mean ... life's short. Is it worth being estranged for ever? And when people don't say things, don't talk to each other, we just grow further apart, you know?'

Cassie had scowled at him, and it was surprising to see her with an expression for once. 'They hurt me. Like, a lot.'

'I know. But maybe they regret it. Maybe ... ' Josh must have caught their curious glances. 'I'm sorry. I guess I'm thinking a lot about my last words to Niamh. Moaning at her about tidying up the kitchen, you know. If I'd known I just would have ... said other things. Asked her things. Told her things.'

Caroline said, 'Mine to Anto were, "All right lazy arse, I'll go to the shops, but it's your turn next time."'

Cassie took a huge gulp of wine. 'I just said, "I'll be back in a minute." I went to the hospital canteen for a coffee. When I came back she was gone.' Lisa had died of ovarian cancer, at forty-one. She and Cassie had been thinking of having a baby before the diagnosis, then it came, and six months later she was dead.

'I'm sorry,' said Josh. 'I'm not trying to do a Sinead, I promise. I know how hard it is. I just ... I've been thinking a lot about it. The things we wish we could have said to them, but now it's too late.'

Caroline drained her wine. 'So Josh, is this thought inspired by *How to Be a Widow*, or is it your own epiphany?'

And then they had to explain Sylvia's book to Cassie, and Cassie wanted her own copy, and hours later they rolled out with a new friend, and Caroline ate a cheeseburger on the way home, a cheap oniony meaty one from the takeaway, and it was gorgeous, and she was actually smiling when she stabbed her key at the lock and went in, kicking off her shoes and switching on the TV in search of something easy, *Family Guy* or something. She was just brushing her teeth for bed when she remembered she'd never asked Josh what it was he'd wanted to talk about.

5. GET OUT OF THE HOUSE

Josh

'City Boy.' Josh looked up, bleary-eyed, to see Maggie at his desk.

'Oh. Hi.'

'Hi to you, too, employee who I pay to write stories for me. No need to ask how you're getting on.'

Josh's computer screen had actually timed out, it was so long since he'd moved the mouse. He'd been staring into space, crumbs of McCoy barbecue flavour crisps down his shirt. 'I'm . . . mulling it over.'

'Well, mull faster, we have space to fill.'

'All right.' He didn't know how to tell her he hadn't even started the article about Niamh. How did you begin to sum up something so huge, a feeling that picked him up and whirled him about like a tornado? 'Maggie?'

'Yes?' She turned back.

'What would you do if you wanted to find out who lived at a particular address?'

'Why?' She cocked her head.

'Oh, just, you know – that expenses story.'

'Well, you could check the electoral roll, or the land registry website – you can sometimes find things there. But you know me, I stick to the old-fashioned ways. They work.'

'And what's that, in this case?'

Maggie snorted. 'Go through the bins, of course. Honestly, what do they teach you in journalism school these days?'

'Ha. OK, thanks.'

'Don't break the law or anything,' she said easily, eyeing him shrewdly. He wouldn't, of course he wouldn't. Was rooting through the bins a crime? It was a good point, though. How far would he go to find out what had happened to Niamh? Maybe that was why he hadn't told anyone yet, not Maggie, not Caroline. There hadn't been a chance to bring it up in the pub, with Cassie there, and maybe that was for the best. He wasn't sure he was ready to have someone tell him it was nothing, just a random address, a picture, a vague sense Niamh had distanced herself from her sister. When they'd first met, he'd told Caroline everything, poured himself out to her. She would always say the right thing, as if she understood how desperate he felt sometimes, how grief seemed to roll over him like waves, up to his neck and drowning him. Maybe he had burdened her too much – after all, she had her own troubles.

Maggie groaned. 'Oh Jesus, here comes Shaggy Doo.'

Oisin, the picture editor, had come loping over. He was from Dublin and talked about surfing a lot. His unwashed fair hair was bundled up in a man bun at his neck.

'Howyeh, guys. Boss.'

'What's that you have there?'

Oisin, to be fair to him, did have mad graphic design skills, and his flyers for his ska band were works of art. Which, all the same, didn't mean that Josh wanted to go and see Killer Clownz perform.

'Another gig. You'll come this time?'

Maggie shook her head. 'Ah, I'd love to, but I have this terrible condition where I can't listen to loud music or be in crowds any more.'

Oisin looked puzzled. 'Yeah?'

'Yeah. It's called "being fifty".'

Oisin frowned. 'You'll come, Josh, won't you?'

He thought of Sylvia's next instruction – *get out of the house.*

You will find yourself tired of looking at the same four walls, and the memories of your loved one will be extra painful there. Why not try going to a place with no associations?

He thought of the long quiet nights in his painfully clean flat, brooding over Niamh and her secrets. 'Sure,' he said, as Maggie raised her eyebrows in surprise. 'Why not?'

As Maggie and Oisin walked off, arguing about using a picture of Jimmy Savile to illustrate yet another child abuse story, Josh put his head in his hands. Why did Niamh have that address? What was she doing there? Was she having an affair with someone who lived there? Why had she been searching for DNA tests on her laptop? Josh had to get out of his head or he was going to lose it. He took out his phone and saw a message from Caroline, apologising for forgetting he wanted to talk the night before. He didn't feel like going into it now – it would hardly help, dwelling on it over and over, retracing Niamh's final steps down the street, onto the main road, off the pavement and into the path of the car.

On an impulse, he typed back: *Doesn't matter. Fancy a gig tonight?* Maybe she'd find it weird, especially given they were supposed to see each other on Wednesday too. Apart from the pizza night, they only ever hung out at the support group or in the pub afterwards. But it would lift his mind from the endless groove it had settled in, at least. Automatically, his eyes flicked to the clock. 11.47 a.m. A weary sadness washed over him. He'd got through it for another day. *Now I'm driving to the hospital. I don't know it, but she's already dead. She's already gone.*

Caroline

A gig. A gig with Josh. All right, it was in a smelly old-man's pub, and there were only about ten people here, but still. She was doing what Sylvia advised, ticking off the tasks like the teacher's pet swot she was. Caroline had never really been into gigs – they were always too loud and there was nowhere to sit down – but maybe that was the point. Do something different. Put yourself out there. She felt like Sylvia would be proud.

But what to wear? She rang Jenny in a panic on her way home from work. Jenny was startled. 'Lord, you're asking the wrong person here, the last gig I went to was Michael Bublé. Jeans, I suppose?'

Caroline was approaching her house; she felt in her bag for her keys. 'But what on top – like something fancy or just a big baggy jumper? That's what the young ones wear these days, isn't it? Like we used to wear in the nineties.'

Jenny was doubtful. 'I think at our age we need some scaffolding, Car, and that's the God's honest truth. I saw a girl in my office wearing dungarees the other day, I swear to God. Nothing underneath!'

Caroline felt a dart of panic. She'd been planning to wear a nice top and heels, but was that too 'ageing auntie on a hen do?' 'Oh God. Maybe I should just stay at home and watch more *Friends*.'

'Ah come on now, he's asked you. That's a good sign, isn't it – he's trying to get out there. And you should try, too.'

She sighed. 'All right, all right. I bet they run me out of the place for being too old. Bye.'

She'd taken ages to get ready, doing her eye makeup properly for the first time in months, trying to remember what she'd been told by the tight-faced woman at the counter in House of Fraser. She blow-dried her hair, put on a nice top she'd bought not long before Anto died. It still had the tags on, even. She dressed it down a little with Converse instead of heels. Even with all this effort, she was still ready far too early. Trying to distract herself as she waited to leave, she leafed through Sylvia's book with a heavy heart. Would these scribbled notes, written by a woman in a dusty old house, really help her? *Get out of the house*. Well, she was doing that, wasn't she? She was meeting Josh, out in the world, for a drink and a gig. It was Sylvia-approved – no need for her to feel so sick, right down to her stomach. And yet she did. Strange.

Josh was already at the pub when she went in, wearing a soft jumper of yellow wool. The air felt oddly charged as she crossed the room to him, not just like meeting a friend.

'Hi,' she said shyly. Why was she shy? It was just Josh.

'Hi!' He got up and kissed her cheek, something he never usually did, and she felt a warm hand on her back for a second and breathed in his aftershave. Oh. Sometimes she forgot that this was an attractive man. 'What can I get you to drink?' Manners, too. He really was a catch. Whoever got him next, if and when he ever moved on, would be a lucky woman. That would be a while still, she was sure.

'Oh! I'll have, um, a pint please.'

She wanted gin, the clean burn of it, but it took too little time to drink and she didn't think they'd have much of a selection here. He went to get it, and she watched as he chatted with the barmaid, who was all of twenty and smiled up at Josh, braided hair, tight vest top, tattoos on her arms. Probably she was eyeing him up, and who could blame her? Somebody should tell the poor girl it was a non-starter – Josh was so far away from being able to think about such things.

Soon, he was back. 'So. How are you getting on with "*How to Be a Widow*"?' He did air quotes.

She sighed. 'Oh, I don't know. I guess it helps a bit. But it seems stupid, doesn't it? Like what difference could it possibly make?'

'I know what you mean.' He sipped his beer, small flecks of foam settling in his stubble. 'But on the other hand, I have to do something. I've been going mad, these last few weeks.'

'Yeah?' That was a shame; she'd thought he was coping OK. Or at least as well as could be expected. 'How come?'

He hesitated. 'Oh, I don't know. I just wish I could ask her why she ran into the street. Tell her not to. I have these mad conversations with her in my head, but of course I never get an answer.'

'I know what you mean,' said Caroline, taking a sip of beer, wishing she'd picked something else. 'It's maddening, that they can't respond.'

'You do it too? With Anto?' It felt strange when Josh said his name, this man who'd never met Anto, a man she wouldn't even know if Anto were still alive. It made her feel guilty almost, which was ridiculous.

'Only all the time. It's like a break-up, I guess, only one you'll never get closure from. You still have all the anger and love and even crossness that they don't change the loo rolls or whatever, but it has nowhere to go, so it just builds up. Makes perfect sense.' Caroline laughed, a breath of tears in her voice, like rain on the wind. 'Oh God. I'm such a mess. Losing it altogether.'

'We both are.' Josh smiled, and his eyes were so kind, so understanding. 'Car, this kind of thing, we aren't supposed to be able to cope with it. Maybe when you're seventy, but not now. So don't ask too much of yourself, OK?'

'And you, the same.'

'I know. Oh look, the work people are here. I'll introduce you.'

And now here she was meeting people from Josh's real life, moving on from just being a site-specific friend, like one you did a night class with then spent the next five years shaking off. That was nice. Maybe they were proper friends after all. She met his boss, an older woman with a missing finger and gimlet stare that Caroline was sure could see right through her, and his colleague who was in the band, who made deep eye contact from under his sandy lashes and said, 'So, what's your deal, like?'

'She's just lost her partner,' Josh said crushingly. 'Leave her alone, Oisin.'

But did Caroline truly want to be left alone? She'd always liked guys with long hair, even if she leaned more to the grungy type than the surfer dude. When Oisin bent over the bar to order a craft beer she saw he had abs you could bounce pebbles off, and a butterscotch tan from being outside as much as his job allowed, and even more than that sometimes. And he'd noticed her. Guys still noticed her, even if she was a tragic widow on the wrong side of thirty-five. It was making forgotten parts of her brain light up. Maybe there were options. Maybe her life didn't have to be over at thirty-six, along with Anto's.

Caroline caught herself. How could she even think that way? One pint of bad beer and some not-good music and she was losing the run of herself. OK, Oisin had given her the eye, but look at him also giving it to the barmaid. It meant nothing. And Anto was hardly cold in his (non-gravelled) grave. Of course she couldn't move on. Not now, probably not ever. In the days after the funeral, she'd tried to reconcile herself to that fact – she would probably die alone now. Most likely, Anto had been it for her. You couldn't expect two great loves in a lifetime.

127

Josh was coming towards her, large hand stretched around four pints. The band, who were called something weird, Killer Clownz, weren't very good, but as Caroline drank more to drown out the bad thoughts, the rough beer did its work, and soon she was giggling, even dancing along a bit.

'Thanks for inviting me!' she yelled in Josh's ear, over the din.

'Thanks for coming. It'll get me out of band duty for at least a year now.'

He was so close she could see the faint sweat on his skin, smell his aftershave. She moved to say something else, probably about how bad the band were, and at the same time he leaned it to say something to her, and for a second her lips brushed his face, just under his ear. She felt him draw in a breath. He hadn't touched her. But he hadn't moved away either. Nervous, trembling, she half-turned to face him, and for a moment they locked eyes. Oh God.

'Sorry. I just – need some air.' And he was gone, stumbling to the exit, as on stage Oisin sang about fracking, with his eyes earnestly closed.

Caroline followed him out, rubbing her arms in the cold night air. 'Are you OK?' God, what an eejit she was. She hoped he hadn't got the wrong idea.

'Yeah, sorry. Too crowded in there.' It wasn't crowded at all. Except for Caroline pressing herself into him with wild abandon. Embarrassed, she was thinking about making her excuses to leave when Josh suddenly said, 'Car? Do you carry actual photos of anyone with you? Like in your bag or purse?'

What a random question. 'Hmm? No, I don't think so. They're all on my phone, like.'

'Not even one of your dad, or your brother or anything?'

'No, but . . . what's this about, Josh?'

'Nothing. Nothing. Just . . . trying to figure out some things.' And he lapsed into silence.

She hugged her arms round herself against the cold of a Belfast night. 'So what did you want to tell me the other day, at the pub? I'm sorry, it went right out of my head.'

Josh paused. 'Oh, it's nothing.'

'You're sure?'

'Yeah.'

'In that case, can I tell *you* something?' She wasn't sure why she was bringing it up now. Maybe to be clear what she wanted, that she hadn't been trying to brush his face with her lips or anything mad like that. 'I'm . . . trying to have Anto's baby.'

'What?' Josh stared at her. 'Car . . . you can't . . . what?'

Haltingly, she explained about the fertility clinic, the IVF they had planned. She hadn't told Josh this before, perhaps not wanting to gross out a new male friend with tales of her malfunctioning insides.

'Oh?' was all he said.

'Oh?' she repeated. The door of the pub opened and Josh's boss came out lighting a cigarette, looking over at them curiously. Now wasn't the time to have this conversation. 'That all you have to say?'

'I'm sorry to hear that,' said Josh politely, stiffly.

Caroline wanted to say he'd got it wrong, that there was nothing to be sorry for, that on the contrary, this was a blessing, a miracle, a chance to have Anto's child when he was gone. 'Well, no need to be sorry,' she said lightly. 'There's a good chance it will all work out fine.'

'But Car . . . ' He tailed off. 'Are you sure it's a good idea?'

'What?' Anger burned in her solar plexus. 'I have to do *something*, like you said. Why would it not be a good idea?'

Josh paused, then dipped his eyes. 'Look, forget I said any-thing. I hope it all works out for you.'

Caroline didn't think he meant that, and she was confused, and wanted to have it out with him despite the cold and his boss watching, but instead she pushed past him into the warm blaring pub. 'Come on. It's my round.'

Josh

Josh sat in his car with his hoody pulled over his face, feeling more than slightly stupid. Various passers-by – rubberneckers, Niamh would have said – had already slowed down to stare at him, and he was sure a call to the police about the black man acting suspiciously on their road wasn't far off. But what else could he do? He wasn't about to bang on the door of the house and demand to know why his dead wife had this address in her handbag.

This was his life now. Staking out a random house in a street he knew nothing about, except that his wife had died near here. It was all he could think of to do, because he had to find out who lived here and why Niamh had the address. He'd turned over all the options in his head, and none of them were good. Had she gone there for a private appointment of some kind – a therapist, or a massage or something? A fortune teller or tarot reader? He knew Niamh set great store by horoscopes and was convinced that a friend of her granny had the second sight, whatever that was. But she'd have told him if that were the case, he was sure. She loved to wind him up by telling him all about the money she'd spent on acupuncture, reiki healing, having her birth chart done, all of which Josh thought was utter bollocks. And there was no business registered at this address, he'd already checked. It was just a nondescript terraced house, bins left neatly outside, window frames in need of painting. He had timed his drive-by for half-five, when someone with an office job would likely be coming home from work. And he was determined he'd see the person who lived in there, and hopefully get some answers. Just for a second. Then he'd go to Caroline's school concert, definitely.

While he waited, he brooded over the previous night, at the gig. Something about it had upset him. He'd been annoyed when Oisin held onto her hand a bit too long, staring into her eyes with the soulful 'Hiya' that reduced young goth girls to jelly. Caroline was thirty-six and reviewed her pension arrangements every six months – she wasn't for Oisin to hit on, even without the little matter of her dead husband. She was far too good for him. But maybe he shouldn't have warned Oisin off. After all, Oisin was good-looking in a scruffy way, and had half the women in the office mooning around him. Maybe Caroline was up for that. They'd not discussed it, but it was the obvious next step, to try and move on with their lives, meet someone else. Except Josh was nowhere near ready.

Then there'd been the weird moment when they'd both leaned it to talk at the wrong moment and brushed faces. He hoped she didn't think he was like Oisin, a sleazebag. She wouldn't think that . . . would she? Then, outside, she'd told him her baby plan, almost as if making the point that she wasn't interested in Josh that way. Which he'd never thought she was! When she'd said, 'I'm . . . trying to have Anto's baby,' a shy smile had broken over her face, one he'd never seen before.

Oh no, Josh had thought at first. *She's gone mad. She believes in magic or God or voodoo.* His 'Oh?' had been polite (he hoped). Then Caroline had explained – the paused IVF, the sample still frozen in a clinic, which the law currently didn't allow her to get her hands on. He hadn't known what to say. Was it wise, when Anto had ticked the box to say not to use it, when his family were against the idea, when she'd have to bring the child up alone, grieving, never to know its father? Was it fair? Caroline was convinced Anto had filled the form in wrong, but how could she be sure? His mother seemed to think otherwise.

A dull ache resonated somewhere in the region of his chest at the thought of a baby. He hadn't thought of having kids with Niamh, not yet, but the vague idea had always been there in the future. Of course, that wasn't an option for him now Niamh was gone. How would it feel if your last chance was in a freezer somewhere? To have that one baby in particular, keep a bit of someone you loved alive in the world? But what if the baby inherited Anto's mental health problems? Manic depression, that could be passed on, couldn't it? He didn't want to say it, but it must have shown on his face, because he'd seen Caroline frown, then suggest they went inside. And of course Maggie had witnessed the last part of the conversation, and would be sure to ask about it at the office. She missed nothing.

He didn't want to fall out with Caroline. Maybe she was just making her last grab at not being alone. To have someone else, to not end up like Cassie, stunned with misery. What chance did Josh have? To take his mind off it, he went through his copy of Sylvia's book, looking for the next challenge. *Get out of the house* – he'd done his best there. He was having dinner with Billy and his housemate soon. He'd finally cleared out Niamh's things, though it had broken his heart, every unravelling scarf and down-at-heel shoe a part of her, a further nail in her coffin. He'd tried to take care of himself, be mindful of falling into ruts, gone out in the evenings. He'd started staying later at the office, to make up for the fact that he still couldn't do anything before half-eleven. He was doing his best! So why did he still feel so awful? Because what would he even say? How could he explain?

It was getting late – he was going to miss the start of the concert, and didn't fancy creeping in late to a hall full of parents. But as he reached for the ignition, he saw someone coming. He'd parked a bit along the street, since he didn't actually want to get in a confrontation with whoever lived there about stealing their spot. A man was walking down the street towards the house. Josh couldn't tell the age in the rear-view mirror – forties, maybe? He wore a smart tweedy jacket, of the kind Josh might have liked himself, and as Josh watched he went up to number seventeen and fished some keys from his pocket. Was this the person Niamh had been visiting? Josh squinted. The man had silvery hair, and looked to be in his mid-forties, though good for it. Trendy. Crinkly eyes. Handsome. He was also familiar. Josh was almost sure that, thirty or so years later, this was the teenage boy in the picture from Niamh's office. The man found the right key and let himself in, closed the door behind him.

Josh sat for a few minutes more, blood thundering in his ears as he tried to make sense of what he'd seen. A man lived there, alone perhaps, and Niamh had the address in her bag, his picture in her desk.

Chest pounding, he got out and crept towards the house, looking at his phone as if trying to find an address. He sneaked a look at the recycling bin in front of the house, which held a few bits of discarded Amazon packaging. The name on it – *Christopher Stone*. It had crossed his mind, of course, but he'd thought he was wrong. He'd hoped he was wrong, because surely it was impossible. Niamh had loved him as he'd loved her. But he had to look at the evidence: was his wife having an affair?

Caroline

'Miss?' A small sticky hand was pulling at her cardigan. Caroline looked down, harassed. The end of term concert was starting in five minutes and it was becoming sadly clear to her that the kids weren't ready. For past concerts, before her husband had killed himself and taken with him any chance of her being a mother, she'd stayed in work late for weeks before, rehearsing until her class were word-perfect on their songs and poems. This year, she had skimped, just trying to breathe and get through each day. It wasn't good enough.

'What is it?' Her heart gave a lurch – the child tugging at her was Davey Magee, whose exercise book had been used by Anto to write his suicide note. Of course, Davey didn't know that and never would, but Caroline did.

'I need to pee, Miss.'

She looked at her watch. 'Well, if you're quick, Davey, and I mean very quick.'

'Miss, I can't get out of my costume.' Davey was dressed as a dinosaur, in a zip-up green onesie with a cardboard head and tail. Caroline sighed. No one else was in sight – Mr Rigley, the accompanist and music teacher, was going through 'He's Got the Whole World in His Hands' with some of the kids, who couldn't seem to remember what else He had in his hands after the sun and moon. She'd have to do it. In the end she barricaded the door and helped him out of his costume as best she could, then waited for Davey by the sinks. She heard the tinkle of his pee, and realised he was reciting his lines under his breath. He trotted out. 'Put it back on, Miss?'

She helped him into the tail and head. 'Um, did you forget something, Davey?'

'Hmmm?' He was on his way out.

'Hands?'

'Oh, yes, Miss.'

She supervised as he washed them. Funny how she'd never done any of this, nappy changes, loo trips, reminders to brush teeth, when some people her age already had teenagers. Girls from her school had four children – five in some cases. And it would have been her doing it – Anto would have been rubbish at all that. He'd have made up bedtime stories, swept the kids away on impromptu camping trips, played at monsters, but likely never made a packed lunch or wiped a bum. Would it be so different doing it all by herself?

Davey finished washing his hands, splashing water all up the mirror, and trotted back out, his tail getting stuck in the door. 'Miss Hooper?'

'Yes?'

'I'm sorry your husband died.'

All at once, in the middle of the smelly boys' loos, Caroline was about to cry. 'Thank you, Davey.'

'Do you miss him?'

'Yes, Davey, I miss him a lot.'

'I miss my hamster. He died too, you know.'

'I'm sorry to hear that.'

'He got sucked up in the hoover.'

'Right.'

'Your husband didn't get sucked up in a hoover though.'

'No, he didn't. Now, off you go, it's almost time for you and the rest of T-Rex.' A joke that many of the parents wouldn't have the faintest idea about, let alone the kids, but never mind.

After shepherding Davey onstage, Caroline rushed to the back of the hall so she could subtly conduct the kids. A sea of faces, mums, dads, grannies, aunties, and she had a sudden rush of loneliness. Maybe she'd never watch her own child on stage, stumbling through an off-key rendition of 'Twinkle Twinkle Little Star'. Even if she did, there would be no dad to watch it with her, film it proudly on a mobile phone, clap till their hands hurt. She couldn't help but look – no sign of Josh. Silly to think he'd come to a kids' concert anyway.

'Hello, dear.' A whisper and pat on her arm. Sylvia had dressed rather heartbreakingly in her best, a long floaty dress in a sea green. There were some holes around her hem that her old eyesight must have missed in the gloom of her house. Caroline wondered how long it had been since Sylvia had had people to talk to. She needed to visit more often.

'You came!' Despite her politeness, she hadn't known if Sylvia would really want to see a load of out-of-tune children murdering various hymns and pop songs.

'Of course I did. How lovely to see the young people sing. How are you, my dear?'

'Oh, I'm ... ' The word 'fine' stuck in her mouth like a too-big pill. She wasn't really fine, was she? 'It's hard. It's very hard.'

'I know. That's why it's so important to lean on your friends. How's Josh?'

'He's ... well, he's not here, I don't think.' She didn't really know how he was, did she? He'd tried to talk to her at the pub after support group, but she'd got distracted and he'd clammed up since. And the night before at the gig had been weird, there was no getting away from it. Was that why he hadn't come today? Maybe he wasn't telling her things. Maybe Josh wasn't fine, either. 'Honestly, I don't know. How did you do it, Sylvia? All these years? Have you family?'

Sylvia was settling into her seat, unwinding the vast sparkly scarf she wore around her neck. 'My family were rather like poor Cassandra's, I'm afraid. They weren't exactly … supportive of my love for Iris.'

'Oh no. I'm so sorry.'

'Don't be, dear, I don't regret my choice. Although I would have liked to see my nieces grow up – my brother had two girls. I imagine they might have children now themselves, even grand-children.' Sylvia smiled as a little girl toddled past, clutching an Elsa doll in sticky hands. 'So lovely to be around wee ones. Thank you for inviting me. It's not something I do very often.'

Caroline had a lump in her throat. Something she took for granted, even resented some days – being around kids, going to a rubbish school concert – had made Sylvia's week, if not her month. She had to remember to be grateful. 'You're very wel-come. I'm sorry I haven't been to visit. I will soon, I promise.'

Sylvia patted her arm. 'I must sit down and let you get started. But perhaps you should reach out to him, dear. Josh. I'm sure he would appreciate it. I feel there are things he's keeping locked up, if you know what I mean?'

Caroline watched her shuffle forward, politely finding her way to her seat, cane flashing. Sylvia had no children, no family any more, and had lost the love of her life. And yet she was still trying to live, to be happy, to help people. Caroline could try too. She would contact Josh as soon as the concert finished. Then, later, she would visit her parents and tell them her plan to go to court. So what if they didn't understand? They also couldn't use FaceTime without pressing it to their ears. She would follow Sylvia's example, and keep striving to be happy as best she could.

6. WRITE DOWN YOUR FEELINGS

Josh

He stared at the screen of his laptop. He'd never had trouble getting words down – you couldn't afford to, if you wrote for a living – but this was different. This was asking him to crack his soul open, talk about the greatest love and greatest loss of his life. He looked around the office. Oisin was waxing a skateboard in the corner, like a parody of himself. He'd already asked after Caroline, sniffing around, and Josh had put him off again. He allowed himself a flicker of wondering why he was so outraged at the idea, then stamped it out. He should text her to say sorry for his no-show yesterday. In the end he'd stayed too long outside the house, waiting to see if anyone else went in.

Josh sighed – he didn't have time for this endless speculation. Maggie was heaping him with stories as well as the article, and good ones – a punishment beating, a child-abuse scandal in a swimming team, stories he would have bitten her hand off for before Niamh's death. It was as if she knew that, with too much time by himself, his mind kept drifting to Christopher Stone. The man Niamh had maybe, possibly been visiting that day, which she hadn't told him or any of her friends about.

Josh had spent hours the night before squinting at the man's public Facebook profile, which he'd found after clicking through various people with the same name. He'd found out nothing useful – Christopher Stone seemed like a normal guy, into football and cycling. Josh couldn't see if he was single or not.

Wasn't he too old for Niamh? He looked to be at least forty-five. He was racking his brains to think of older men she'd ever fancied, 'silver foxes' as she called them. Brad Pitt was fifty, wasn't he? And George Clooney. She had a crush on the weatherman from UTV Live as well. She always said, *It doesn't matter that it's been raining every day for three months, because you're my sunshine, babe!* Pretending to kiss the TV.

Again, it was a joke, a safe one because he'd never thought for one second Niamh would have looked at another man, in the same way he'd not noticed any other woman since he'd met her; they'd just receded to background colour. But maybe he'd been wrong. Maybe it hadn't been that way for her at all. How would he ever find out? He'd already decided to ask her family again, press harder this time. He couldn't think what else to do.

He went back to the article, of which he felt partly proud and partly ashamed. He knew what Irish people were like – they might find it maudlin, or even tawdry that he was getting paid to write about her death. He had thought long and hard about it, and decided that Niamh would have said go for it, and sure we'll have a night in a nice hotel or something. But he had no one to take to a hotel.

Caroline flashed across his mind. He bet she knew all the secret deals, had discount codes coming out of her sleeves, had compared the cleanliness and value for money of every hotel in Ireland already. Probably she had a spreadsheet. For a second he imagined it – walking in the woods with her, having breakfast together. Separate rooms, of course. Or maybe a twin. He could imagine the soft murmur of her voice saying goodnight. He shook himself. Caroline wasn't his mother or his girlfriend, she was his friend, someone as broken as he was. He had to just get on with this, stop leaning on her.

Maggie was pacing around her office yelling into her phone, an indistinct hum of annoyance drifting out. Perhaps she was on with her ex-husband Javier, a war photographer from Colombia. They'd had no children, and instead led a glamorous, dangerous life, being run out of countries and escaping over borders, embedding themselves with guerrilla fighters in the mountains. On his wedding day, Josh had looked over at Maggie, getting stuck into the Prosecco with his Auntie Phyllis, and had the thought – *I'll never have that life now.* Yes, he'd loved Niamh, with all of his heart and body and bones, but she'd meant settling down. A quiet life. Buying furniture, growing herbs in pots on the window. He had accepted it, because he loved her, but now she was gone and he was still stuck in the same old safe life, alone in what felt like a foreign country. Even her family seemed foreign to him now, without her. Siobhan had been acting strange when he'd seen her, smoking like that, evading his questions. Did she know something more than she'd said? Why would Niamh stop talking to her adored eldest sister, who'd practically brought her up? A bit ungrateful, wasn't it?

Feeling guilty at even this slight negative thought, he gazed at her picture again. A smile frozen in time. Sand on the floor of the car, the tang of salt on the back of her neck when he kissed her there, her hair bundled up, damp from the sea. He began to type.

What can you say about a thirty-two-year-old woman who died? I'm copying the first line of Love Story, a film that Niamh, my wife, absolutely hated. I remember we watched it one rainy Saturday and when it got to the bit where Jenny is diagnosed with leukaemia (spoiler alert, sorry), and the doctor tells her husband but not her, Niamh just stared at me and then burst out laughing. *Oh my God. If I ever have leukaemia and you agree with some sexist twat doctor not to tell me I'm sick, I will kill you, and then we can both die, OK?*

At that point it was just a joke. We never thought either of us would die, not for at least sixty years, and who can think that far ahead? But as it was Niamh died at thirty-two, when she ran across the road without looking and was hit by a car. The driver – I'll call him Gerard – technically was the person who killed her, though it wasn't his fault. Everyone agreed, police, paramedics, onlookers. Gerard was in bits, shaking and crying and saying how sorry he was. He came to her funeral and had to leave in the middle, because he was crying more than her family.

Josh broke off, lifting his wrists from the cool metal of the MacBook. He was doing it. He was writing about Niamh's death, something he would very recently not have thought possible. Feeling galvanised, he took out his copy of Sylvia's book, dog-eared and crumpled after being carried around in his bag for weeks, and leafed through it. What was the next challenge? There it was, one of the handwritten bits, in Sylvia's shaky cursive. *Write down your feelings. This will help you get clarity, and understand the process and different stages of grief.* Well, he was doing it, and maybe he'd get paid extra and could take his mum away somewhere nice for the weekend.

That was another issue about losing not just your partner, but the person you lived with. Suddenly he had to pay all the bills and rent by himself, because of course Niamh hadn't had life insurance, because why would she? She was thirty-two. He had some through work, because journalists were considered still at risk here. Ironic. If he'd died instead of her, Niamh would have been quite well off. *Sure I'll go on a Caribbean cruise,* she'd said flippantly, when he got her to sign the forms. A joke. A routine admin task. Not something they would actually have to face, or so he'd thought at the time.

Almost without thinking about it, he'd picked up his phone to tell Caroline about the article, but he stopped himself. Maybe he was asking too much of her, bringing her every little win and failure of his day. Instead he texted: *Really sorry about the concert. Something came up at work.* He felt bad lying to her, but could hardly tell the truth.

She texted right back, as was her way. Efficient, reliable.

No worries. So sorry to ask this but I could really do with a hand dismantling some furniture tomorrow night. I will pay you in pizza??

Josh thought about his weekend. Niamh's family on Saturday again. Dinner with Billy Sunday. If he went to Caroline's that evening, that would fill the space up nicely. He could avoid the deadly silence of traipsing around the house, watching the dust suspended in mid-air, obsessing over Niamh and Christopher Stone. *Sure. As long as there's no goat cheese on it.*

He waited. The little dots appeared that showed she was replying, and Josh was amazed at the way his heart, so recently down in the region of his stomach, soared up, to know she was on the other end. That she wasn't annoyed about the gig, or him not turning up yesterday.

Great! Thank you so much!

Feel free to wear pyjamas again though.

Excuse me, they are not pyjamas, they are lounge pants, highly acceptable garments to wear to corner shop or for dinner engagement.

Josh sent back a laughing-face emoji.

As he put the phone down, he found he was feeling lighter. Maybe it was just the idea of not being alone all weekend, wondering over and over about the man Niamh had maybe been meeting. Maybe it was finally writing things down, getting some clarity. Damn it, Sylvia was some kind of witch.

Caroline

Once again, Caroline spent ages getting ready for Josh to come round. She wasn't entirely sure why – he'd already seen her at her worst, trekking to support group in a tracksuit and Anto's old jumper, her hair unbrushed for weeks, weeping in the car park after a particularly hard-hitting session with Sinead, snot smeared over her face. But he'd never come to hers before. It was years since she'd had someone over on her own, and she'd become so used to slobbing about the house, letting her true self leak out, the one who picked at dry skin on her feet and watched endless *Don't Tell the Bride* episodes in a tea-stained tracksuit, that it was hard to find Outside Caroline in there. A woman who'd smile, and laugh at unfunny jokes, and hide her crazy, pack it all away like a tent into a bag.

It was half-term as of next week, and she felt the dangerous sag of too much time around her. To think. To obsess. She'd tried Sylvia's next tip – write down your feelings – but she'd felt silly, like a teenager with a diary. Instead she'd made a list of what she was going to say to her parents when she saw them, how she would explain what she wanted to do. Anto's baby. How she was chasing that possibility, going further and further every day. Putting the house on the market! She even had some viewings booked in. They would be sure to find that out soon, so she needed to tell them herself or she'd never hear the end of it.

146

She was carefully toning down her eyeliner, thinking of intelligent things to say about the news, when she remembered it was Josh. Not some random man who was trying to get his band/stand-up comedy career off the ground, and whose main aim would be to communicate how little he wanted to commit right now. Josh was like her – smashed up behind the eyes, bumbling through life. She wouldn't have to try and impress him. She didn't need to impress anyone, in fact, because she wasn't looking to move on. Of course she wasn't! Anto was hardly dead. There was nothing to play for here at all, just spending time with a friend who would understand. The thought was unexpectedly cheering, and she found herself smiling into the mirror.

Coming into the living room, she surveyed the place. She'd been to the shops twice already, once for a variety of tasty snack options, and once for healthier ones and almond milk, in case Josh had dietary restrictions. Shouldn't she know about that? What if he didn't even drink tea? She tried to think had she seen him drink it at group. God, it was exhausting, having to start all over again, learn the operating instructions for a new person, with no manual provided. But that wasn't what was happening! It was just a friend, helping her out.

Josh arrived on time – of course he did – just as she had taken the mad notion that he'd judge her for serving shop-bought pizza, and started making her own dough, forgetting what an almighty mess it created. Her hands were coated in thick globules, the kitchen and her apron and her hair were shrouded in flour, and every bowl and chopping board ruined, when he rang the bell. Damn. Caroline caught sight of herself in the kitchen window, looking like a crazy woman – *What is wrong with you?* It was just Josh. It made no difference what she looked like.

'Hi!' She answered the door to him.

Josh looked puzzled at her flour-spattered appearance. 'Am I early?'

'No, no, I just . . . I've had a dough-related emergency is all. Give me two minutes?'

He followed her into the house. 'Wow! This place is great.'

'Ah, thanks.' It *was* great. That made it so much harder to sell it.

'Show me where the furniture is?'

She led him into the living room. 'It's just this old bookcase, I wanted to take it apart and throw it out. Make the place look nicer. I'm getting rid of few things, minimalising.'

'How come?' Josh was moving around it, assessing the dimensions.

'Um . . . I've put the house on the market.'

'You have?' He looked around him. 'But it's beautiful, Caroline.'

Sudden hot tears stung her eyes. 'I know it is. It's my dream house.' And it was – apple tree in the garden, red brick, stained glass around the door, antique parquet floor. 'I love it so much. But . . . Josh, it's haunted for me now. Every time I come in I . . . '

Josh knew what had happened to Anto. She saw his gaze shift subtly to the ceiling. 'I understand. Sometimes I feel that way about the flat, and it's just rented, temporary. Like she's still there, all around me. I keep finding her hair and her tissues everywhere. So many tissues – you have no idea.'

It wasn't just the presence of Anto's ghost, of course, that meant she was selling. She needed the money for the legal case, although something made her not want to mention it to him again. His reaction at the gig hadn't been exactly supportive. She moved into the kitchen, changing the subject. 'Listen, I saw Syl the other day. She came to my school concert.'

Josh took off his jacket. 'Oh?'

'God love her, I think she actually enjoyed it, too. She's lonely, Josh. No family about, Iris gone. I was thinking – what if we tried to find her family for her? She has nieces and they probably have kids; they might like to get to know her.' The idea had come to her while clearing up from the concert. Maybe Sylvia didn't have to be so alone, not for ever.

He frowned. 'You think she would like that? Didn't they sort of reject her for being gay?'

'Surely they wouldn't still be so bigoted – her nieces, anyway? They'd be in their fifties now. I mean she's ace, who wouldn't want to get to know her?'

Josh frowned. 'I guess.'

Again, Caroline had hoped for more enthusiasm. 'You don't agree? You were the one who told Cassie to contact her parents, and they're bigots, too.'

'I know. I guess you're right. It's just . . . I don't want to see Syl hurt. She seems so fragile, you know?'

'I wouldn't tell her until I found them. If I even did.'

'Sure, sure. Let me know how I can help. You must have your hands full, with the court case and selling the house.'

Caroline shrugged. 'Got to keep busy. You know how it is – if I have to be alone with my thoughts I might lose the head altogether.'

'If you're sure.'

A pause between them. What now? The air felt charged somehow. Caroline pushed her hair back with her forearm. 'I'll just . . . finish up in here.'

'I'll get started, then.'

As Caroline manhandled the dough into a bowl and began to clean up – easier said than done, since she'd coated the place in the stickiest substance known to man – she heard him moving about in the next room, opening the tool box she'd left out, taking out bits and pieces. Josh was here in her house. It shouldn't have been strange, and yet it was. Anto had been here, sat on that sofa, walked across that floor, leaned against the counter to talk to her while she cooked, stealing bits of food from the pots. And now he was gone and Josh was here instead.

'Do you need a different screwdriver?' she called. She had her own set of tools, of course, because she was a practical woman, and there was no use depending on Anto for anything like that.

'I brought my own.'

Of course he had. She peeked into the living room, watching how his faded red T-shirt rode up as he bent over, showing his smooth brown back. Then she caught herself. Leering over Josh like a pervert! Yes, *sure*, he was lovely, a real ride, as Jenny had said when she'd seen his picture, but that was no excuse for eyeing him up like some mad horny widow. She hid her burning face in the sink, scrubbing until everything was clean and the dough rising neatly. It would be ready in an hour or so. Next door, Josh was now wielding a screwdriver with quiet confidence.

'How did you learn to be so handy?' she asked, leaning in the doorway to watch him.

'My dad died when I was eleven, so I kind of had to. My mum wasn't about to do it.'

'I didn't realise you were so young when you lost him. What about your brother, he was just a kid then?'

'Sam, yeah. He's the classic youngest child. He was five when Dad died, so I guess that's some excuse, but ... it's also not, you know?'

'He didn't come to Niamh's funeral, you said?' She felt bad

saying his wife's name, here in her house. They'd been closer than this before, leaning over tables in noisy bars to shout in each other's ears, but this was much more intimate. The silence of the house around them. Anto's books still in the bookcase, his photos on the wall. Her shoes kicked off by the door, Josh's jacket hanging on the back of a chair. She would only have to cross the room to slide her hands under his T-shirt; four steps would do it. God, what a thought to have.

Niamh, a woman she had never met and never would, hovered on the edge of her thoughts a lot. She'd been messy, warm, funny, expansive, it seemed, from Josh's stories and what Caroline had seen on her occasional deep-dive into his Facebook pictures (a perfectly natural thing to do when you made a new friend, she told herself). Given to exotic hats and floral prints. Whimsical, sweet, untidy. All things Caroline wasn't. But that didn't matter, of course. They were just friends, her and Josh.

He removed one of the bookcase shelves with a small grunt of effort. 'The funeral was really fast. That's a thing you do here, I guess. But all the same, he could have tried. Mum came.'

'Yeah. All the same. Have you been to visit them?'

'Not for a while, no. You know how it is.' Josh stood up, palming a handful of wooden bits, whatever they were called. Dowels? She had a strong flashback to moving in here with Anto, assembling their bed, a task they had naively started at ten minutes to midnight, already worn out by moving all day, their first home together. *I'll take a dowel please, Carol.*

Hysteria had quickly set in. 'Where's the bloody Allen key?'

'How the hell would I know? What are all these little wood bits? What are they *for*?' That night they'd slept on the mattress on the floor, wrapped around each other, and in the morning Caroline had gone to the hardware store and taught herself how to do it. Oh, Anto. She found sudden tears in her nose, sharp and stinging.

Josh, of course, noticed. He noticed everything. 'You OK?'

'Yeah.' She wiped her face with her hand, leaving trails of flour. 'It's just ... I've not had many people here since ... him. You know? I think they get spooked because it happened here. It's just weird.'

Josh was nodding. 'I know what you mean. Even when you came round for pizza I felt guilty. It's daft – Niamh would have been delighted I had female friends.'

Friends. Of course, that's what they were. She ducked into the kitchen. 'Tea while we wait for dinner?'

'Thanks, I'm OK. I don't understand this Irish tea mania you all have.'

See? She knew nothing about him. Just because they were both suffering, it didn't mean she understood him. 'I've got some Orangina?'

'Sure, that sounds good. I basically have the tastes of a small child.'

Not in everything, I hope. She'd almost said it – overtly flirtatious. Words that would take them to another level. She stood in front of the fridge, staring blankly into it. What was going on with her? Why had she asked him over to help with a task she could easily do herself? Was it just the sheer insanity of being alone in her house, the house where he husband had died, night after night, for the rest of her life?

'Car?' Josh came up behind her. The kitchen was so small she could feel the warmth of his skin fighting the fridge air. 'Can't find it?'

Her shoulders were shaking. 'I ... I'm sorry, Josh.'

'Hey, hey, what is it?'

'I don't know?' There they came – choking sobs. 'I'm sorry. I'm so sorry.'

'Hey, hey, you haven't done anything to be sorry for. Come here.' He folded her against his shoulder, the red T-shirt smelling of fabric softener, and she wept against him, her arms around his strong, lean back.

'It's just so hard. Every day, it's just so hard.' Anto had left her, she was allowed to live her life. But even a brief taste of it, even having Josh here as a friend – he'd even said they were just friends! – was enough to fill her up with guilt, like a sinking boat.

All the same she might have done something, touched his face maybe, because Josh was so kind, so understanding, so handsome and so very much in her arms right now, if he hadn't pulled back from her slightly. His eyes on hers. Was he going to kiss her? Oh God. What would she do if he did? 'Car, you know that . . . '

'Hmm?'

Neither of them said anything. The moment went on and on, she had no idea how long for.

Josh

There was a space between people where things were understood, without ever being put into words. He'd had it with Niamh, when they'd met in that café in London and she'd been late and chaotic, as was her way, but all the same they'd both known at once that they would be a part of each other's lives, that in a city where people walked out a door and you never saw them again, the bonds stretched too far through tube lines and tunnels and underpasses, he would keep hold of her for ever.

He had it to some extent with Caroline, their unspoken under-standing of each other's grief. It had felt natural to take her in his arms when she was crying, but as soon as he did it was just like at the gig – he was too aware of her breath on his neck, her perfume, the rise and fall of her body as she wept against him. Something was there. But she was in bits, she couldn't even stand to have a man here in her house, even when he'd made sure to point out he saw them just as friends, in case she got the wrong idea. Or thought he'd got the wrong idea, really. In case either of them had the wrong idea, whatever that was. It was the first time he'd been in Caroline's house, and he'd been surprised by it, how wild and untidy it was, ivy poking through the red brick, a fruit tree shedding apples over the garden. He'd imagined her living somewhere neat, modern. It made him see her differently. And that was . . . dangerous.

Standing there, hugging her as she gulped in sobs, Josh realised something he'd never acknowledged before. There are women you can genuinely be friends with, that you'll never be attracted to, that you can hug without being aware of their breath on your skin and holding your own. He'd thought Caroline was one of those, his buddy in grief, his rock, but now, holding her in the kitchen, in her jeans and soft cardigan, her eyes red, her fair hair falling over her face, he knew the truth. She wasn't one of those women, and if things had been different he might be here hoping for something. If her husband hadn't died upstairs, if his wife had looked both ways before running across the road, or more likely if he'd never met Niamh in the first place, never gone to that café or got up and left sooner, impatient at her lateness. But Anto *had* died here, and Niamh *had* existed. Those things could not be undone, and here they were, a widow and widower, standing in each other's arms in her kitchen.

Just for a second, it might have happened. Then they both moved.

'I think the Orangina's in here ... '

'I'll just get on with ... '

Josh moved back into the living room, picking up the screwdriver again, and he thought she must have been relieved the moment was over, despite the awkwardness of how they'd pulled apart. He called back, 'I'm the same you know. Sometimes it just hits me, any little thing that reminds me of her.'

'Yeah,' mumbled Caroline, fiddling around with the dough. 'It never gets easier, does it?'

Josh finished off the bookcase in record time, reducing it to a pile of chipboard slats and screws. Broken. Just like both of them.

Caroline came back into the room. 'Pizza's almost ready.'

The words were out before he knew he was going to say it. 'I should go.'

She frowned. 'What? But you haven't eaten yet.'

It was terribly rude. All he knew was he had to get out of here, the weight of silence. The ghost, perhaps. Another man, one he had never met, tall and blustering, an artist, a drinker. Nothing like Josh. 'It smells amazing. I just ... I have to finish this article I'm working on for Maggie.'

'On a weekend?' Caroline folded her arms, and he saw he had offended her. God. What a mess.

'I'm sorry. Really I am.'

'It's fine. Thanks for your help with the bookcase.'

'No problem.' Josh fumbled with his jacket. 'I'll see you on Monday?'

'At the Heartbreak Club. Yes.' She gave him a weak smile, lifting her chin bravely. 'Sorry I cried.'

155

'Hey, remember the rules. No apologies for crying. Remember I punched the wall that time, at my second support group?'

'True. Your hand came off worse than it did, though.'

'Also true. OK ... see you.' Hesitantly, he crossed the room to her. She felt at once too close and too far away. He pressed a kiss to her cheek, holding his breath. There was a smear of flour across her forehead and he wiped it off, without thinking. Caroline blinked, looking briefly shocked. 'Um ... bye,' he stammered.

'Bye. Thanks again for the, eh – for helping.'

Josh was outside and halfway down the street before he could breathe again.

7. SPEND TIME WITH CHILDREN

Caroline

'Peadar. Peadar, pet, don't lick the windows.'

Peadar gave Caroline a beady-eyed stare, then put both sticky palms to the window and wiped his spittle into an artistic swirl. Caroline sighed.

'He doesn't listen,' said Maddie, who was five and glued to her iPad watching a YouTube video of someone playing *Minecraft*. *Peppa Pig* was on the TV at the same time, ostensibly for Peadar, who was ignoring it. Peadar was three. The baby, Ryan, was two months, and had just been sick down Caroline's back. Inspired by Sylvia's advice of spending time with kids – *their ability to live in the moment and be joyful will lift your heart* – she had offered to babysit while Matt had some 'time to himself', but had regretted it the moment the door closed and Peadar immediately daubed her good Oasis cardigan with red poster-paint. At least it was distracting her from Josh leaving in a hurry the night before. She was still smarting about it. Why had he run off like that? Had she said something, done something wrong? Was it because she'd cried all over him? But he'd hugged her first, hadn't he? He'd taken her in his arms, not the other way round?

Why does it matter anyway?

Because. She didn't want any misunderstanding between them.

Are you sure that's all it is?

'It's a hard time for all of you,' she said to Maddie, jiggling the baby and trying to judge how far the sick had gone down her back.

'Peadar's always bold,' said Maddie, sounding world-weary. 'Mammy said he was a holy terror.'

Caroline had done courses on how to talk to children about death. 'I'm very sorry about your mum, Maddie.'

Briefly, Maddie looked up from her swiping. 'She's not coming back, you know.'

'That's right. It's very sad.'

'Daddy said your husband died too.'

'Yes.'

'How did he die? Mammy bled. She bled on the floor over there.' Maddie inclined her head to the kitchen. 'After she came home with Ryan. It was all blood and she was crying and went to the hospital and she never came back.'

'I'm so sorry. That's awful.'

'So what about your husband?'

'Um . . .' She was just working out how to explain suicide to a five-year-old when the door went and Matt was back, earlier than arranged.

'Daddy!' Peadar launched himself at his father's legs. Ryan began to howl. Maddie went back to her iPad. Caroline wondered if she was detaching from her father, from fear of losing him, as well. She'd seen it before in kids who'd lost a parent. Should she recommend therapy? Talk to Maddie herself? Talk to Matt?

'You're early,' she shouted, over the screaming.

Matt sighed. His hair was sticking up, his shirt rumpled and missing a button. 'I was just wandering round Castlecourt staring at shops and not going in. Christ, I've no idea what to even do with myself when I have free time these days.' He held out his

160

arms for the baby. 'I'm better off here, at least I can keep busy. But thank you, Caroline. You're a star, you really are. Do head off now, I don't want to keep you.'

'Oh. I could make some dinner, if you like?' Suddenly, despite the din and the smell coming from Ryan's nappy, she didn't want to leave, walk out the door into the dark and go back to her own clean, lovely, quiet house.

'Ah no, you've done enough. Thank you. I'll see you Monday at the group?'

'Yeah . . . Monday. Come for a drink with us after, if you can.'

Matt took off his jacket. 'Isn't that you and Josh's thing?'

Caroline frowned. 'No! Cassie came with us last week. You're all very welcome.' Was that what people thought? That she and Josh were some kind of *Mean Girls* grief clique? *On Wednesdays, we wear black.*

Matt held out his arms and took the smelly, howling baby from her. Caroline watched how Ryan calmed right away, laid his head against his dad's chest, so trusting. Her heart twanged. She knew it was hard having a baby, even with two parents around, and she knew her life would likely become disordered and sleepless and a lot stickier than was optimal. But would she never have that, a little head resting on her shoulder? Falling asleep with total confidence that you'd hold them, never let them go. Matt said, 'Well, we'll see. Thank you again. You've been brilliant. Say bye to Caroline, guys?'

Peadar squinted up at her from his dad's legs. 'No. Don't like her.'

Maddie's gaze didn't lift from her iPad. 'Bye Caroline, thank you.' She was polite, but there was something not right with the girl, all the same. Of course there was. Her mother had gone into hospital to have a new baby, then come home full of joy and

161

bounce and within hours started to bleed all over the living-room floor, and very soon after she was dead. No one could be right after that. Ach, it was exhausting, all this loss and pain. Josh, brooding over Niamh, and she knew there were things he wasn't telling her. They hadn't spoken since the night before, when usually they messaged several times every day. Then there was Sylvia, alone in her dusty house, and Caroline made a note to go around with some food, give the place a spruce-up. She also had to see her parents and Jenny and Skype her brother and nieces and talk to the SENCO at school about that kid in her class who'd started wetting herself. So many people to carry, but before this she'd been able to hold them all up, and Anto as well, with his many needs. Now she could barely hold herself up.

Back home, Caroline unlocked her front door, noticing the smell of the daffodils she'd bought earlier that day, already unfurling in the water. The sheen on her antique furniture. The clean kitchen with the dishcloth folded on the draining board, where Josh had stood so recently, holding her in his arms. The silence.

'Baby,' she whispered, setting down her keys with a clink. 'Baby, I'm home.'

But Anto wasn't there. Not even his ghost.

Josh

'I want so sit next to Uncle Josh!'
   'No, I want to! It's not fair!'
   'I hate you.'
   'I hate you, smelly poo!'

162

'Hey, hey, you can both sit beside me if I go in the middle, OK?'

The kids – Liam's daughter and Clare's son – subsided as they were served up their dinner, apart from several gripes about what cup they wanted for their orange squash, what fork they would use to eat, who got the place mat with the burn mark on it from where Niamh had lit a tealight without putting anything underneath.

Josh waited until they were all sitting around the dinner table, the best chance of getting the Donnelly family to actually shut up and listen, if only because their mouths were full of Irish stew. He'd never understood the enthusiasm with which the family all ate Niamh's mother's food, which to his mind was bland and stodgy, nothing like the fiery flavours of his own mum's cooking. But at least it kept them quiet.

He'd come to the regular Saturday-night dinner again in the hope of answers, although it made him think non-stop of Niamh – Niamh sneaking a second glass of wine in the living room, Niamh moaning about the choice of Irish stew for dinner, which she hated, Niamh hugging her nieces and nephews and even her great-niece, Siobhan's grandkid. The whole family was gathered around the table, almost. There was Siobhan and her husband Gerry, her daughter Lucy and Lucy's baby Darcy, eighteen months. Siobhan's son Ciaran was at university in England. There was Liam, his wife Marie, his daughter Sadie, six, his son Mark, twelve and monosyllabic. There was Clare, pregnant with her second child, a baby Niamh would never meet, her husband, an accountant, and her toddler son Jimmy who was smearing his stew carefully all over his place mat. There was Darragh, the career-girl sister, with her long-term 'partner' Steve, who cycled everywhere and didn't eat meat, to Mammy's disgust (he was having potatoes and carrots for his dinner). This was a family Josh was no longer entirely part of, now that only an empty space was left where Niamh should have been. On top of that he was trying not to think about Caroline, holding her in her kitchen the night before. The idea of that moment made his pulse flutter, as if he'd escaped some terrible disaster by the skin of his teeth. All the same, he couldn't help but wonder what might have happened next if she'd lingered there a moment longer, her wet face so close to his . . .

'Hey,' he said, casually. 'Do any of you know a guy called Christopher Stone?'

A silence fell around the table. People had stopped chewing, even, everyone except for the kids, who carried on splattering potato and fighting over who had the most squash in their plastic cup. Josh looked from face to face – Clare and Darragh and Siobhan, Niamh's frail mother and silent father, Liam shushing his noisy daughter, Liam's wife, Siobhan's husband, Clare's husband, Darragh's boyfriend with his top-knot that Niamh had so enjoyed making fun of. So many people to consider in this family.

It was Clare, three years older than Niamh, who spoke, hands on her rounding bump. 'Where did you hear that name, Josh?' Too casual.

'I can't remember. I saw it on Facebook, maybe, and I think she mentioned him one time.' He'd decided he couldn't tell them about his stalking, finding the address in Niamh's bag or going to the house. He couldn't tell anyone. 'Who is he?' Clearly, they knew him, whoever he was.

In the same casual tone, Darragh, the middle child, said, 'Did he not go to school with you, Liam?'

Quickly, Liam said, 'Oh aye, he was the year above. Kind of a cool dude, knew all the bands before anyone else did.'

Josh looked between them, feeling firmly like an outsider in this family he was no longer really part of. 'So . . . would Niamh have known him?'

Clare began to clear away the plates, although not everyone was finished. Their dad was eating steadily, staring at his stew, and their mother was looking around the room uneasily, her eyes resting on the grandkids. Clare said, 'Don't think so. You're sure you saw it on Facebook? Her Facebook?'

'I don't know. The name just jumped out at me for some reason.'

'That's weird.'

'Dunno what that's about now, right enough.'

'Mammy, is there Viennetta for afters?'

'Sure the weans aren't done yet, Clare, leave it be . . . '

'I'll just get it out so it's not so hard to cu . . . '

'I'll put the kettle on . . . '

A suspicious bustle had erupted, everyone talking over each other and doing tasks that didn't need doing right now. Josh watched them carefully, aware that he was being lied to, or if not exactly lied to, kept in the dark. The only person still sitting down, not meeting his eye now, was Siobhan. Aware that he was passing the bounds of polite behaviour, he looked square at her. 'Do you know the name, Siobhan?'

Siobhan tapped her nails on the table. He noticed they were nicely done, as always, in a bubblegum-pink gel. She had time to get manicures, since she didn't work. Her husband Gerry was a lawyer, her children grown. She'd done well for herself, people said. 'From Liam's school, aye.'

'And you can't think of a reason Niamh might have known him? Not at all?'

The kitchen went quiet. Darragh stood with the kettle in her hands, and Clare with the freezer door open, a transgression that would ordinarily have kick-started a row about electricity usage, and even Daddy had stopped shovelling food into his mouth, and Mammy's hand fluttered to her throat, and Liam picked up his daughter and bundled her out, to cries of, 'But why Daddy? What's happening? I wasn't finished!'

Siobhan looked right back at him, then picked up her wine glass and drained it. 'No, Josh. I can't think of any reason at all.'

Caroline

It had taken some time for Caroline to find out about what Anto's family called his 'wee problem', i.e. severe mental illness. The first time she'd stayed over at his – the hovel he shared with four other guys, the bathroom littered with bottles of supermarket shampoo with an inch of scum in the bottom, the shower curtain peppered with mould spores, the one towel he seemed to own – she'd seen him pop some pills from a silver blister packet and swallow them. 'What's that?' she'd asked, half-asleep in the unmade bed, the covers pulled off by their exertions.

'Just some tablets I take.'

She'd sensed from his tone that she shouldn't ask more, but it had been there at the back of her head. A concern. Something on the negative side of the columns she was totting up – his untidiness and drinking and lack of a steady job paired up with his extraordinary sexiness, his honesty, his sense of humour and unashamed admiration of her. The pro side was winning, despite some fairly big cons, she had to say. Which was why she wasn't expecting it when he suddenly ghosted her.

They'd been on a date to the cinema – some stupid superhero film – and Caroline had wanted to go for a drink afterwards, since they'd hardly spoken all night. Anto had stood some way away from her, scuffing his holey trainers on the pavement. 'Eh . . .I have to work tomorrow.'

She had gaped at him. 'At what?' She had assembly with a hundred children at 8 a.m. If anyone had to work, it was her.

'Stuff. I'll . . . I'll call you. Sorry.'

And he went. No kiss. Caroline felt her heart slowly sink until it was somewhere in the region of her stylish boots. She'd allowed herself to get complacent this time, to believe that this one was different. That he liked her, because he so clearly did. That he wouldn't just vanish from her life, leaving her to wonder for ever what she'd done or said or worn that had driven him away. That had ruined it.

She told herself he'd call over the weekend. Then Saturday came and went, and Sunday. She tried to keep busy, marking, seeing Jenny, going to a spin class. Always the gnawing, growing anxiety was there – he wasn't going to call. Each day that went past made it more likely. Her phone was empty, silent. Like my heart, *she thought, then laughed at herself for being an eejit over a man.*

On Monday, a strange woman was standing outside her house when she came back from work, having been unusually snappy with the kids all day.

'You Caroline?' The woman had streaked brown hair and a cheap leather jacket; she smelled of smoke.

'Yes?'

'I'm Antony's sister. Mary Anne. I would have called but . . . it's easier if you just come with me.'

She ground her cigarette out on the pavement, littering outside Caroline's home. Caroline could have said no – she didn't know this woman, and certainly didn't want to get into her fag-smelling car. But she did. And they drove in silence to the hospital, and as the woman – Anto's middle sister, she would later learn – grumbled about parking charges, Caroline saw that they were at the psychiatric ward.

*

167

It took a while to get inside. Things to be signed, doors to be unlocked. The squeak of feet on industrial flooring, a smell of cleaning fluid and sadness. Everyone in here seemed to smoke, as well. Anto was in a bed in a room by himself, wearing soft grey clothes, watching a small TV that was chained to the wall. Escape to the Country. *Mary Anne had melted away, no doubt for another cig, and Caroline was on her own with him. Part of her was relieved, she had to admit – he hadn't dumped her. But this – what the hell was this?*

'Hi.' Anto sounded exhausted. 'I'm sorry I ... I threw my phone in the river, so I didn't have your number.'

'Oh?' Caroline wasn't sure if she should sit down or not. The room was so depressing, with its chipped cream walls and the remote control bolted to the TV stand.

'Yeah. I – Car ...' He'd never called her that before. Her heart imploded, melted between her ribs. 'I'm so sorry. I'm sick, you see. I get like this sometimes.'

And he told her about his clinical depression, his bipolar condition, which sometimes saw him stay in bed for weeks, sometimes try to climb on the fence around the Lagan (where his phone had ended up) and get arrested until some kind police officer realised what was really up with him and found him a hospital bed.

Anto fiddled with the edge of his sheet. 'Most of the time I can manage it. But ... there's always a risk. This is the first time in five years. I think it was ... I think it was meeting you. Because, Car, I think I love you, and it's sent me reeling a bit, and reeling is not good for me.'

There was a lot to take in there. Caroline, a sensible person, weighed up her options. If she stayed now, this might be for good. She might have kids with this man, take on his illness. Worry about him all the time. Lose him the next time he thought it was a good idea to jump into the river or walk through traffic. She could walk away now, go back to her ordered and comfortable life, meet someone dull and safe who worked in a bank, maybe.

But she couldn't, could she? Not really. She stepped forward and took his hand, noting the cuts and bruises on it. 'I love you too,' she said, and that was it. She'd made her choice. Four years later, the illness had taken Anto from her, and she wondered every day had it been the right one. If she should have simply hugged him that day – the planes of his shoulder blades, the soft back of his neck – and wished him well and left, cried on her sofa for a night, moved on. If she'd be married with kids by now. Happy, numb, insulated from the world. Instead, she felt like all her skin had been torn off.

Her parents looked at her, then at each other. Her mother set down her teacup with a tinkle. Her father took off his glasses and polished them.

'Well, say something.'

She was irritated. She'd made the drive down here, sat through a viewing of not one but two sets of local news, the same stories told in slightly different ways, and endured a dry meal of mashed potatoes – just potatoes, no butter or milk – and a defrosted chicken breast. She knew her presence was sending their food calibrations for the week out of whack. There were sixteen breasts in the pack, but they'd had to use three, so now there were uneven numbers. She'd heard her mother fretting about this when they thought she was out of earshot. Earshot to them, in their seventies, being a bit different than it was for her.

Her father cleared his throat. 'I don't know now, love. Is it even possible?'

'Of course. That's the whole point of freezing … it.' If for nothing else, she would never forgive Anto for making her say the word *semen* to her parents. She was pretty sure she'd just shaved five years off her father's life.

Her mother said, 'But love, maybe it's just not meant to be.'

Silence. The carriage clock, which had belonged to Caroline's grandmother, ticked. 'What's that supposed to mean?'

'Just, if it didn't happen all those years . . . maybe that's a sign.'

Bloody Irish people, with their signs and symbols. 'Meaning what? I wasn't supposed to be a mother?'

'Pet, you'd have been a great mother,' her dad said, weakly. Caroline noted the tense. Not *you would be*. You *would have been*. They'd already given up on her.

'Don't you want grandkids?' she tried. Her mum's eyes went to the framed pictures over the fireplace – Keegan and Kelsey, their existing grandchildren. Their father was Paul, Caroline's brother, who'd buggered off to Australia ten years ago, leaving Caroline to take care of their ageing parents. His life appeared to be one long round of barbecues and beach trips, with his sun-kissed, long-limbed wife Gilda. Anto called her Aussie Rules, since she had so many regulations around food. *Had called*. Her heart ached. She'd found in Anto an ally against her family, a Trojan horse she'd smuggled in who would always be on her side. Now she was alone again. 'I mean, grandkids in this hemisphere.'

Her dad muttered something about maybe they'd come back one day, as if Paul and Gilda were really going to trade barbecued steaks on the beach for the drizzle and all-you-can-eat carb buffets of his home town.

'We'd have loved it if it had happened for you,' said her mother simply. 'But it didn't. And this . . . it seems like it's not natural, Caroline.'

'How's it any different to IVF?' She hated the huffy tone of her voice, a straight throwback to 1999 and the protracted battles over her A level choices.

'Because, pet, he's gone. The baby, if there was one – it would never know him. He'd have no say over it. I don't think it's right.' Her mother's voice wavered. Caroline was surprised she had such a sophisticated understanding of medical consent.

'He'd have wanted it. I know he would.'

Another glance. How she missed that, the looks only a long-term couple could share, which only deepened with each year. Her parents had forty-plus to go on, whereas she and Anto only had four. So little in the scheme of a life. 'But pet, he didn't tick the wee box, did he?'

There it was. The same thing everyone was going to say – doctors, lawyers, maybe the judge, too, as if a tiny misjudged pen mark on a page was what mattered, not Caroline's years of knowledge of her husband's wants and wishes. She realised this particular battle was lost. Her parents weren't going to support her.

'Well,' she said, her own voice shaking now. 'It doesn't matter. I'm doing it anyway. I just wanted you to be on board, but I can see you're not.'

She had vaguely hoped there might be some money knocking about that she didn't know about, but she could see that, even if there was, it wouldn't come her way. Likely it would go to Paul to fund his imminent trip over, Mammy and Daddy now having decided they were too old to travel all that way, what with her father's bladder and everything.

'Pet, don't upset yourself,' said her dad. Same thing he'd said to her when Take That split up, and she had been absolutely inconsolable. She'd definitely cried more then than on the day of her husband's funeral.

'Why not?' Furious, she whirled around. 'My husband is dead and this is my only chance to have a baby, and no one wants me to take it.'

She pounded up the carpeted stairs to her old room, the gesture deeply familiar. It was all the same. The single bed, the patterned wallpaper, the built-in chipboard wardrobe that had been the envy of her friends in 1993. There was even – was there? Yes. She bent down to peer at what was clearly the corner of an old Take That poster, taped up to the door. Her mother's eyesight wasn't the best these days, and her cleaning was getting slapdash, she who'd once been the most house-proud woman in Ireland. Any money they did have should go on a cleaner, and then, maybe, more and more care as time went on. There was no point in asking Paul to help out, he'd only complain about his surfboard business suffering from El Niño or something like that. Nope, Caroline was truly on her own here. A cold dread crept up her back as she realised she was the spinster daughter everyone would expect to sacrifice her life to care for her parents. Only not a spinster, a widow, so she couldn't even argue that she'd not had her chance at a family. It was her own fault she'd not been sensible enough to have a baby right away, or persuade her husband to stay alive with her.

As she lay sprawled on her bed, she picked up her phone, about to text Josh and tell him she was in purgatory, aka her family home. Then she remembered. Friday night. The awkwardness. How quickly he'd left, and she'd had to eat all the homemade pizza by herself, even though it didn't agree with her and she'd had to get beat into the Gaviscon all that night. He hadn't messaged since. Maybe he thought she'd thrown herself at him, a desperate older woman. Luring him to her house under false furniture-dismantling pretences so she could pounce on him. Well, she couldn't have him thinking that. Better put a little distance between them. Caroline put her phone down and lay back on her childhood single bed again, a wave of despair crashing over her.

Josh

Josh hadn't been sure what to bring round to Billy's the next day. Was wine weird? Billy didn't seem like a wine kind of guy, with his Rangers tattoos and shaved head, but maybe Josh was just being snobby. In the end, he settled for a selection of craft beers, and made his way to the address Billy had texted. It was one of those areas of Belfast that always surprised Josh when he stumbled into them. The kind with murals, and the kerbs painted red, white and blue, tattered Union flags flying above rundown streets. Places you'd see on the news that he'd assumed didn't exist any more.

At least he was English. He'd be more popular here than on the other side of things. Billy's house looked ex-council, with a neat square of lawn outside and red geraniums around the door. Not what Josh had expected. He wasn't sure what he'd expected. Billy answered the door – he was wearing a smart blue shirt and smelled of aftershave. Josh had only ever seen him bearing down the pitch in sweaty football gear, or with a towel in the changing rooms, whacking people good-naturedly on the arse.

'Sorry, am I early?' It was a bad habit he'd developed, unable to sit alone in the house any more. The visit to Niamh's family had only made things worse, because now he was convinced they were lying to him. But why? Who was this man, Christopher Stone?

'You're grand, you're grand, in you come.'

'Er ... I brought ... ' Josh handed the beers over awkwardly in their carrier bag. 'I didn't know what we were ... '

'Ah lovely, I love a drop of IPA, so I do. Padraig!' A slight Asian guy came into the room, wearing an Ireland football shirt. 'This is Josh.'

'Hello, Josh.' Padraig shook his hand. His accent was solid Ireland, maybe Kerry, Josh thought, with his limited knowledge. 'Glad you could come.' Billy's flatmate, he assumed.

'We're on the Merlot, Josh. Will you join us, or would you like a beer?'

Josh already felt ashamed of his assumptions about Billy. The room was cosy, candles burning on the mantelpiece, framed photos of various kids – relatives, he guessed – and cookbooks on the shelves. The furniture was cheap but sparkling clean. 'Wine's great, yeah, thank you.'

'Hope you like Thai,' said Padraig. 'It's an awful cliché, but I took a class when I went over and turns out I really like it.'

'A wee prawn cracker, I call him,' said Billy, and, in passing, he planted a kiss on Padraig's mouth. Josh tried not to blink. He'd really known nothing about his teammate.

Over a fiery hot Thai soup, then a green curry that stripped away the roof of Josh's mouth, Josh learned several things about Billy. One, that he was gay, had come out when he was seventeen to his UVF-member dad, who'd walked in the Belfast Pride march with him last year (Josh teared up at that, though it could have been the chillies). Two, that his husband Padraig had been born in Thailand, adopted by Irish parents, a couple now in their late seventies struggling to keep a farm going. 'God love them,' he said, in his thick country accent, filling Josh's glass. 'Not only a wee brown baby, but a gay one to boot. They've done their best.'

'We'll get them to Pride next year.' Billy squeezed Padraig's hand.

'Ach, sure Mammy can hardly walk without her Zimmer.'

They were friendly company, keen listeners, affectionate to each other without freezing Josh out. As the wine and then beer and then whiskey took hold, he marvelled that he'd almost turned down the invitation. That Sylvia, she knew a thing or two. He thought of her alone in her darkened home, and was saddened. He'd go to see her soon. Take her something nice to eat, instead of the tins and bottles she seemed to live off.

'How do you find our backwards nation then, Josh?' Padraig sat back, crunching a last prawn cracker. 'Are they funny with you?'

'Honestly, less than I thought. Or if they say stuff it's just stupid, not unkind. Like they ask are people still starving in my country, or say I look like Idris Elba or something. I guess it's meant well?'

'I get a lot of, *But where are you really from?* Especially growing up on a farm in the middle of nowhere. People hardly knew what to make of me.'

'You went to Thailand to trace your family . . . I mean, birth family?' Josh hoped it wasn't rude to ask.

'Aye, I did. Turns out I've a daddy still living over there. I wasn't even an orphan, they just couldn't afford to keep me.' He didn't seem bitter about it. 'I suppose I'd have a very different life if I'd stayed there. I wouldn't know this one.' He smiled at Billy, with his tattoos and shaved head, who smiled back so sweetly it threatened to make Josh cry again.

'You got married?'

'Civil-partnered,' said Billy. 'No equal marriage here. We're working on it.'

'And your families were . . . OK?'

Billy laughed. 'Well, my family are pretty special. Nearly all of us have been inside, me included.'

Another thing he hadn't known. Josh was shocked. He didn't know anyone else who'd been to prison. 'You?'

Billy took a casual swig of beer. 'Oh yeah. Membership of a banned organisation.' He rolled up his sleeve to show a red hand tattooed there, which Josh knew was a symbol of Loyalist paramilitaries. 'Also breaking and entering, burglary. All in the past now. A misguided youth, and sure I married a Taig and all. The family took that harder than him being a fella. But . . . well, we lost my younger brother to it ten years ago. Shot in the head. So I suppose they thought life was too short to be dicks about it.'

'I'm sorry.' So that explained how understanding Billy was about grief. 'So you know how to break into houses and stuff?' He tried to keep the question casual, though an idea was forming in his mind. A terrible idea.

'Oh aye. I can get a door lock off in under a minute.' Billy sounded proud. 'Not that I would these days. On the straight and narrow now. Well, not straight exactly.'

Josh said: 'That's great your family accepted you both. It's nice to be married, civil-partnered. It means something, doesn't it?' The words sounded thick in his mouth – maybe he was more drunk than he realised.

'I'm sorry about your wife,' said Padraig, straightforward. 'Billy said it was recent. What was she like?'

'She was . . . the most fun of anyone I knew. Always up for a hooley, as she called it. First on the dancefloor. Shoes off, handbag down, drink in either hand. So untidy. So nosy, so interested in other people. She'd have loved you guys.' He felt embarrassed after saying it, hoping it wasn't patronising.

'She sounds a dote,' said Padraig, clearing the plates.

'She was. A dote is right.'

Josh stared into his beer for a while, until Billy asked if he wanted to play FIFA, and they got out the Xbox, and the madman Billy, scourge of the East Belfast Five-a-Side Friendlies League, emerged, and more than one bottle got broken in the process, and despite it being a work night, Josh rolled home at 1 a.m. with a pounding head, raging thirst and wobbling step, reflecting hazily that it was one of the best nights he'd had since Niamh died. *Thank you, Sylvia.* She'd been right – it was surprising, the people who came through for you if you just let them.

On the way in the taxi he had taken out his phone to text Caroline and tell her what he'd been up to, see how her weekend had been, when he remembered things were weird between them, and just like that his good mood evaporated.

Caroline

She'd been expecting the doctor to say, I'm sorry, *or something at least vaguely sympathetic. But he didn't. He spent a lot of time clicking at their results on the computer in the bare little hospital room, asking questions they had already answered, like how much they drank each week (Anto lied with a straight face, and Caroline tried not to frown); how much did they smoke (again, he lied); were they having sex enough. 'I mean . . . as far as I know,' Caroline ventured. The truth was, it was like everything – dependent on how Anto felt. In an upswing he couldn't get enough of her, until all she wanted was to go to bed with a book. On the downward trajectory he could barely touch her, so cocooned in the fog was he.*

Then came a question they had to answer honestly. 'Are you taking any medication?'

Caroline leaned forward and listed the contents of Anto's medicine cabinet, knowing he would probably fudge this one too if she let him answer. It was a lot, designed to keep him from another hospital admission, from trying to jump into the river or off a high building. As she listed them, she watched the doctor's bored expression gradually turn more and more serious.

'Ah,' was all he said when she'd finished. 'Ah.'

Caroline was brooding over it, as she sat in the law office. She'd been asked to come in early but they wouldn't tell her why. She was turning the last few days over in her mind. Her parents. Matt and his terrible situation, but how she'd even felt a strange stab of jealousy because he had his kids, he had a noisy and messy house to distract from his grief. And Josh. What was she going to do about Josh? Neither of them had messaged since Friday, unheard of for them.

Just then Jane Adams came out, interrupting this unwelcome thought. She was dabbing at her nose with a tissue; she must have near-constant hay fever, or a cold that wouldn't shift. Caroline itched to offer her Sudafed.

'Caroline. Come on in.' Already the office was familiar to her, the posters in the waiting room, the faded impressionist prints on the walls, the law books on the shelf. So many words, so much paperwork, just to give Caroline the thing she wanted most in the world. 'How are you?'

Caroline was taken aback at the question. These sessions were costing her two hundred quid an hour – there wasn't time for small talk. 'I'm fine.' A lie, but it would be too expensive to explain that things had taken a weird turn with her best grief-friend and she was for some reason raging mad about it.

'Listen,' said Jane Adams, and in those two syllables Caroline heard the end of her hopes.

Her stomach plummeted. 'It's bad news?'

Lawyers didn't like to talk in black and white. 'As you know, the clinic was amenable to your request, provided we could get a court ruling on the permission form.'

'But?'

Jane sighed. It was a very human sound, and made Caroline warm to her, even as the woman was ruining her life. 'There's been a challenge to the case. Someone claiming to speak for Anto, to uphold the fact he did actually know his wishes when he signed the form. We can still try for the judge's ruling – but it's going to be much harder, I'm afraid.'

'Who is it?' said Caroline, her voice too high, although she already knew the answer.

Jane Adams slid a piece of paper across the table, and Caroline saw the name *Petitioner: Mary Carville*. Anto's mum.

There were downsides to being considered incurably sensible, almost from birth. It made it hard to rage and scream, kick the door, punch the wall. Instead, Caroline walked stiffly away from the lawyer's office. She found a coffee shop, ordered a latte in a robotic voice, remembering to pay and to ask for almond milk (dairy tended to bloat her), and she sat down.

What now? Mary didn't want Caroline to have Anto's baby. Why? Mary had never been her dream mother-in-law, but Caroline had thought they got along OK – afternoon tea on her birthday and a meal on Mother's Day, thoughtful Christmas presents chosen by Caroline, since Anto wouldn't bother his arse. Even once or twice going to a film together, usually a nice costume drama. And now this. Had the Carvilles never liked her? Did they think she'd be a bad mother? Or were they just somehow convinced that this was what Anto wanted? But how could anyone who knew him think that? He loved kids. They'd been planning their own family since they met, practically.

Caroline drank her coffee, cursing her own practical frame of mind. Jane the lawyer had said they could fight it, but if they got turned down it would cost more to have a full trial hearing. Caroline had asked how much more, and Jane had made some worried noises and hinted it could be 'around the six-figure mark'. Jesus. Who had that kind of money sitting around spare?

Oh, Anto. Could you not have ticked the right bloody box? A memory rose up from the froth in her coffee. Anto tossing his first-born niece Carly up in the air and catching her, to the horror of her watching mother. Carly shrieking in delight. Anto's sister Mary Anne saying, 'You'll have one of your own soon enough,' as people tactlessly did, not knowing your situation, but Caroline hadn't minded it then, because she wanted one of her own, and they hadn't started trying yet so they naively thought it might happen right away, as it did for other people. She'd looked over at Anto, the child in his arms, and smiled, and he'd smiled back, and she knew they were on the same page: *This'll be us soon.* But *were* they on the same page?

No. She couldn't think like that. Of course Anto had wanted the same as her. Mary was just getting into her head. She sighed. What she really wanted to do was buy four slices of the Victoria sponge on the counter, oozing with cream and shiny-sticky jam, and shove them in her mouth. But she was too sensible for that. It was very annoying.

Josh

This was so stupid. This was maybe the stupidest thing he'd ever done, worse than trying to skateboard down the Tube when he was seventeen and breaking his front teeth. Worse than setting fire to his mum's kitchen making pop tarts, age twelve. Caroline would not have let him do this. She'd have talked him out of it if he'd told her about it like he'd originally planned. Unfortunately, they weren't talking as usual right now, so there'd been no one to lead him gently away from the precipice, and so he had jumped off it and now here he was. At the bottom.

The idea had come when talking to Billy, a casually mentioned gift fallen into his lap. He now had a friend who knew how to get into houses. And there was a house he desperately wanted to get into, to see what was going on and how the resident had known his Niamh. The morning after the dinner, he'd casually texted Billy and said he was writing an article about avoiding burglary. Was there any chance Billy might show him some techniques, so he could tell readers what to be careful of? The *Chronicle* readers, being mostly in their sixties and seventies, were absolutely terrified of being robbed, as if hordes of rampaging thieves were desperate to lift their H Samuel jewellery and medium-sized TVs.

Billy had duly shown up at Josh's flat that day and shown him how to pick a lock using just household appliances like pliers and wire. He'd told Maggie he was working from home on his article, and though she wasn't happy – she stuck to the old-fashioned ways of sleeping under your desk and dying from a heart attack at fifty – she'd agreed.

As Josh asked more and more detailed questions, Billy had begun to frown.

'Josh, pal ... I know better than anyone grief can send you off your head. But it's not worth doing anything stupid over it, like, you know?'

Josh had forced a laugh. 'God, no, it's for a piece! I'm just interested. My life's so boring compared to yours.'

Lightly, Billy had said, 'Ah no, I'm just your average gay ex-paramilitary with a criminal record is all.'

But he'd looked worried, and declined staying for lunch. Josh worried he had ruined the friendship before it was even begun, but he couldn't think about that. He had to push on. The alternative – giving up, never finding out the truth about Niamh, letting her fade away into the night – was not an option.

He'd been watching Stone's house for an hour now, and no one had come in or out. It was getting on for five, so Josh reckoned he had a good hour and a half window, based on the time he'd seen the man coming home on the other days he'd swung by here. It was amazing how easy it was to slip into full-on stalker behaviour. Facebook did half the work for you, and then you just had to casually pass by wherever you thought the person might be.

The article for Maggie was in truth almost finished. It had flowed from him, coming from some strange wellspring inside. He had no idea if it was good or mawkish garbage, so he was afraid to send it in. He'd have to soon. But Josh was getting quite good at putting off thinking about things. Like the fact that he was about to break into a house, and for the first time in his life commit a crime.

He sauntered as casually as he could up the pavement. He'd thought to bring a cardboard box with him, like a delivery man, and was part-pleased, part-alarmed at his criminal mindset. Someone like him would stand out on a Belfast street, but maybe if they thought he was a courier they'd overlook it. He went up to number seventeen and knocked on the door. No answer, as he'd hoped.

He went round to the side door of the house, which he'd already scoped out. No one would see him pick the lock from there. Then he laid out the items Billy had suggested – a pair of pliers, a length of garden wire, some of Niamh's eyebrow tweezers. Jesus. Was he really going to do this? He thought about getting caught. Going to prison, maybe. His mother's devastation, when she'd fought so hard to shield him from the crime in London. He'd lose his job, lose everything. But he'd come this far, he had to at least try. It took him a lot longer to pick the lock than it had Billy – almost twenty minutes kneeling on the cold stone path, twiddling and fiddling, all the while sure someone would see him or Stone would come back. Finally, the lock tripped with a tiny click and he was in. He couldn't believe it. A surge of adrenaline ran through his body, almost frightening in its power. He was breaking and entering!

The house was messy. Clothes dried on a rack, and shoes were heaped up by the door. He saw that some were a woman's – so this guy was married, or at least in a relationship. What was he doing with Niamh, then? The breakfast dishes, a surprising number, sat out on the table. The butter not even put away in the fridge, which was exactly the sort of thing Niamh would do and almost took Josh's breath away for a second. He was imagining all kinds of things. She'd got bored living with a neat-freak stick in the mud like him. She'd found a man who was easy-going, someone her family would understand, an older man who knew about the world. An Irish guy. A cool guy who was probably in a band and brewed his own beer in the shed.

What was he doing here? What did he hope to find out? There'd hardly be evidence of an affair lying around – pictures of Niamh naked or a pair of her pants or whatever.

Josh was about to leave, and hopefully recover his senses from wherever it was he'd left them, when he heard a noise. The sound of feet, and voices raised: 'Mummy it's not fair, why can't we have biscuits?'

A woman. 'Because, they're bad for your teeth.' And then, in a flash, he saw the signs he'd somehow missed. The child's shoes in the hallway. The daubed drawing on the fridge. The framed photo on the mantelpiece of Stone and a pretty woman in her thirties, and a little girl aged maybe six or seven. He had a family. And they were about to walk in the door, where they'd find the strange man who had broken in, and scream, and call the police and his life would be over.

Josh didn't believe in an afterlife – he'd have felt much less hopeless about losing Niamh if he did – but just for a second he prayed. *Niamh, babe, if you're up there, please help me out, yeah?*

Caroline

Sinead stood by the whiteboard, tapping her marker against it aggressively. 'And where's Josh?'

Caroline glanced at the empty seat in the circle. He was late. He was never late. Where was he? 'Hmm?' She'd missed something Sinead had said to her.

Sinead was staring at her. 'I *said*, you must know, Caroline. You two are as thick as thieves.'

Everyone – Matt, Cassie, Ruma, Sylvia – looked at her too.

'Um, no, I don't actually. He didn't say he'd be late.'

She felt Sylvia's eyes on her, appraising. The woman missed nothing. But Caroline really didn't know where he was. And why not? Why wouldn't he tell her?

Sinead sighed. 'You know, I *do* give up my time to run this group. It's not some *drop-in* service where you can come and go as you please.'

Matt grimaced at Caroline in solidarity, and she smiled back uneasily. Why hadn't Josh said he'd be late? Wouldn't he normally text her? Of course, they hadn't been in touch all weekend.

'Anyway, we better get started. Today's topic is rituals. Is there anything that you've found helpful at all? Caroline. You start.' Sinead glared at her.

'Um . . . ' God, she couldn't think of anything. Her head was filled with the baby, and Josh, to the point where, she realised with a nasty lurch, she'd hardly even thought of Anto for the last few days. She'd *thought* of him, of course. Just not . . . every waking minute.

'Well?'

Sylvia said, 'One thing I found very helpful was visiting the grave once a week, taking her favourite flowers – not irises, funnily enough, but lilies. Having a little chat and a catch-up.'

Sinead glared. 'Yes, thank you, but I wanted to hear from Caroline. She's hardly shared anything in weeks.'

'Well . . . ' Did she have any rituals? Or was she just trying to hold herself together from one moment to the next?

Luckily, at that moment the door crashed open and Josh practically ran in, wild-eyed and sweating, far from his usual cool.

'Finally,' said Sinead frostily. 'I *have* said before you may as well not come if you're going to be late.'

'Sorry,' he muttered, sitting down beside Caroline and wiping his forehead, which gleamed in the harsh lights.

Caroline tried to catch his eye to ask what was wrong, but all through the meeting he just stared at the floor, and didn't look at her once.

On the way out, Sylvia caught up both their arms. 'Well, my dears? What progress this week?'

Josh was staring at the ground. 'Oh. I don't know, Sylvia. The same, I guess. I went out a few times, wrote something, saw her family again. Saw a friend from football.'

'But that's wonderful! You're doing so well.'

He'd been with Caroline two of those times, which apparently they still weren't telling Sylvia about, and both had ended so strangely.

Caroline tried to put on a hearty voice. 'Same here, I went out, saw my parents, and I babysat for Matt, even. The kids are so sweet.' Bloody Peadar. She would never get that paint out of her good cardigan.

Sylvia squeezed her arm. 'More children, when you're with them all the time at school! You are good, isn't she, Josh?'

'Oh. Yeah.' He still wouldn't meet her eyes. What was wrong?

'You're very quiet tonight.'

Josh had barely spoken all through support group, and now they were in the pub he was still monosyllabic, nursing a pale ale. Matt and Cassie were chatting about Sylvia, who had gone home, waving her stick cheerfully at the end of the street. Cassie wanted to help clear up her house – she played on a netball team who together apparently had strong enough shoulders to shift the entire houseful of junk. Caroline had turned to Josh, determined to heal the weirdness between them. She'd hoped to speak to him before the group started, but he had of course been late, earning a stream of caustic comments from Sinead all night. *It might be good to think about why you're late, Josh. What are you avoiding?* Whenever Caroline had tried to catch his eye to commiserate, he'd turned his away.

Josh started. 'Hm?'

Caroline repeated, 'You've barely spoken all evening.'

'Sorry. Lot on my mind.'

'Such as . . . ?'

Josh didn't answer, and Caroline felt obscurely annoyed. Weren't they friends? Why wouldn't he tell her what was up? She knew he'd been to his friend Billy's the day before for dinner, and had wanted to ask how it went. He'd also been to see Niamh's ones. Maybe something had happened there? But if he didn't want to tell her, that was up to him. Maybe he was embarrassed at how she'd broken down in his arms on Friday. It sucked. She wanted to tell him about Jane Adams and the bad news about Mary, about her parents and their baffled reaction. He wasn't the only one suffering.

She leaned in, touching the edge of his sleeve to get his attention. His hoody was soft, well-washed. He jumped back, and she saw how on edge he was, coiled tight with nerves.

'Josh, what's up with you? You're like a bear with a sore head. Is this about Niamh?'

He frowned, toying with a beer mat, and she saw that she was right. 'How can it not be? She died, just like that and I don't even know why she was there, why she wasn't at work. And I've *found* stuff, Car.' He told her about it then, in an urgent whisper underneath the noise of the pub – the photograph in Niamh's desk, the address in her handbag. The Google search. Her family acting strangely.

Caroline's worry grew as he spoke. 'But that could mean anything, the address. A work contact. A house she wanted to view. Anything at all! You haven't gone there, I hope?'

Silence.

'Josh!' she hissed. 'Promise me you won't go there. You could get in a lot of trouble.'

He tore his beer mat to shreds. 'But it's just so hard! I can't ask her what she was doing there, can I? And her family, they were so weird.'

'I know, but they've lost her, too, haven't they.' She sighed. 'I know it's hard, Josh. But we have to accept there are things we can't know, and move on. That's what I'm doing. Niamh probably didn't think it was worth mentioning, wherever she was that day. I bet it was something totally innocuous. Did you tell her every single wee thing you did every day, is that it? Of course you didn't.'

Josh said nothing for a moment. Across the table, Matt and Cassie looked at them curiously, noticing their intense tête-à-tête. Then Josh said, 'Are you, though? Moving on?'

'Well, yeah, I'm trying to have a baby.' And selling her house and throwing all the money into a court case. It was a lot more movement that she was comfortable with, in fact.

'With your dead husband. Car – you said we can't know what they were thinking or doing. But Anto left you a strong sign – he ticked the box for no. Don't you ever think maybe he meant it?'

She gaped at him, the noise of the pub washing around her. 'He didn't know what he wanted! He was sick. Really sick.'

'Exactly. And he knew about that, didn't he? What it was like to struggle, year after year, and never get better? Car – what if he didn't want a child to ever feel the same? It's hereditary, right, what he had? Or it can be?'

The sounds in her ear were like a roaring sea. This was Josh saying these things, her lovely kind friend. 'Wow, Josh ...'

'I'm sorry. I just think someone needs to tell you, before you waste all your money and end up with nothing. Your house, even! Your lovely house that you fixed up so nicely – do you really want to lose that? Even Anto's family don't want this – they don't want their own grandchild. Doesn't that tell you something? Maybe they respect his wishes. Maybe you should do the same.'

She was stunned. Sure, her parents had been resistant, but they were old and conservative, and Anto's family weren't keen, but they were just control freaks, and yes, the doctor had clearly thought she was crazy, and the only person on her side was Jenny, but then Jenny always thought whatever Caroline did was fine, and had done since they were kids. But she'd never imagined Josh would be against it too.

'Don't you *dare* say that.' Caroline was at first shocked by the harsh tone of her own voice, and then she was pleased. *Good. Show him how wrong he is.* 'You don't know what you're talking about. I lived with Anto for four years. I knew how he was. What he struggled with. You never even met him! So don't you dare try to tell me what he felt.' She stood up, almost knocking over her half-drunk glass of wine. Who cared? She'd leave it behind. 'You're out of line, Josh. I know you're upset because Niamh maybe wasn't the perfect little fairy you thought, but we're all bereaved. Grow up.'

Matt and Cassie gaped as she pushed her way out, struggling with her bag and coat. God, she'd never known the joy of a good storm-out. She'd always been too polite, too easy-going to do such a thing. Not any more. It had gone to her head, the thrill of it, turning everything upside down, burning it to the ground.

The air on the street was cool and she gulped it in like cold water. What now? Was she no longer speaking to Josh, her best friend of recent months, her partner in the wasteland that was grief? So what? He deserved it.

'Caroline!' Cassie was standing by the pub door, arms hugged round herself against the cold air. 'Jesus, what's the matter?'

Matt was peering round the door too, looking dismayed. These people who Caroline had felt sorry for, sure that she was at least doing better than them – here they were looking at her with pity and concern. She couldn't stand it.

'Ask Josh. Seems he thinks he's the expert on my life now.'

Josh was coming out into the street now too, his expression thunderous. 'I was just being honest. I thought you valued that.'

'Not when it's *wrong*. You're wrong, Josh.'

'I'm trying to help! Anyone can see you don't have a legal leg to stand on. He ticked the box, Caroline! It's what he wanted! There's not a court in the country will go against that. And you know what, maybe that's for the best. Look at you! Do you really think it's a good idea to have a baby now?'

An even worse feeling swamped her, a black shadow falling over her. Anger, and rejection, and something else. Josh, of all people, thought she wasn't fit to be a mother.

Why do you care? You don't like Josh that way.

It was just ... the betrayal of the thing. That was all she needed right now.

She swallowed down her rage, her sorrow. 'I thought we were friends, Josh. Guess I was wrong.'

She turned on her heel, letting the bitterness seep in till it filled every pore. She understood at last, at least partly, Anto's urge to ruin everything. The grim satisfaction of losing it all. Of hitting rock bottom. A quick look back showed her Cassie was retreating into the pub, zipping up her hoodie, and Matt followed, looking confused, scratching his head. Caroline sensed she was being judged, that she and Josh had gone from being the cool kids of support group to a drama-riddled car crash, a bit like Fleetwood Mac but without the amazing songs.

As she looked back at the junction of the road, Josh stood

outside the pub, tense, angry. His eyes locked into hers – judging her, maybe, for being angry, for fighting Mary, for trying to get what she wanted at any cost. For not being perfect, a sunny blonde princess like Niamh. And then Caroline realised exactly what the other feeling was. A nasty stomach pain of an emotion that she hadn't felt in years, not since she'd met Anto's eyes across the dancefloor and they just belonged to each other, from that moment until the morning he'd gone into that bathroom and let go of his fragile hold on life.

Jealousy. That was what she felt. She was jealous of Niamh, who would always be perfect in Josh's eyes.

Josh

'Well? Say something.'

'Can you give me a second, do you think?'

Maggie had been reading the article for more than ten minutes now, peering over her glasses at her computer screen. Josh paced up and down in her office. What if she hated it? In the end he'd only sent it because what happened at Christopher Stone's house, followed by his horrible fight in the street with Caroline, was so awful that, whatever Maggie thought of the article, it could hardly be worse. He still jumped every time there was a knock at his door, convinced he was going to be arrested.

When he'd heard the voices at the door in Stone's house – a kid, a woman – he'd almost thrown up right there in the hallway. The whole horror of the situation had come slapping down on him, as if he'd just woken up having sleepwalked into a busy road. Shit. They were coming in. He saw dark shapes through the glass of the door, heard keys jangling. The lock turned in the door, but it didn't open – of course it didn't, because he'd unlocked it already.

The woman's voice said, 'Hm, we must have not turned the big lock. Silly us.' The key was turned the other way, and without thinking about it, Josh ducked into a cupboard in the hallway. It was very small and stuffed with coats, welly boots, a bike. He was sure he felt the handle of a tennis racket poking into his back. Stupid, stupid. What if they took their coats off and put them in this cupboard? He was going to prison. Was grief an acceptable defence?

'It's not fair, Mummy, he always gets to do water play, and he's not even the goodest, he drew a bad face on my exercise book.' The child was a girl, and sounded about six maybe? Josh didn't know much about kids but that was the age of Niamh's niece Sadie – his niece, too? Was she – oh God, *not the time Josh, not the time!*

'Well, that's how life works, sweetheart.' The mother. Christopher Stone's wife. Did she know he'd maybe been cheating on her, with a woman who was now dead? Dark thoughts crowded Josh's mind. Could Stone have pushed Niamh into the road somehow, to cover up the truth? No, all the witnesses said she ran out without looking. He must have upset her in some way. Dumped her, perhaps. It made his heart hurt with too many different feelings – rage that someone would do that to Niamh, sorrow that she would cheat on him, bewilderment that he hadn't spotted it.

It might not be true.

Why else would she be here, then?

He was so wrapped up in these thoughts that he hardly noticed it had gone quiet outside, and when he did, he allowed himself to let out a breath. Unfortunately, in doing so, he knocked the tennis racket from its precarious perch on top of a pile of random things, a yoga mat, some dumb-bells, a mini-trampoline. Oh God. Oh God. He listened for footsteps, coming to see who or what was in the cupboard. Nothing. Pressing his ear to the door, he heard the sound of a TV. A cartoon, he thought.

Very gently, he eased the door open. The hallway was empty. There were four steps between the cupboard and the door. He took them at a run, not looking round, and then he was outside and very very softly shutting the side door and running to his car, all the while expecting to hear shouts after him. A shot, maybe – the police here carried guns, after all. But there was nothing. He reached his car, drove off at speed, buckling his belt as he did. His heart rate was through the roof and he likely wasn't safe to drive. But he had escaped, and hopefully they'd never noticed anyone was there. Christ. He could have gone to jail, or been killed, even. His nerves had been on fire all through support group, which was maybe why he'd been so brutal with Caroline. He felt bad about that. But someone had to tell her, and she hadn't exactly been understanding of his situation, either. Telling *him* to move on! As if *she* had! Needless to say, they hadn't spoken since.

Now, Maggie slowly took off her glasses and began to polish them.

'Done?'

'Done.' She said nothing more.

Josh burst out, 'Are you doing this on purpose?'

'I'm just ... trying to find the right words.' She paused. 'Josh ... this is the best thing you've ever written. It's the best thing anyone at this paper has written, probably. We have to publish it.'

He blinked. 'Oh. You like it, then?'

'Like it? I'd be crying right now if I weren't a cynical old hack who hasn't shed a tear since Bambi's mother died. I'll talk to Layout about getting it online right away.'

So that was it. They would publish Josh's article about his grief over Niamh – no mention of course of how he'd lost her, the mystery surrounding the accident. He wanted to keep it pure, his memory of her unsullied by suspicion. Suddenly, he realised that if the article was published, there was a good chance Christopher Stone would read it. Did he even know Niamh was dead? Would he care?

8. CHERISH YOUR FAMILY

Caroline

She was coming off a flight from London, a hen do for a work colleague she didn't like all that much, and was strung out on cheap Prosecco, passive-aggressiveness, and the sheer disorganisation of the weekend. They'd gone all the way to Soho, centre of the entertainment industry, and ended up in a bad Irish pub (was there any other kind?) She was planning to subtly phase out Mary-Therese, the bride, before the wedding, and maybe not even attend, and was already putting the strategy together in her head (First, miss her birthday. Invent a medical complaint requiring minor surgery. Kill off an imaginary aunt of Anto's . . .) as they trailed down the ramp at Aldergrove Airport, bumping their wheelie cases over the carpet. She remembered the girls starting to mutter around her.

'Isn't that . . . '

'Wonder who . . . '

Mary-Therese gave a small shriek. 'Jaysus, Car, it's your husband. What's he doing here?'

Anto was standing in Arrivals, clutching a huge banner with her name on it, and a vast bunch of red roses (thirty quid's worth at least). When he spotted her, his face broke out in smiles, and he ran at her, chucking the banner and thirty quid of roses to the ground. 'There she is! Love of my life!' And he scooped her up in a big hug, and Caroline was mortified, but also pleased at the boot-faced look on the bride, whose intended, a GAA-playing culchie, was nowhere to be seen.

'Come on,' he said, taking her bag, not lowering his voice at all. She'd been texting him all weekend with the grim details of their bike tour through

197

London, the hen who'd thrown up in her handbag, the endless competition over whose 'hubby' was the most romantic. Well, look who just won that one. 'I'm taking you away from all this.'

'Bye, girls!' Caroline took his arm, waving cheerily. Thinking, thank God, that's me sorted for life. There's no one else I need. *If only she'd known.*

'Is that them?'

'For God's sake, Daddy, you've said that about the last fourteen people through. That's two wee boys.'

Caroline's mother tutted. 'Have you not your glasses with you, Donal?'

'I can see just fine, thank you, Kathleen.'

Caroline thanked God she had driven them to the airport, otherwise they'd likely be dead in a ditch. All the same, she was having to do a lot of offering it up. Sylvia said it was good to cherish your family when you'd been bereaved. But her father never stopped going on about the parking charges at the airport and her mother was still in a sulk because Caroline wouldn't let her buy a ginger and toffee muffin from Costa Coffee, which with her diabetes could kill her stone dead. She was also doing her best not to think about Josh, the terrible fight, the silence on her phone ever since, the bad news on her legal challenge. Oh, and Anto's death, of course.

'We'll get food when they arrive, I told you. I have it all in hand. Look, that's them.'

A loud Australian voice filled the lobby: 'Deeddddy, I don' loike this ployce!' And two little blonde girls trailed sulkily out, one sucking her thumb. They were both wearing pink frocks, matching, and had ratty fair hair that Caroline itched to brush. Dresses, for a flight across the world? What was

198

Gilda thinking? Gilda, their mother, was in yoga wear, as per usual, and looking around Belfast International Airport as if she might catch cholera. There was Paul, Caroline's brother, red-faced and balding, in surf clothes better suited to someone twenty years younger.

She sighed deeply, then pasted on a smile and plunged into the fray. 'Keegan! Kelsey! There's my wee dotes, let me see you. Gilda, looking lovely. As always.' She dispensed kisses and hugs – Gilda had a back like an ironing board. Her mammy and daddy were still standing, bewildered, Mammy clutching her handbag like an evacuee in wartime. She directed the tired little girls to them. 'There's Granny and Granddad, you remember them? Go and say hello.' Finally, she turned to her brother, who, despite not having seen him for a year, she didn't hug. That was the mark of real family. 'You made it then.'

'Jesus, those budget flights are shite. Nowhere to charge my iPad, even! And they were right snippy about giving Gil hot water for her home-grown mint.' She'd forgotten how much Paul liked to complain.

'Ah well, offer it up.' Had she really said that? She was turning into her mother at a visible pace.

Gilda came over, all tanned skin and taut abs, nasal Australian accent. 'Can we get a snack for the kids? They're starvo.'

'They've muffins in that Costa,' said Caroline's mother hopefully.

Gilda shuddered. 'Oh my God. Refined sugar and carbs. What about some avocado or sprouted seeds?'

Her mother looked blank. 'Brussels sprouts, you mean?'

Caroline's smile grew even tighter. It was going to be a long two weeks.

Josh

'You wrote this? I can't believe it.'

'What, you don't think I have the talent?'

'Of course I do, you eejit, it's just . . .' Niamh gestured two-handed at his laptop, which was sitting in the triangle of her crossed legs. She was wearing a T-shirt of his, a baggy cotton one printed with the names of his GCSE leavers' class and the stupid nicknames that had seemed hysterically funny in 2000 – Josh 'Wassuuuuup' Mkumbe. Because he'd said 'Wassuuuup' a lot back then, presumably. They all had. 'Josh, this is so good. Really.'

'Ah, it's nothing special. Give me.' Josh took the laptop from her, and replaced it with his head, nestled on her thigh. Secretly, he was delighted. Journalism increasingly seemed a mad career choice, as magazines and even monoliths like the Independent *folded around him. But it was all he wanted to do.*

'It is so special. You're gonna win awards one day. I'm already picking out my fancy dress, so I am.' And he loved her for that, not just for her casual confidence in him, but also for the assumption they were going to stay together.

Josh was thinking about that as he listened to the head of ad sales talk about his article, which had gone live the day before. He'd done his best not to obsess about it, actually turning his phone off and putting it in a drawer in the kitchen, although his fingers kept inching for something that wasn't there, like a phantom limb. He was afraid of what Niamh's family might say, whether they'd like it, or make fun of him. What Caroline might say – if he'd accurately represented grief or if she'd get out her teacher's red pen and correct him. Not that she was talking to him. They hadn't spoken at all since their row after support group.

'We've not had anything like this before. Not even the piece about which city councillors look the most like dogs, and people *loved* that one.' The head of ad sales was a guy called Joe who wore trendy clear-rim glasses, the kind Niamh called Deirdre Barlow glasses. *Had called.*

'So ... it's OK?' Josh was having trouble following Joe, so accosted was he by memories of Niamh.

The article seemed to have stirred them all up, like sediment. Maggie was on the other side of the table, flicking through the stapled sheets of figures. She hadn't said much in the meeting, which wasn't like her.

'It's amazing. The engagement is off the charts. Ten thousand retweets, estimated reach of ... ' Josh saw Maggie wince as Joe spoke. She thought Twitter was the death of journalism, and of truth in general. 'We've even had syndication enquiries. And the advertising click-through will keep us going for months.'

'All right then.' Josh was still watching Maggie. 'That's great.'

'It really is!' Joe the sales guy pushed his trendy glasses up his nose. 'I'm scheduling a whole rack of tweets to maximise exposure. Are you on Twitter, Josh?'

'No,' he said quickly. 'And no plans to be.' Some journalists found it useful for tracking down stories, but Josh used Facebook for that, and he hated the negativity of Twitter, the trolls and the outrage mobs.

Joe looked disappointed. 'You're getting some awesome praise on there at the moment. People love it.'

Maggie finally spoke. 'Apart from the ones who think it's mawkish and exploiting his tragedy for money.'

No extra money so far, Josh wanted to point out, but didn't. 'Hmmm.'

Maggie said to Joe, not looking at Josh, 'Don't make him go online if he's not keen. Why don't you go and send a few more wee tweets, son?'

'There's more to it than—'

'Now, maybe?'

Joe gathered his papers and left, casting curious glances at Maggie. Something was definitely up. Josh's stomach sank away. As the door shut, he said, 'Look, if this is about the councillors' expenses story, I'll get to it, I promise.'

'Forget the expenses story. I already have Bob on it.' Bob was a super-antiquated reporter of the beer-belly door-stepping ilk, who existed in a cloud of smoke and had a face as red as a Christmas ham.

'OK. So . . . ?'

'IT sent me something this morning.'

'Oh?' Where was she going with this?

Maggie slid a piece of paper over the table. It took Josh a moment to realise he was looking at his own search history, on his work computer. *Christopher Stone. 17 Morris Street Belfast. Who is Christopher Stone. Christopher Stone Niamh Donnelly.*

Oh God. He'd been rumbled. 'So what, you spy on us now?' He stalled for time, panic coursing through him.

'Only when you spend all your time doing things that aren't work. What is this, Josh?'

'I just . . . I needed to find out what happened. She ran out in the road, Maggie! Something had upset her. And I found out she was at this guy's house, Stone . . .'

'How did you find that out?' Her voice was low and controlled, and he remembered that she'd been the one journalist to break 'Mad Badger' Cassidy, head of the IRA punishment squad in the 1980s. She'd even made him cry.

'I . . . there was an address in one of her old bags. I found it. And she had this photo as well . . . '

'Josh, did you go to the house to see who lived there? That it was a man?'

No point in lying – she was like his mum in that regard, she'd see right through him. He nodded.

'Did you . . . Josh, please tell me you didn't go inside.' It was almost what Caroline had said.

He needed to make her understand. 'Maggie, I had to! This guy, I have to know who he was to Niamh. He's married, has a kid. What if they were having an affair? What if he did something to her, and she ran out because of that? What if he *killed* her?' His voice cracked on the word.

Maggie let out a deep breath. 'You broke into his house.'

'Yes.'

'A place where a woman and child live.'

'Yes, but I didn't know—'

'Let me ask you something, Josh. Have you completely lost your mind?'

'Of course I have!' he burst out. 'Did you not read my article? My wife died. She was thirty-two years old and she died, and no one can tell me why, and all I know is she was visiting some guy that day, someone she never even mentioned, a place she'd never told me about, and no one, not me, not her friends, not her family, knew anything about it, or if they do they sure as hell won't tell me. Of course I've bloody lost my mind. That's what grief is.'

Maggie took the piece of paper, and removed a pen from behind her ear, and wrote a number on it in blocky writing. She pushed it across the table to him. A London phone number.

'What is this?'

'An editor at *Dude* magazine read your piece. They'd like you to write for them. Could be a staff job in it, even.'

He gaped at her. This conversation was taking so many strange turns. 'In London?'

'In London. They want you to go over for an interview.'

Josh didn't know what to say. 'You want me to *leave*? Because of this?'

She sighed again, exasperated. 'Of course I don't. You're my best reporter – I mean who else have I got? Bob with his halitosis, who can hardly walk two paces? But you're not right, Josh. This place . . . you only came here for Niamh. Now she's gone, and your family, your own life, are back there. You're spiralling, love. Look at you. Maybe you'd be better off leaving.'

'Oh.' He let that sink in. Maggie thought he should go back to London. 'Am I fired?'

'Of course you're not fired, you eejit. The paperwork'd be too much hassle. But I'm strongly advising you, as your boss – and your friend – to reconsider your life here. Is this what you want, writing about endless sectarian scandals that have nothing to do with you? Trying to figure out nine hundred years of tribal warfare? You're young. You're talented, you're "diverse".' She did ironic air quotes. 'There's plenty of stories you could tell that matter more.'

'But . . . a magazine? I'm a news guy.' He'd never really considered himself a writer, if he was honest, never thought about features or magazines. He was hard news. Bringing down the corrupt, lifting up the voiceless. Even if, increasingly, people only wanted to read lists of celebrities who looked like cats, and vice versa.

'Just think about it,' said Maggie. 'Get them to pay for your flight and go and see your mammy. I bet she worries. I know I do.'

That hit home. He'd rather Maggie was angry with him than have her worried, Maggie who'd faced down hardened terrorists without turning a hair. If she was worried, he must be in a bad way. Josh took the piece of paper and went out. He glanced at the clock, more out of habit than anything else: 11.52 a.m. Niamh had died for another day.

'Mum ... Mum! Please stop crying. I might not even get the job, OK?'

It made no difference. Eventually, he had to hang up because her weeping and wailing showed no sign of ending. He'd no idea she wanted him home so badly. His flight to the interview was booked for early the next day – he would go, anyway, and see what they said.

Sitting in his car in the *Chronicle* car park, he let himself think about it. Finding a new flat in a housing market that would only have gotten worse – he wouldn't survive living with his mum and Sam for long, he knew that. But Sylvia's next tip had been cherish your family, and he was hardly doing that staying in Belfast by himself, dodging his mum's calls. He thought about having somewhere to go on weekends, for dinner and TV. Having friends that weren't Niamh's, family that wasn't hers. Eventually, perhaps, starting to date again, though the idea made him want to sleep for a hundred years. Maybe leaving behind this dangerous obsession with Christopher Stone, whoever he was, and how he'd known Niamh. Did Josh even want to look under that particular stone? Would it just ruin his memories of her, bright and clean for ever?

Leaving would also mean saying goodbye to Caroline. His dear friend, the person who'd got him through these last months. Could he really leave her? Of course, she wasn't talking to him. Josh itched to apologise, but resentment blocked up his throat and he still hadn't messaged her. He knew he was acting a little crazy at the moment, obsessing over Niamh's secrets. But she of all people should understand that he had no choice. To end the silence of the grave, to try and see into Niamh's final hours, he would do anything for that. And wasn't she the same, trying to second-guess what Anto might have wanted? Flying in the face of all the evidence? No, she could say sorry first, and then maybe they'd be friends again.

On his way home, Josh drove near to the street where Christopher Stone lived. He wanted to turn into it, go up to the door and knock and demand answers, but he knew that was madness. Instead he made himself drive home, back to his empty flat.

Caroline

'Daddy! I don't loike this stuff!' Kelsey was crying. It was, at Caroline's count, the seventeenth time that day. Earlier it had been because the floor was too slippy. Then because her glass of water was too warm. Then she couldn't find her toy kangaroo (bit on the nose, that one, for an Australian kid), then she couldn't see anything she wanted to watch on TV (Caroline's parents refused to pay for subscription channels, thinking it a wicked indulgence; you'd watch what was on and be thankful for it). Now it seemed to be about the white bread ham sandwich she'd been offered for her lunch. The kids were used to a totally different way of eating – avocado slices, salads. Caroline didn't think her parents had ever seen an avocado up close, and certainly wouldn't dream of buying one, assuming such a thing could even be found in their nearby Spar.

She laid her head against the sofa in the Good Front Room, where she had escaped for five minutes of peace, though it was frowned upon to be in there when it wasn't Christmas. She sighed. She was expected to come up every day to visit when her brother was home, and since it was half term, she had no excuse, because as far as they saw it she had no other life and no calls on her time. She felt drained, sad that she didn't know her nieces better, depressed that her parents were getting so old and slow. She was doing her best not to think of Josh, who still hadn't got in touch. Was that it, then? They weren't friends any more?

The sound of the door opening ended her moment alone. It was Paul. 'Oh! Are you allowed in here?'

'I'm thirty-six, Paul, I can go where I want.'

All the same, she stood up, careful to smooth down the cushions on the sofa. 'Is Kelsey all right?'

He sighed. 'It's hard for them. They're jet-lagged, they're freezing all the time – this is spring? – and they can't eat any of the food.'

'You used to love this kind of food,' said Caroline pointedly, even though she too thought her parents' strict regime of white carbs and processed meat was not the best.

'Not you as well. "Oh Paul, you've changed! You're so Australian now!" Well, guess what, people are allowed to change. We don't all have to sit here drowning in rain and, I don't know, sausages.'

Caroline glared at him for a moment, then started to laugh. He smiled, running his hands through his thinning hair. Her brother was beginning to look old, and that meant she must be too. 'So you love it out there, huh?'

'It has its drawbacks. Skin cancer, spiders, racism . . .'

'Sharks, jellyfish, crocodiles,' she continued.

'Yeah. But it's sunny and everyone's happier than here. More hopeful, I guess. You should come out and visit.'

She knew she should have before, but they'd always been saving, first to patch up the ridiculous house Anto had bought for them, then for IVF. 'Yeah. I just . . . might not have the cash for a while.'

'Because of this court case?'

She was surprised. 'Oh. Did Mum tell you?'

'Yeah. She's worried about you.'

Caroline gritted her teeth. She was worried about *Caroline*? The sensible daughter, not the son who'd gone haring off around the world, losing his passport and all his money in various pyramid schemes, contracting malaria once, even? 'There's no need to be. I have it all figured out.'

'Mum said you were selling your house.'

'Yes. Well, it doesn't have the best associations for me now.' It came out tartly.

'I know, I get that. Christ, Car, I'm so sorry for what happened. Anto was . . . I saw how happy you two were. But do you really want to sink it all into this court thing? What if you lose? Where will you live then?'

She stared at the mantelpiece, trying not to lose her temper. The framed photos of the kids, of her and Paul when they were little, posing in a studio. The one of Caroline and Anto's wedding was gone. To avoid upsetting her, or because they'd never really approved of him? 'What else can I do?' Her voice wobbled.

'I don't know. Maybe it's just not meant to be.'

That phrase again, the one that was guaranteed to send her off the rails with rage. 'Oh piss off, Paul, it's easy for you to say, with your two healthy kids. You can't understand what it's like, knowing you might never have them. So don't you dare talk to me about money, the amount of times Mum and Dad had to bail you out over the years! Just don't talk to me at all.'

And she stormed out, slamming the door of the Good Front Room so hard that it started Kelsey off crying again.

Josh

'Are you all right, dear?'

'Oh! You're awake.' Josh had been sitting on Sylvia's dusty sofa for a while now, but since the older woman had fallen asleep in her armchair midway through an anecdote about Iris, he'd drifted off into memories, dissecting once again his last few days with Niamh. Not that he'd known they were that. Had she said something? Acted differently? Was there a giant red flag waving right in front of his nose and he hadn't even noticed? Why had she been visiting a handsome man in his forties? Why were her family lying? 'Sorry, I was just thinking about . . .'

'About your young lady?' Sylvia's face was thin and lined, dark circles round her eyes, but she was smiling.

'Yes. Niamh.'

'You moved over here for her?'

'Everyone thought it was mad, leaving London for Belfast. But . . . we just knew.'

'I met my Iris when we were seventeen. At school, still. But we knew, too. Luckily, no one suspected – we could live together quite happily, as friends.'

'And how did they . . . your family, they found out?' They must have, since they'd disowned her.

Sylvia sighed. 'Iris was an orphan – she'd been left some money, so she was fine. But my parents . . . my father was a

209

landowner, quite wealthy. They wanted me to marry. It all came out when I went home for a visit and the neighbour's son was there. Our fathers planned to join the estates, you see. They said they were stopping my allowance, and I was moving home. No more teacher training. No more Iris.'

'So you told them?'

'I said I wasn't marrying anyone, and I wasn't leaving Iris. We never used the words ... well, people didn't in those days, but they knew what I meant.'

'And they cut you off.'

It was so unfair. So many people never found a love like Sylvia and Iris's, one that would last a whole life, and yet her family couldn't be happy for her.

Sylvia's cold, papery hand touched his. 'Don't be sad for me. We had a wonderful life, Iris and I. That's what it makes it so hard now she's gone. You feel that way too, don't you?'

Josh wondered how Sylvia could see that, when she'd only met him a few times. 'It's just ... I moved here, I gave up my own life, left my family, my flat. I thought I was building a life with Niamh, but now that won't happen.' He swallowed hard. 'I don't know what's left for me, if I don't have her. I changed myself so much for her.'

He hadn't needed anything else when he had her, not hobbies or friends to go drinking with or his mum or even career progression. Just Niamh and their evenings of films and music, their holidays to America and Australia, camping in Donegal, the tent collapsing onto them with the weight of rain, running laughing down the hill to take shelter in the pub. So many memories that only the two of them knew about. There was nothing lonelier than a memory no one else shared.

Josh shook himself – he was supposed to be cheering Sylvia

up, not bringing her down even more. 'You said you have some relatives left?' Josh remembered Caroline's idea to look for Sylvia's nieces. He'd said he would help but then done nothing, tangled up as he was in Niamh and her secrets. He was a bad friend, and now of course Caroline wasn't even speaking to him. He so wished they could make it up, but still couldn't bring himself to message first. He hadn't even told her he was going to London the next day for his job interview.

'I had a brother; he inherited the house, I imagine. He and his wife had two girls. My nieces! They'd be in their fifties now. I've never met them. My brother passed some years ago, I saw the funeral notice.'

It was so sad, the way she said it. Accepting a terrible loss that never needed to happen. Death took people all the time – took them and wouldn't give them back, and however much progress the human race made, it still kept taking. Road accidents, like Niamh's. Diseases, cancer. Even if all of those could be avoided or cured, there was still suicide, people sending themselves into the darkness like Anto had, because life was just too painful to keep on living.

'You've never tried to find them?'

'Oh, they wouldn't want to bother with an old woman like me! I would love to have met them, though. Just once, even.'

'Iris, she died two years ago?'

'That's right. Cancer. I nursed her to the end.'

Two years almost totally alone, in a house full of memories. Josh had done his best to tidy up discreetly while Sylvia napped, but the house was dirty, and cold breezes came in from the draughty window panes. 'It's lonely,' he said, half to himself, 'when you lose the one person in your life.' Caroline was right, Sylvia needed more people.

'I know, dear. It's like half of yourself dies with them. Or more.' She hesitated. 'You can still change that, however. Your family, you're close to them?'

'Kind of. My mum, yes. My dad – he's dead. My brother – he hasn't really been there for me. It's . . . disappointing.'

She was nodding. 'That's how it goes. It's often the people you wouldn't think of who'll be there for you, and carry you through. That's why I say in the book to reach out to people.'

'Yeah. I'm trying.'

'And you have Caroline. A wonderful young woman.'

'Hmm. Yeah.' Except she wasn't talking to him, no word of apology for screaming at him in the street. What if that was it already, an end to their growing friendship?

'I'd hang on to her if I were you. She's a good one.'

He looked up sharply. How could she know these things? For a moment, he wanted to confide in Sylvia, thinking that maybe she would understand the strange thoughts he'd been having about Caroline, the way your partner died and you still had to go on living, and it could hardly be cheating if you felt a momentary pull to someone else, when their fair hair brushed your cheek and you smelled their perfume, and yet it still felt like cheating, it felt terrible. 'Sylvia . . .'

Soft breathing. Sylvia's eyes had drooped closed, and she was asleep again. Josh crept into the kitchen, where he washed up some of the dishes in the sink, plus others on the draining rack that hadn't been properly done. Poor Sylvia. Was this what awaited him, if he couldn't find a way to move on? Stuck in this city where he didn't belong? Or would this interview be a way out?

Caroline

She lowered her head to the keyboard in frustration. Why couldn't Sylvia have had a nice, distinctive surname? She'd finally had time to do some searching for the relatives, amid the mayhem of the family visit and court case and the house sale. After casually picking Sylvia's brain as much as possible, Caroline had learned that the nieces were called Heather and Lynn, also hardly unusual. Sylvia had once known the names of their kids, but she had temporarily lost them, like a misplaced pair of glasses. Caroline returned to her shortlist of Heathers (why did so many women have to change their names when they got married? Didn't they know how hard it made it for amateur genealogists?) and copy-pasted her little spiel.

> Hi, my name is Caroline and I recently got to know a lady called Sylvia Smyth, in her eighties. She's getting on now and would love to see her family once again – there was some kind of rift, I gather. If you're her niece I would love to hear from you. Thank you!

She was tempted to add a bit about her own sad story, to show she knew what she was talking about, but how to explain it without sounding mad? Anyway, it wasn't relevant. She added a smiley face so she looked friendly. Then she sent the same message to ten other possible Heathers of around the right age. Even if it went nowhere, it was good to have a hobby, something to distract herself from the fact Anto was dead and Josh wasn't talking to her.

Hating herself, Caroline clicked on Josh's Facebook page. There was a recent update – he had checked in at Gatwick earlier that day. What was he doing back in London? Visiting his mum, or more than that? It was mid-week, a strange time to go. Normally he would tell her something like that, and it lodged in her chest that they really weren't talking now. How long would it go on for? She'd kind of expected an apology, she had to admit, but none had come.

Caroline found herself going through each of his photos all the way back to 2007 when he'd joined Facebook. She even looked at the wedding photos, Josh so handsome in his electric-blue suit. It was an unusual choice for someone so quiet and resolute, hinting at an underground lake of fun in his character, when he wasn't bereaved and grieving. She wondered if that person would ever resurface. She looked at each of his 547 pictures, careful not to click anything that would leave grubby prints on them. Deep-liking, they called it. She'd be mortified if Josh thought she was into him in that way. God, it was such a mess. How could she take back what she'd said to him at the pub? Should she say sorry? He should apologise to her, really. He was the one acting crazy, obsessing over Niamh's last moments, and yet he'd treated her like she was losing it. All the same, she desperately missed him, being able to text him any random thought she had, any time someone was insensitive about her grief, any time something was darkly funny. Any time she got distracted for a second and forgot Anto had killed himself, only to have it take her breath away again when it all crashed back to her.

An hour later, Caroline stopped, a crick in her neck and wrist aching, eyes burning. She'd spent too much time alone lately, surfing the internet, looking for answers that weren't there. It wasn't good for her. She needed to get out and do something, see people. And she would. Tomorrow. Maybe.

Since she was in a self-loathing self-harm-by-surfing mood,

she googled Josh's name. Just a whim. A list of his old articles came up. And something new. She clicked. *What can you say about a thirty-two-year-old woman who died?*

The next morning, she still couldn't stop thinking about it. The beauty of Josh's words, the pain he felt over Niamh. How could you ever get over something like that?

As she drove to her parents' down country lanes, numb to the beauty of the spring flowers poking through cold earth, listening to songs that reminded her of Anto, Caroline wondered was she going ever so slightly mad. Yes, she had her parents, and her brother, but in some ways that made it worse – they clearly didn't approve of how she was handling things, so she couldn't talk to them about her loneliness. Seeing their worry and disbelief just made her feel crazier. Jenny tried to be there for her, but being perennially single she couldn't really relate to the pain of a once-loving house gone quiet as a grave. And the only person who had understood, she had pushed away, fought with, screamed at. Caroline couldn't think of a time when she'd felt more alone.

9. AVOID BIG LIFE CHANGES

Josh

'Jesus, I hate travelling. We have to do something about this, so we do.'
Niamh spoke into the side of his neck. She'd run straight through arriv-
als at Gatwick and into his arms. They'd been apart for five days and it
was agony.

'How's your mum?'

She twisted up her face, bent down for her case. 'She'll be OK, they
think. Very weak. Everyone's so afraid they're sniping at each other right left
and centre, and Daddy's become obsessed with trimming the hedge. It's the
best-trimmed hedge in all of Ireland, three times this week. And Siobhan's
the queen of the castle, bossing everyone round, making us eat her horrible
low-fat, low-taste dinners just because she's on Slimming World. She makes
the chips with cooking spray, *for the love of God!'*

As they made their way to the train, Josh let Niamh's chatter wash over
him like a bath. His little flat, which had once felt so peaceful after years of
a house share, seemed so quiet without her. They weren't even living in the
same place at this point, had been together less than a year when her mum
got sick. Breast cancer. Niamh had broken the news to him – she'd have to
go home for a few months to help out. It was just expected, never mind that
she had four siblings still at home. And Josh would have to give her up. As
she came over less and less frequently – flights were expensive, and she'd quit
her headhunter job to be at home – his uneasiness grew. He was horribly
afraid that one day she would just stay there. It was her home, her family.
She'd never liked London that much anyway, had confided she was on the
verge of leaving when she met him. Josh wasn't confident he was enough of

an anchor to keep her there, against the counterweight of her sick mum and family and friends and home. He was also afraid that he didn't know how to lose her, not now he'd finally found her.

Now, he made the same journey through Gatwick himself, going the other way this time. It felt wrong. London had always been his anchor point, the place he returned to. It was strange being back – the city seemed so loud and busy, people jostling him as they streamed through the gates to the train and out into Victoria at the other end. Josh had to smile, knowing what Niamh would say if she saw him. *Looks like we took the city out of the city boy, so we did.* He made his way to his mum's house in Peckham, noticing all the changes in the year since he'd been here, trendy themed bars opening up in disused African grocers, craft beer breweries, even what he thought was a bar themed as an African grocer (it was hard to tell). In between were scattered hairdressers, nail parlours, everything the existing population here still needed, at least until the hipsters eventually drove them out. His mother's neighbours on either side of her little terraced house were large house-shares of creatives, photographers, writers, comedians. The house down the street had sold for a million pounds the month before, but still Josh's mum stayed firm.

He stood outside for a moment, thinking how strange it was to come home and have to ring the bell. His mother took her time getting to the door, moving as she always did with a sort of slow bustle. 'There you are! I've been waiting.'

'It's a long journey, Ma.'

'Let me look at you.' She drew him into the kitchen, which he could see groaned with cakes, pies, stews. Niamh had always said his mother was trying to make her fat with her cooking – though they'd got on well, both of them addicted to gossip, their mutual chat streams meeting and merging like in *Ghostbusters*. 'You look tired.'

He shrugged away. 'I got up early.' *And you know, the whole dead wife who might have been having an affair thing.* Josh wished there was someone he could open up to about it, who'd understand but wouldn't try to talk him off the mad path he'd set himself on. He knew it was mad. That wasn't the point. He thought yet again of Caroline. Why couldn't they have helped each other through all this, instead of falling out? 'Where's Sam?'

His mum turned to the counter, busying herself with food preparation to cover any awkwardness, a thing she had in common with Niamh's family. 'You want a sandwich? I made some cake, too. Or a cup of tea?'

'Mum.'

She sighed. 'He . . . went out.'

That was nice. His only brother hadn't seen him in six months, hadn't even come to Niamh's funeral, and now he wasn't here to say hello. 'Big surprise. Did the new job pan out?' Sam had been working in a trainer shop, last he heard.

She chopped some cucumber with vigour. 'It's hard right now.'

Sam was twenty-eight, but bounced continually from low-paid job to unemployment. Why would he need to get a job when he lived quite happily in his old room at his mum's, where he didn't have to cook or clean or learn to take care of himself? Josh felt a rush of anger. 'Well, I have to get ready for this interview, anyway.'

'You really think you might move back?' She kept her tone light, as she buttered bread for the sandwich he hadn't said he wanted. She was hiding how desperately she hoped he would return. Josh thought of being back here, his dad's picture on the wall, never older than Josh was now, sharing a room with Sam again, listening as his brother's phone buzzed all night with messages from his girls and his mates, as if he was a teenager still. Don't make big life changes for a while, Sylvia had said in her book – it was too risky to do it in the midst of grief. And this would be one, for sure. London was home. But returning would feel like taking several big steps back, to being a man with no place of his own, and most importantly no wife. Single again. It was a bleak thought.

The magazine offices were impressive, he had to admit, after the dingy 1970s block the *Chronicle* was housed in. Smoked glass, a lobby full of plants, shiny lifts with a complicated control panel. He was met by a young woman in clear-rim glasses and baggy dungarees. 'Josh! So happy to see you. Calvin'll be along in a tic, OK? Can I get you a kombucha?'

What in the name of god is kombucha? muttered ghostly Niamh, over his shoulder. 'I'm fine thanks. Maybe some water.'

Josh had done his homework, of course. *Dude* magazine had been somehow thriving in the difficult market for print, with a combination of hard-hitting reportage and emotional first-person features, plus a popular website full of lists about cats. They weren't the old-fashioned 'boobs and negging' type of men's mag, but were 'unashamedly male', whatever that meant. Spending twenty quid on a razor, from what he could tell from the advertising spread.

'Josh! Mate!' The greeting was so friendly he wondered for a second if he'd already met Calvin McCready and just forgotten about it. But no. The editor was young, hardly older than Josh, surely, with a shaved head and buttoned-up lumberjack shirt. 'Oh man, we're so pleased to have you here. Loved your piece. Didn't we, Malandra?'

'OMG, I had all the feels,' said the dungarees-girl, who must be Malandra (was that a name?), clasping a fist to her chest.

'Come, come, let's chat. You want a coffee? Cold brew?'

Josh had expected to go to an office, but instead they went to a central coffee area, set up like a hip café, with views over East London. Josh looked out at the hot, swarming city, and wondered if it was still home. He accepted something called cold brew, which hadn't quite made it to Belfast yet. *What's wrong with a nice Barry's tea?* whispered Niamh.

'So! Josh! Your piece was just …' Calvin mimed his heart exploding. 'And the engagement online – wow. We need some of that here at *Dude*. We'd love you to write for us.'

'Did you have a piece in mind?' Josh had a list of ideas he'd scribbled down on the flight over, feeling a bit of a fraud mining his own boring life for pitches, instead of chasing down news stories as he'd been trained.

'Mate. We want you on staff. I'm offering you a job.'

Through the window, London roared around them, oblivious to whether Josh came back or stayed in Belfast. It was all the same to the city.

Caroline

'God love you, is it mad with them all here?'

Caroline and Jenny were drinking wine in a bar in the city centre that was far too noisy and crowded for Caroline's tastes. She was going to have to face it – she was too old to be out on Friday nights. Her mind went to her pizza evenings with Josh. She'd seen him check back into the airport on Facebook earlier, during what had become an hourly stalk of his feed (Why? So stupid) so it was just a short trip to London. Was he moving back there? It would make sense. His mum was there, and there were more journalism jobs. There was nothing really to keep him here. The thought made her pick up her drink, glug it hard before answering Jenny.

'Yeah, Mum and Dad are too old to cope with the kids, really. Dad goes mad if anyone changes the radio station, and Mum can't get her head around "clean eating" at all. She keeps telling Gilda she scrubbed the dirt off the potatoes, and Gilda just makes a face like someone's trying to murder her with carbs.'

'And how long are they here for?'

'Ten very long days.' Caroline felt bad. She hardly got to see her brother, and when he was here all he did was wind her up, just like when they were kids. The girls were sweet, but inclined to be whiny and picky with food (like their mother). Caroline couldn't help but think of her dream-child, amenable and chatty, who alternated between being a boy and a girl, who would never whine or complain but be cheerfully grateful all the time, like Pollyanna with an iPad. Their name would be Patrick if a boy, after Anto's dad, or Louisa if a girl, after Caroline's granny. Maybe she could have more than one, even, if she won the case. The brief spurt of hope died in her. No one else thought she could do this. There was no guarantee of having any child at all.

'Ah, now,' said Jenny philosophically, which made Caroline think of Josh, too. 'And how's it going with the legal stuff?'

Caroline traced the condensation on her glass, as a loud burst of laughter came from a group of office workers to her right. 'Not so good. Mary's challenged my application, so that means the judge is less likely to rule on it. It might have to go to a full trial.'

Jenny frowned. 'Why would she do a thing like that?'

'Jenny, your guess is as good as mine. Spite. Religion. General madness. I don't know.'

'She's grieving too,' said Jenny quietly, and Caroline nodded irritably.

'I know. But that's no reason to make my life harder.'

'What did your ones say about it?'

'Ach, you know how they are. It feels so embarrassing,' Caroline winced. 'Making a fuss like this. About sperm, of all things. I may kill my mammy and daddy with sheer embarrassment.'

'Sure Irish mammies and daddies are embarrassed by everything. Mine still haven't forgiven me for being sick in the neighbour's leylandii hedge when I was fifteen that time and we got pissed on peach schnapps.'

Caroline sighed. 'God! I miss peach schnapps. It was so delicious. Why do we have to drink all these bitter drinks now? Gin and wine and what have you. Those were simpler times.'

'I know,' said Jenny, nonetheless guzzling down her dry white wine. 'So what's the next step? Legally?'

'See what the judge says. Then go to court if I need to, have a full trial. Challenge it.'

'Mary won't like that.'

'No. I imagine she won't.' Caroline sighed again. Why did life feel so flat and dreary? Sure, she was bereaved, but she'd felt all right before, like there was still some hope in the world. Now she just felt grey. She caught sight of herself in the mirror over the bar and realised she looked sour and tired.

'And how's the support group?' Jenny was full of questions as always, a good listener. Caroline felt guilty for talking about herself all the time, but she couldn't seem to muster much interest in the outside world.

'Ah, you know. Everyone's got their own burdens. Cassie's doing a bit better, I think. Matt's barely keeping his head above water. Also, I think Josh might be moving back to London. Or thinking about it, anyway.' And of course they weren't speaking, but she was too ashamed to tell Jenny that. She knew it would sound childish.

She said it lightly, but Jenny's face clouded over. 'No! Why?'

'Well, it makes sense I suppose. His family's there, plus there's more jobs.'

'But . . . I thought, like, you and him . . . ?'

'Me and him what?' Her voice was sharper than she meant.

Jenny blinked and back-pedalled. 'Ah, nothing. I always just thought, in time, there might be something there.'

'He'd hardly be interested in me,' Caroline said lightly, taking a large gulp of her drink. The wine was sour in her mouth. 'I'm older than him, he'd be off with some young hot thing if he was up for moving on, which he isn't.'

'Ah, Car, sure how could he do better than you? Maybe he doesn't realise it yet, and sure neither of you are ready, but in time . . . '

'We're both grieving,' Caroline said, again hating her snippy sarcastic tone. 'Neither of us could even think of something like that.' She squashed down the memories of the kitchen, his arms around her, the beat of his heart against her own.

'I know, I know, but later . . . '

Caroline had always hated that approach to her grief, like it was a bout of the flu or a case of fungal nail infection that would grow out in a few months. It was more like a life-altering injury, Anto gone for good, never coming back. The chance to have his child had been the only thing keeping her going, because that too was permanent, a part of him that could never be taken

226

away. 'Listen . . . ' She stopped herself. She'd been about to snap at her oldest, dearest friend, her rock when Anto had died, who'd spent the whole evening asking Caroline about herself. All because Jenny had dared to suggest something that had been playing shamefully around the edges of Caroline's own mind for weeks now. Her and Josh. Josh and her. One day. Maybe she'd even allowed herself to think it, in some distant corner of her mind. But not if he went back to London. 'Jen, I'm sorry, this place is getting on my wick. Everyone looks fifteen. I can't hear myself think. Do you want to come back to mine and we'll pick up a nice bottle of wine? Or even better, a bottle of Archer's?'

Jenny looked surprised. 'Well, sure, if that's what you want. It's expensive here, right enough.'

'And then you can tell me what you've been up to, and I'll stop going on about myself so much, like the selfish old bag I'm turning into.'

Josh

'So . . . they want me start as soon as possible. If I take it, of course.'

Silence. Josh looked round at the Donnelly family. They were having dinner at Mammy's, as they always had on weekends and always would. Had Niamh been alive, had she not run into the road that day, Josh would have been doing this for the rest of his life, or at least until one of Mammy and Daddy died. Probably then Siobhan would take over, as matriarch. She was staring at him now with a curious expression. Hostility? Sadness? Relief, maybe?

'Well, that's great,' said Darragh nervously. 'Is it a good job?'

'Yeah. Pretty good.' *Dude* had offered him more money than the *Chronicle* ever had, the chance to work on long reads, everything he should have wanted. He didn't know why he wasn't more excited.

'So you're leaving?' said Mammy, who seemed a bit slower every time he saw her. What would happen when they eventually passed on, Mammy and Daddy? Would Josh go to the funeral, or was he out of the family now?

'I think so. I haven't totally made my mind up but ... I think so, yeah. For now, anyway.' That was a stupid thing to say – what possible reason would he have to move back to Belfast again? Niamh was dead. This was the final nail in her coffin. 'I ... I hope you all understand.'

'Of course we do,' said Siobhan briskly, rising to her feet. 'I'm sure your mammy will be glad to have you back. Now, who's for dessert?'

And that was it. As the children scattered, the adults covering their feelings with bustle as always, Niamh's daddy hung back. For a moment, Josh thought he was going to say something meaningful, perhaps about how Josh would always be part of the family, even though Niamh was gone. Instead, he clapped Josh's shoulder once again. 'You're all right, son.' That was all he said. *You're all right, son.* Josh felt like crying.

'I'll just ... excuse me.' There was one thing he had to do before he left this house, possibly never to return, never again to bash his head on the low ceiling of the bathroom or awkwardly pass by the holy-water font in the hallway. Probably nothing. There were most likely no more clues to be had in the mystery of Niamh and Christopher Stone. But he just had to check one more thing.

*

'What the hell are you doing?' Siobhan stood in the doorway, her phone in her hand.

Josh paused, caught red-handed. He was in the front room, on his knees in front of the cupboard with the photo albums. He had snuck in during the general hubbub of cleaning up dinner and getting dessert out. The albums, fragile items with printed leatherette covers and crinkly plastic infills, were scattered all around him, careless. A few faded pictures had already fluttered out. But he didn't care. This family, they were nothing to him without Niamh. He'd burn that to the ground along with everything else, if he had to. 'I'm looking for answers, Siobhan. Because you've not given me any, have you?'

'What are you talking about?' She came in, closing the door after her. Josh found this suspicious; the doors in this house were never shut, a source of great irritation to him.

'This guy Christopher Stone. The name meant something to you, I could tell. And look.' He held out a picture he'd found in the album labelled *1987*. A 'formal' picture of a younger Siobhan in an unflattering salmon-pink dress with puffed sleeves, arm in arm with a young guy in an ill-fitting tux. The same one from Niamh's picture – taken at the same time, by the look of it. The two of them beaming, happy despite their terrible haircuts and Siobhan's black-eye makeup. 'That's him, isn't it? With you.'

Siobhan took the picture from him gently, almost reverently. 'You shouldn't take the pictures out of the albums. You'll damage them.'

'For God's sake!'

'OK. Fine, yes, that's me and Christy.' *Christy.* 'I told you, he was friends with Liam. I had to take someone to my formal, so why not him?'

'And did you go out with him for a while?'

229

She winced. 'Maybe. It was years ago. So what?'

'But ... why would Niamh have his picture, or his address written down?'

'I ... ' Siobhan threw up her hands. 'I told you, I didn't know any of this. Niamh would get notions. You know that. We were talking one time, before she ... before we lost her. About past boyfriends, all that. Christy maybe came up, and I told her we'd lost touch. Maybe she took it on herself to bring us back together or something like that. Not that it's very fair on Gerry, but she wouldn't have thought like that. You know what she was like. Romantic, daft.'

Josh ran it through his mind. It kind of made sense – Niamh did indeed get notions, and had been impractically romantic. But still he didn't trust Siobhan, who was clutching the photo tight to her chest now. 'Really?'

'As far as I know. Like I said, I'm as in the dark as you.'

'Why did you break up, you and him?'

'Oh, who knows. Mammy didn't approve. He was a bit wild, Christy, or what she'd have thought was wild. Drank the odd beer, smoked, that sort of thing.'

'Right.' Was that really it? No affair, no big mystery? Just a crazy idea of Niamh's, to get her sister back in touch with an old flame? Maybe she thought Siobhan and Gerry weren't happy, or maybe she hadn't even considered that. Why then had she frozen her sister out those last few months? Siobhan wouldn't meet his eyes.

'Put these away now. I won't tell if you don't.'

That was suspicious too. The Donnelly kids, all in their thirties or forties, were usually only too happy to run to Mammy telling tales about each other.

Siobhan stooped to help him with the albums, and as she

did, another picture floated out. A younger Siobhan, holding a baby on her lap – it must have been Niamh, based on the age of Siobhan, and taken not long after that formal shot. She picked it up and stared at it, her face shifting. 'Ah God love her. She was a beautiful baby. A beautiful woman, too.' Siobhan's voice thickened with tears. 'Sorry Josh. It's just very hard.' And she walked out of the room, leaving Josh surrounded by the memories of a family he no longer felt part of.

Caroline

Finally, after ten very long days indeed, it was time for Paul and Gilda and the kids to leave. Back they went to Aldergrove, paying an iniquitous amount for parking that shocked Caroline's father so much he didn't speak for a full ten minutes. 'Gougers,' he muttered. 'That's what they are, bloody gougers.'

Caroline already felt guilty about having fought with her brother while he was here, knowing she'd miss him until she saw him again, not for two or three years at least, at which point he'd immediately start to annoy her again. That was family. She kissed the girls, aching at their little arms around her neck. 'Bye bye, Auntie Caroline!' She'd bought them things for the plane, colouring books and healthy snacks and even some sweets that Gilda swiftly confiscated. She would have to go and visit, find the money somehow – they changed so much at this age, and she didn't want to miss it. If she never had a baby, at least she had them.

'Bye Gilda, take care.' She patted her sister-in-law's bony shoulders. She wasn't such a bad stick, Gilda. At least she kept Paul in line, stopped him asking for handouts, had got him wearing proper trousers instead of shorts all the time. Caroline couldn't take a grown man seriously in shorts.

Finally, she turned to her brother, as her mother fussed over the girls and her father muttered more about the nefariousness of Belfast International Airport and all who ran her. 'Well, this is you, then. Take care, bro. Hope the surfboards do all right.'

'I'm doing OK, you know,' said Paul, surprising her. 'I know you think I'm still your fuck-up little brother, but I'm not. Not any more. The business is doing really well – I took on four staff members last year. Gilda's given up the yoga teaching to help me, though she still gets in an hour every day minimum, of course.'

'Of course,' muttered Caroline. 'Well, that's good. I'm happy for you.' Typical Paul. All these years she'd been the dutiful one, and here he was with a lovely wife and kids and a thriving business, too. She'd have to get some cats, that was her only option. Never mind that the hair would get all over her good sofa.

Then Paul said something that astonished her. 'Listen. I know you need cash, for this legal case.'

She blushed at the idea of her brother knowing the ins and outs of her reproductive struggles. 'Hm, yeah ... '

'I can lend you it.'

'What?'

'Honestly, I can. It's no problem.'

'You would do that for me?'

He shrugged. 'Always wanted a little niece or nephew.'

'What about Gilda's lot?' A vast brood of barefoot bohemian children streamed forth from Gilda's family every year. No fertility troubles there.

He grimaced. 'They're all still breastfeeding at six. It's a bit much, ya know? But a little mini-Caroline, who can learn the ways of bossiness ... '

'Eh, it's efficiency, not bossiness.'

'Potato, potahto ... Seriously though, the offer's there.'

Caroline didn't know what to say. 'Well ... thank you. That's very generous.' Could she really borrow money from her feckless little brother? Money that might very well go straight down the drain, if the court upheld Mary's wishes? What would Anto have said about that? 'I ... let me have a think about it. But thank you. Really.'

Caroline dropped her parents off, still muttering about the parking charges, then drove home, already dreading the empty house, the neatness and silence. Instead of going straight there, she stopped her car outside a red-brick house with spring flowers in pots outside.

'Sylvia?' She leant hard on the bell, waited. Nothing. She tried rapping the door. 'Syl? It's me, Caroline. Just popping by to see how you are!'

Nothing. Caroline peered through the dirty window, a growing sense of unease in her stomach.

Josh

Josh was at home, wrestling over his resignation letter. He had to take the job. Didn't he? What did he have here? He liked Maggie and the people at the office, but she was right, he'd never fully understand Northern Ireland no matter how long he stayed here, and there was nowhere for him to progress career-wise. Niamh was gone, and her family were hiding something from him. He still wasn't happy with Siobhan's answers, which made less sense the more he thought about them. Even his new friends,

Billy, Matt, Cassie (and Caroline but he wasn't thinking about her, no), they weren't enough to justify staying in this wet, grey town. Not when his mother, his brother and this shiny new job were waiting across the sea. All the same, he was finding it hard to sign off the letter, when his phone went. Caroline. At the sight of her name, his heart leapt in his chest. Why was she calling now? What if something had happened to her too? He'd been so harsh on her, so cruel . . .

'Josh?' Caroline's voice sounded brisk, serious. As if something bad was happening but she was handling it. She was the sort of person who did that. She didn't apologise for the fight they'd had, or what she'd said in the pub, just got straight to the point. 'Sylvia's had a stroke, she's in the hospital. I went round, I found her– the place is such a mess, Josh. She's not been coping.'

He looked at the unfinished letter, which was giving him a queasy feeling in his stomach. Thought of how much he'd have to do if he left as planned this week – the packing, giving up the lease on the flat. Then at the phone, thinking of Sylvia alone in hospital, her trembling hands, her sparkling beads, her kind eyes. 'Where are you now?' He was already moving.

'Hospital – the Mater.'

'I'll meet you there.'

Josh was so worried about Sylvia that the name of the hospital didn't even resonate. But as he drove up and parked, he remembered – he'd done this journey before, looked around for a parking spot before, been briefly shocked at the charges before. This was the hospital where Niamh had died. For a moment he wanted to bolt, experiencing as a deep muscle memory that day of running in, looking desperately for the right ward, following signs, dodging past people on drips and in wheelchairs, afraid to be too late but also afraid to get there and hear what had happened, perhaps already knowing that his life had changed for ever and he just hadn't been told yet. But he had to go in. Sylvia needed them, she had no one else.

Caroline was fighting with a vending machine as Josh jogged up. A flash went through him – anger at what she'd said last time, awkwardness, pain at not being friends with her. 'You OK?' he said cautiously.

'Bastard machine won't give me my ... there!' A shove dislodged a Snickers bar. 'I didn't have any lunch.'

'I'm not judging. Is Syl OK?'

Caroline shook her head. 'She's broken her hip. Fell off the wee bookcase steps looking for something. They think it might have been a stroke, her speech is a bit slurred. She's asleep now – they said she'll have to stay in a while.'

'You found her?'

Caroline looked down at her Snickers. 'Yeah. I don't think there was anyone else, to be honest. She'd ... been there for a day or two. Lucky she keeps a key under one of the plant pots.'

'Oh.' Josh thought about that. Lying alone in a dusty house, not able to get to the phone, not sure if anyone would come to the door. Thank God Caroline had thought to visit. 'I only saw her a few days back – I should have gone round again.'

'Don't. I feel awful. We'll do better now, OK? Visit her in shifts. Bring her grapes and that.'

'Can she go back there? Into the house?'

Caroline shook her head, making her fair bob swing. 'I don't think so.'

Josh thought of everyone he had in his life. He'd lost Niamh, yes, but there was still her loud family, his own mum and brother, Billy and the football lads, Maggie and Oisin. Cassie,

Matt, Ruma, even Sinead in her way. And Caroline. Watching her unwrap the chocolate bar and bite off a huge chunk, getting some on her face, he thought how grateful he was to know her, to have her in his life. He had to hold onto that, try to smooth over the cracks between them, not take the friendship for granted as he sank under the dark waves of Christopher Stone. 'We'll look after her,' he said. He knew he should tell her about the job, not make promises he couldn't keep, but their friendship was so fragile, and he was so happy to have her talk to him again. He'd tell her later.

She smiled, chocolate in her teeth. 'I'm so glad you said that. And listen, I'm so sorry about … the night at the pub. What happened. Screaming at you in the street like some kind of mad fishwife. I've been feeling so bad about it.'

'God, me too. I was way out of line. If you really want to do this, the baby thing, I'll back you all the way. I hope you know that.'

'Ach, I was just mad at you for what you said. That I'm making a fool of myself. You don't really think that?'

'I … of course not. I was just worried for you, about the money, the stress of it all.'

Caroline sighed. 'Unfortunately, it just got a lot more complicated.' She told him about Mary's challenge to her case, and Josh shook his head.

'I'm so sorry. Have you any idea why she's so against it?'

'She seems to think it's what he wanted. I guess it's like you said – if he ticked the box, maybe he meant to tick the box.'

'But you don't think so?'

'I just can't make sense of it. He loved kids. We'd already taken years to get that far. I suppose he might have panicked, told Mary he wasn't sure. He wasn't the most consistent of people.'

236

Josh didn't understand it, either. Why would Anto agree to IVF, all that effort prodding one cell towards another, the tiniest speck of humanity that could exist, if he didn't want it in the first place?

Caroline sighed. 'It's maddening. Trying to imagine what he'd say. Having all these conversations with him, when he can never answer back. You have that with Niamh, you said?'

'All the time.' Oh God. He had to tell her the truth. It was building up inside him. 'And listen, Car – what you said about me digging into it, the accident – you were right. I, um . . . I did go round there. To the address I found.'

She stared at him, mouth slightly open. 'Oh Josh! You didn't. Did you talk to him?'

'No. I . . . Caroline, I broke into the house. His wife was there, at least I think she was his wife, and their kid.' Saying it out loud made it sound even more crazy than in his head.

She gaped at him. 'You could have been arrested! The police have guns here, you know!'

'I know. I know. I managed to get out, but God, I've been bricking myself ever since. It was like I totally lost my mind for a while.'

Caroline blinked. 'How did you even *know* how to break in somewhere?'

'Um . . . turns out Billy from the football team has a few skills from before his time in prison.'

'Jesus, Mary, and St Joseph.' She shook her head slowly. 'What does Sylvia have to say about all this?'

'Let's look.' Josh reached into his bag for his copy of the book. 'Maybe this bit: "Setbacks and Meltdowns". Do you think we're in that area?'

'I screamed at you in the street, like we were in *EastEnders*. I'd call that a meltdown, yeah.'

He read the page. 'She says be kind to yourself and to others. It's to be expected. Two steps forward, one step back is still progress.'

'That's nice. And, hey, maybe we can get a pizza after this, even. Maybe there's even some really violent film online, ideally with zombies and people getting eaten all over the show. That would cheer me up.'

'I'd like that.' Josh didn't quite know why, but he lifted his hand and flicked the bit of chocolate from her cheek. 'You just had . . .'

'Oh.' Caroline stepped back, putting her hand to the spot he'd touched. A weird moment stretched. 'Um . . . we better go in and see her. Also, I think we should go and clean out her house. It's a bit of a state.'

10. HELP OTHERS

Caroline

The next day, the two of them arrived on Sylvia's doorstep at the same time. Caroline was in paint-stained jeans and had a big plastic caddy of cleaning products. 'I asked did she mind if we got the place nice for her. Not that I'm at all sure she'll be coming back here.'

'She was OK with it?' Josh peered in the dusty window.

'She seemed a bit surprised – I don't think she knows it's dirty. Her eyesight's not great. But she was OK, yes.' Caroline sighed, rooting in her pocket for the key. 'She was so bloody grateful, Josh. Sitting there in bed, like a little broken bird. I think she's been lonely for such a long time.' She thought about that. About being in hospital, all alone, no one to visit and bring you nice food from M&S. Your family long lost. The love of your life dead for years. She too felt desperately lonely at times, even though Anto had only been gone a few months. She had to find a way through this, or the rest of her life would be grey and empty, stretching on for ever.

Caroline forced the door open, and they stepped into the dusty space. A sour smell greeted them – boiled food, and damp, and a bin that needed taking out. Josh wrinkled his lovely nose. 'Where do we start?'

Caroline took a piece of paper from her coat. 'I've done us a plan.'

'Of course you have.' He glanced at her, amused.

'What?'

'Nothing,' said Josh, shaking his head, smiling. 'You could run the world, you know that?'

'I could, but sure who'd be bothered with that? Now, let's start with the kitchen.'

Caroline had always been practical about houses, as with everything else. But all the same she had grown very attached to her home with Anto, and it was hard not to draw comparisons, clearing out Sylvia's similarly lovely, slightly run-down place. Caroline was already getting viewings on hers, though so far she'd left that to the estate agent, not able to bear the sight of strangers poking about her home. Someone might make an offer soon, and then it would be real. She'd have to find somewhere else to live. She'd have to leave Anto's ghost behind, pack up their life together. Accept that there was no going back. She hadn't yet decided if she needed to tell prospective buyers Anto had died there, in the bathroom. And would the money from the sale even be enough, now that Mary was challenging her appeal?

Sylvia had evidently not followed her own advice about having a clear-out, because the spare rooms were jammed with dresses, shoes, coats and accessories, all dusty and musty as long-unworn clothes are. Caroline and Josh took the bins out, then threw away multiple old containers of food from the fridge. Sylvia had saved everything, little nubs of cheese in freezer bags, Tupperware full of old stews. It was heartbreaking, and Caroline resolved to get her a big shop if she did come back home. They scrubbed the fridge out, till it lost that nasty chemical smell of old, uncleaned appliances. Next were the cupboards, stacked with ancient tins and boxes, stained with treacle and spilled rice and drifts of cinnamon. Someone had once been a keen cook – Iris, maybe, since Sylvia now seemed to live off tins of stew and toast. It was oddly satisfying, filling binbag after binbag with rubbish, getting right into the dirty corners with the Marigolds Caroline had supplied. Josh was doing the high cupboards, since he was taller, and Caroline the low ones. They worked in a companionable rhythm, sometimes humming along to the radio that played from Josh's phone.

From time to time he'd ask things like: 'What the hell is Fray Bentos?', unearthing an old tin. Or: 'Wow. Wagon Wheels. I haven't had those in twenty years.'

'I love this song,' she said. 'Don't Look Back in Anger' had come on the radio, and she sang along. She glanced at Josh. 'What?'

He was staring at her. 'Nothing. It's just ... you have a nice voice, is all.'

'Oh. Thanks.'

Josh ducked his head, wiping the sink. His shoulders, the lovely lines of them, were tense. 'This was – Niamh. It was her favourite. Our first dance song. At the wedding.'

'Oh.' She went back to scrubbing, a fine foam of Cif filling the cupboard. She could feel Josh watching her, and the back of her neck flamed. He was just so *nice*. It would be easier if he weren't so nice. She took refuge in briskness. 'Come on, we still have loads more to do! I've dusted all the living room and got rid of about fifteen spiders. Cobwebs in hanging beads, let me tell you, are not a good thing. No slacking off.'

'Yes, ma'am. Sorry, ma'am.'

'You think that's an insult,' she said airily to Josh, 'but in fact I just love the power. Keep going, soldier.'

Much later, their work was done. The kitchen sparkled with

Caroline's favourite smell – bleach – and the bathroom, too, which had been dauntingly grotty with mould. The carpets were hoovered, every bit of furniture polished, the windows thrown open to let in the cold spring air. Spiders and cobwebs were chased from every corner. The house was clean now, but really it could do with a total refurbishment if it were to be sold – wallpaper stripped and carpets ripped up, doors and ceilings painted. She'd seen Josh eyeing the curtains, as if he wanted to take them down and dry-clean them. She approved deeply of his clean habits. Anto would have left dishes to grow mould if she hadn't nagged him to wash up.

The saddest room was the bedroom, a large double bed with an embroidered quilt on it, homemade in patches of patterned fabric, a rainbow of colours. On one side was a copy of a lurid true-crime book, some reading glasses on top, and a glass of water and some hand cream. On the other side was a framed picture of a woman who had to be Iris, taken some time around the 1970s on what looked like a beach in Europe. She was beautiful, with glossy dark hair and green eyes, and she beamed out, in a polka-dot swimsuit and sunglasses. The dead. They always looked so happy in pictures. Impossible to know the truth behind those smiles. Caroline wondered how it was to go to bed every night for two years, with the place where your partner used to be empty and still. Like sleeping with a ghost.

'Those sheets need a wash.' Josh came in, shaking her out of her gloom.

'I'll take them to a launderette. That washing machine belongs in a museum.'

'You don't mind?'

'God, no. I love launderettes. When our machine broke down I was actually happy, because I got to use fluff and fold.'

'Ah, fluff and fold. Don't tell anyone, but sometimes I use that when I just can't be bothered to do a wash.'

'It is amazing. I never knew clothes could look so neat.'

They smiled at each other, and although it was a nice moment, and they were friends again, somehow Caroline's heart felt as heavy as ever. How could she have thought, even for a second, there was something between them? Maybe she'd had some feelings herself, for a moment or two, but was all too clear that, like Sylvia with her Iris, Josh would never get over Niamh.

Josh

He was surprised how much he enjoyed cleaning out Sylvia's house, even as someone who generally liked to tidy. In fact, he was feeling strangely better at the moment, despite his near run-in with Stone's wife and child, the ongoing mystery of Niamh, the looming decision about the London job, the need to pack up his life here if he took it, and poor Sylvia's fall. He'd made up with Caroline, at least, and that seemed to make everything brighter.

They tried to see Sylvia every day, so she wasn't alone for too long. Josh was going to pop by in his lunchbreak today, so he was rushing to get his work done, busy and focused. So much so that, for the first time, he actually didn't notice the clock inching round, and it was half twelve before he looked up from his computer, and realised that on that day almost three months ago Niamh was already dead and gone. It was a long time since he'd let himself get lost in something.

It was a nice day, finally, something he hadn't been sure actually existed in Northern Ireland. People told stories about glorious summers past, days when the tarmac melted on the road, the July the reservoirs dried up, revealing sunken villages, and when Niamh's brother got so sunburned he was hospitalised. But since Josh had lived here, it had been non-stop drizzle and wind. Matching his mood now Niamh was gone, grey and bleak. But today the world seemed overcome with joy, blossom on the trees, students walking by in shorts and summer dresses, people sitting on every patch of grass they could find. Even at the hospital, workers in scrubs and shirtsleeves sat on a small square of lawn in the car park, faces turned up to the sun, desperately trying to soak up what vitamin D they could before the rain returned.

When he went into Sylvia's room, having picked up some chocolates – he didn't like to go empty-handed, but with the two of them visiting so often, as well as Matt, Cassie and Ruma all dropping by, her room looked like a gift shop – Caroline was there. 'Oh! Hi.' He was hit by a wave of something at the sight of her arranging flowers in a vase, her fair hair pulled back, strands of it falling loose. Something like joy at seeing her, but also some kind of complicated fear and sadness. He was leaving this place. Wasn't he? So why make it harder by deepening his ties here?

She seemed awkward too. 'Sorry, I didn't say I was coming today.'

'Why are you sorry? It's nice to have company. How are you, Sylvia?'

'I'm OK, dear. How nice of you to come.'

Her voice was tiny and slurred, her eyes barely open. She still didn't look good. Her leg was in plaster, and the rest of her seemed to have shrunk and shrivelled since being in hospital. He realised how much makeup she must have worn that first night at the support group, and the reason for the darkness of her house. She might even have worn a wig, because now her hair looked grey and wispy, the scalp showing through. Her skin was dry as dead leaves, her pulse fluttering when he took her hand. A sinking understanding went through him – she wasn't ever going to get better. Maybe she was all right with that. Maybe she thought she'd see Iris again. Maybe she would. Josh smiled at the thought of how pleased his mother would be that he was even entertaining the idea of an afterlife. He saw Caroline watching him.

She looked away as he caught her eye. 'How are you?' she asked, neutral, as if to a distant acquaintance.

'Oh, I'm all right. Lots to do at work. I guess that helps. You?'

'I'm . . . ' Caroline shrugged. 'I don't know. I've been feeling really lonely in the house by myself this past while. It's weird but I suppose it just . . . hit me.'

'I guess that's how it happens, in waves. I'm sure Sylvia had something to say about that.' At her name, the old lady's eyelids fluttered. 'Isn't that right, Syl?'

'Hmmm? I'm sorry, dear, I can't quite keep up. But do chat. It's lovely to hear your voices. It makes me feel . . . not alone.'

Josh got a lump in his throat. 'You're not alone – we're all going to visit every day, as much as we can.'

'You're both so good. Such wonderful, brave young people. I just hope you aren't *too* brave.'

'Hm?' Josh looked at Caroline, who shrugged. Sylvia had sunk down in her pillows. 'Syl, what do you mean?'

'I think she's asleep,' whispered Caroline. 'She keeps doing that.'

They sat in silence for a moment, listening to Sylvia's faint bird-breaths, her chest barely rising. She had four tubes going into her body. Josh remembered his grandmother dying in hospital in London, how the kids and grandkids and partners had filled the room, so the nurse just gave up trying to enforce visitor protocols and joined in with their cake and ginger beer parties. Sylvia had no one. Maybe this was why you had kids. To avoid dying alone, in an empty room.

'Car?' he said, after a while.

She jumped again. 'Yeah?'

'How are you doing really?'

'Oh. This stupid legal thing. It's so much tougher than I thought. And the house sale . . . it's hit me hard. I know something awful happened there, and it should be a sad place, but it was ours. Me and Anto's. And if that's gone, it's another step away from him.'

Josh chose his words carefully, thinking of their row last time. 'Are you sure you want to put all your money into this case? I mean, the court could still say no, couldn't they?'

She bit her lip, which, he couldn't help but notice, was very full. 'It's hard to explain. It just feels like . . . the only way to keep him here on earth.'

And there was no chance of that for Niamh. He reached over Sylvia's bed, her twig-like legs hardly making a bump under the sheets, and took Caroline's hand. She was shaking. 'It's OK. I'm not trying to tell you how to grieve. I'm not Sinead, OK? I just hope it works out for you.'

Slowly, she nodded. Her voice was thick with tears. 'Thank you. If it doesn't . . . I don't know what I'll do. My parents think I'm mad already. It feels . . . lonely, I suppose, having to do this on my own. Like a giant wedge between us.'

Josh sighed. 'I'm still angry at my brother for sending a text on the day of the funeral. A text! Like, spring for a phone call if you aren't coming to the actual thing, you know?'

'He should have been there.'

'Yeah. Well, Sam's always been good at making excuses. Spoiled younger brother. You've got one of those too?'

'Yeah. But you still talk to them, your family?'

He shrugged. 'It means enough to me to stay close with them, even if they suck now and then. Everyone sucks sometimes, I guess.' He realised he was still holding her hand, and suddenly felt embarrassed, so he made an excuse, got up to look out of the window, but when he glanced back at her she was staring at her fingers, which he had so recently been touching.

'They must miss you, all the way over here.'

'Yeah. Mum does.'

Oh God. He had to tell her about the job offer, it was ridiculous that he hadn't. Say that they wouldn't need to miss him soon, as he'd be most likely be back over there before too long. That he probably wouldn't be around to help take care of Sylvia, because he was leaving, abandoning them both. That he'd made his decision, because it was the only sane one, and he had to just get on with things now. Why was it so hard? She'd be happy for him, surely. *He* should be happy for him. All he had to do was turn around and say, *Caroline, there's something I have to tell you.* But as he stood there by the window, looking out at the sparkle of Belfast Lough, the green mountains in the distance, he found that, for some reason, he couldn't.

Caroline

'I'm so sorry. I know we'd hoped for a better result.'

Caroline had just known it was going to be bad news. Something about the tone of Jane Adams's voice on the phone when she asked her to come in, the apologetic way she walked into the room. And it *was* bad – the court had rejected her petition, so it would have to go to a full trial if she wanted to get any further. 'You really think it would cost that much?' The figures for taking a case to court were horrific. More than her house was worth, almost.

'It's just that with Mrs Carville's testimony that Antony ticked the box on purpose, the case against you is considerably strengthened.'

Caroline looked down at the patterned carpet, the dusty skirting board, and felt the disappointment hit, percolate through her. She'd hoped. That was her first mistake, allowing herself to think there was a way out of this. 'What if I win the trial, though?'

Jane Adams made a lawyer's face. A tinge of *God help you, poor stupid layperson*. 'It would still cost thousands, Caroline. And to be honest, if his mother's against you, there's very little chance of success.'

'But ...' Her mind was frantically searching for another option. A Hail Mary pass. There had to be something. Break into the clinic. Petition the HFEA. Go on *This Morning* and cry and wait for the outpouring of public sympathy. But wasn't this denial? If it looked like denial and sounded like denial ...

She thought of the looks her parents had exchanged when she told them. Of Mary's face when she first broached the subject. Paul's bafflement. Jenny's supportive but worried stance. Josh's harsh words – *I just think someone needs to tell you, before you waste all your money and end up with nothing.* No one thought she should do this. Not even Anto himself. 'There's really no other option?'

'Maybe if Mrs Carville would change her mind and support your petition. That's the only thing I can think of, legally.'

'All right,' she heard herself say, and her voice was as heavy as her legs as she pushed herself out of the chair. 'Let me think about it, OK?'

'Of course. I am so sorry it's not better news, Caroline.'

'No, you're doing your best.' And humouring a madwoman. 'Thank you, Jane. I really do appreciate it. Oh and . . . try eating some local honey for that hay fever. It should help.'

In school that day, Caroline sleepwalked through her lessons, and the kids picked up on that, leading her a merry dance. The head even had to poke her nose in to see what the noise was. The shame of it! Caroline was usually called in to quell other classes. She had to get a grip. She'd go to the hospital after work, see Sylvia and take her some spring flowers, brighten up her sad room. There was always someone worse off. Caroline had her family, her friends. She was talking to Josh again, thank God. And the case wasn't dead yet – she just had to decide if she wanted to put all her money into it. Give it everything she had, for the chance to have Anto's baby. And it was only that, a chance. Not even guaranteed – there was only a 30 per cent success rate or something like that, even if she overcame all the legal obstacles.

At the hospital, she relaxed into the feeling of calm activity. Anto had been brought to hospital after he died, of course – it was standard practice – by the ambulance she had called when she found him. She had known he was already gone, although a crazy part of her believed maybe they would save him, that he'd miraculously start breathing again. It's too hard for the human brain to accept death right away, and so it had been some time before it hit – he wasn't coming back. She didn't know if she had fully accepted it even now. Wasn't this baby thing part of it – trying to keep part of him alive?

251

The door to Sylvia's room was closed as she approached, and a doctor stood outside it, updating a chart. She was young, with tired eyes and a granola bar sticking out of her white coat pocket. 'Are you family?' she asked as Caroline came close. 'For Miss Smyth?'

'No – there isn't any family.' There'd been no response to her messages looking for Sylvia's nieces. 'I'm her friend – we're taking care of her.' Her and Josh. A *we*. 'How is she?'

'She's quite weak. This thing is, I'm afraid there's a very high chance of another stroke.'

'Oh.' Caroline let that sink in. Somehow, she had pictured Sylvia coming out of hospital and moving to a nice care home, where she and Josh could visit. Every few days, maybe. The two of them. 'Is there anything you can do?'

'We could operate. But it's a very invasive surgery.'

'Oh no. Will she . . . make it through something like that?'

The doctor's face twisted. 'We don't know. To be honest, Miss . . . ?'

'Ach, call me Caroline.'

'OK. You see, Caroline, Miss Smyth may not wish to take extraordinary measures. She is eighty, after all, and I understand she has no one close. She might prefer to simply be made comfortable. Do you understand?'

She did. They were talking about letting Sylvia die. The vision of that care home evaporated. Maybe she would never come out of here at all. 'Oh,' she said again, stupidly.

The doctor took off her glasses and wiped them on her coat. 'You didn't realise how sick she was?'

'No. I – she never said.' How like Sylvia. Not wanting to make a fuss. 'What does she want, has she said?'

'Well, we were hoping someone might talk to her. Find out, as gently as possible.'

Caroline looked through the glass of the door to where Sylvia lay in bed, tiny and frail. Somehow, she hadn't imagined losing her altogether, despite how frail she was. But perhaps the doctor was right – Sylvia had been alone so long, without her Iris in a house full of memories. Maybe she wouldn't want to be kept alive, with surgery and tubes, and then live on in a care home, tended to by strangers. Maybe it wasn't always the worst thing, slipping away, even if it felt so bad for those left behind.

'I'll find out,' she said, her heart heavy.

Josh

Despite everything – Caroline's shock at how far he'd gone trying to figure out what Niamh had been up to, Sylvia's illness, the new job – Josh was still thinking about Christopher Stone as he finished up his last few stories for Maggie. He'd had an explanation from Siobhan – it was just something innocent, Niamh trying to connect her sister with a long-lost love. And the thing was, it almost made sense. It was the kind of sappy, rom-com, not-at-all practical idea that Niamh might have had, never thinking about the consequences, or the fact that Siobhan was married and Stone likely was too, or that not everyone would even want to be reunited with their teenage boyfriend or girlfriend.

But the other thing was, he didn't believe it for a second. Because Niamh would have told him. She'd have outlined her plans, full of excitement, and Josh would have talked her out of it, pointing out how crazy it was, how intrusive, all the innocent children and even grandchildren involved. That it was hardly fair on Gerry, who wasn't a bad stick, even if he practically lived on the golf course and hadn't washed a sock in his life. Raining on her parade, as was his way. And it also didn't explain why Niamh had fallen out with Siobhan before she died, or the search for DNA tests on her laptop.

Had Siobhan not said that, told him this obvious lie, he might have let it go. He had more or less made up his mind to take the job. Maggie asked him daily what he was doing, since she'd have to fill his post somehow, and he was almost sure he was going, yes, although he hadn't booked a flight or told the rental agent he'd be leaving the flat. He hadn't told Caroline. He assured himself this was just because of Sylvia being so ill, but the truth was he wasn't sure why. Maybe he just couldn't stand seeing her face when he said he was going. Seeing her crushed. Or maybe worse, seeing she wasn't bothered at all. So yes, he was probably leaving and none of it mattered any more. But as it was, he couldn't quite give up the question of Christopher Stone. Why had Siobhan lied to him? Was it that lie that kept him here, in limbo, the date for his supposedly new job fast approaching?

Josh stood up, closed his laptop. He was almost out of this job, so surely they wouldn't mind if he slipped off early to see Sylvia.

Caroline

When Josh arrived at the hospital, Caroline was sitting in the waiting room, clutching a stone-cold cup of coffee that she hadn't taken a sip from. She was just staring into space, while a TV played *Homes Under the Hammer* in the background. Her mind full of the conversation she'd just had with Sylvia.

'You OK?' said Josh. He was wearing a soft yellow jumper, tucking an umbrella into a case. He was so neat. So lovely.

'Not really.' She stirred herself.

'Is it . . . ?'

'She's dying, Josh. The doctor said she'll have another stroke and then . . . if she doesn't get surgery, anyway. But she says she just wants to go home. Be near Iris and their things. All the memories.'

'Oh.' Josh sat down heavily beside her. 'She won't have the surgery?'

'She says there's no point. She's ready to go.'

'Oh. Well, that's – I guess if that's what she wants . . . if she think she'll be at peace. Oh shit. I can't believe it.'

Caroline let out a long sigh. 'Who's going to take care of her, Josh? She'll need nursing, and we don't know how long it'll be till the end. Can we manage it?'

Josh said nothing for a moment. 'Car . . . I'm sorry. I don't know if I'll even be here. I . . . there's something I need to tell you.' She looked up at his stricken face. And there it was, the same feeling she'd had in Jane Adams's office. Bad news. This was going to be bad news. 'I've been offered a job. In London.'

Just as she had suspected. When he hadn't told her, she'd assumed he didn't get whatever it was. But he had, he'd just been keeping it from her.

'Oh?' *But he won't go, of course. He'll stay here, and we'll keep going to support group every week, and nothing will change.* Except it had already changed. 'And?'

'I think I should take it.' He wasn't looking at her. 'My family's there, my friends, this great new job. And here it's just – I see her everywhere. Round every corner. And Niamh's family, Siobhan, I don't know if I can look them in the eye now they've lied to me.'

Of course he was going. It made perfect sense, and Caroline

liked it when people were sensible. This was great. Good for Josh. 'That's brilliant,' she said, taking a huge gulp of air. 'So happy for you.'

'Are you?'

Around them, the noise of the hospital washed. A wave of desolation hit her. No, she wasn't happy for him. She wasn't happy for herself, either, losing Anto and the dream baby and now Josh, too. Caroline squinted at the floor until she could be sure she wouldn't cry. 'Of course. I'm still worried about Sylvia, though.'

'I . . . I'm so sorry. It's terrible timing, I know. I just can't stay here. I'm done, with the whole bloody place.'

'Can't be helped. It's a shame we didn't find her family in time.'

'There are nurses, aren't there? End of life ones. People who come round and do the caring? I could look into it.'

'Yeah.'

They were sitting very close, the sleeve of his wool jumper tickling her wrist. She could see the rise and fall of his chest, and knew he was abandoning her, and Sylvia, and even if it was the right choice for him it still hurt so much. As close as they were, she'd never felt as far from him as she did now. 'She's letting go.' Caroline could hardly believe it.

'Yeah. I guess it's . . . what she wants.'

'But what about us?' Her voice broke. 'You're going, she's probably going . . . what about me?'

'I . . . I'm sorry.' He reached out a hand towards hers, as if he wanted to take it, but then he didn't. The tiny space between them seemed like miles.

Suddenly, she stood up. 'I'm sorry, Josh. I can't do this.'

'What?'

'Let her go. And Anto. All without a fight. I have to try. I'm sorry.' And she fled, running down the corridor of the hospital, putting up her own umbrella as she went.

Josh

'I'm really sorry, Syl. I wanted to be here to take care of you, but they need me to start right away.' He'd gone in to see her after Caroline fled, and he felt terrible, and even worse when Sylvia was so understanding about it.

She patted his hand with her weak one. Her voice was croaky. 'Don't be silly, dear. You don't need to hang around here taking care of an old woman. I wanted you to live your life – that's why I gave you the book in the first place.'

'So . . . you think this is the right decision for me? Going back to London?'

Her eyes were shrewd in her pale shrunken face. 'Only you can know that, Josh.'

'It's a great job. More money, more opportunities. And my mum's there, my brother, my friends.'

'Not *all* your friends,' she said quietly, and he knew exactly what she was talking about. Who she meant.

'No.' But he couldn't stay here just for Caroline. She wouldn't even want him to.

'Josh, my dear, before you go, there's one more thing I'd like your help with. You've already done so much, but I just need this one thing.'

He squeezed her hand, careful not to knock the catheter. 'Anything.'

'Caroline – she's such a dear girl, but I don't think she'll let me go without a fight. And Josh, I don't want a fight. I'm ready to go, I truly am. I believe I'll see Iris again, in some sense, anyway. I've lived a good life, I've met you lovely young people. But Caroline – I'm not sure she's ready to lose someone else. Will you watch out for her? See that she's all right?'

'Of course,' said Josh, but even as he said it he knew he couldn't fulfil the promise. Because how could he watch out for her when he lived in a different country?

11. FACE REALITY

Caroline

An hour later, Caroline snapped back to herself. She was driving down the motorway, fighting rush-hour traffic on her way to her mother-in-law's house, with no real memory of leaving the hospital, getting into the car, or indeed making the decision to come here. Why was she doing it? Because she still hoped she might be able to change Mary's mind, convince her she didn't have any idea about Anto's wishes? Finally get an answer as to why she was doing this?

Sylvia was dying. Josh was leaving, done with the whole bloody place, he'd said. And Caroline hadn't known how to convince him to stay. How to say, *But what about me? Are you done with me?* So she was doing this instead.

Mary was surprised to see her, of course, at that time of the day and unannounced, but manners demanded Caroline be asked in, offered a choice of biscuits (fancy or plain), made tea.

Once Caroline had the tea in front of her it burst out of her. 'Why, Mary? Why won't you let me have this?' Her voice broke. *Don't let them see you cry, damn it.* 'I just want his baby. That's all. I tried and tried and it didn't happen. Why did you have to block it? I mean, what happened? Did Anto tell you he changed his mind?'

Mary's face was impossible to read. She set down her bourbon biscuit on her place mat and took off her glasses on the jewelled string. The house was empty otherwise. Anto's dad had died years ago, before Caroline ever met Anto, and it struck her now that Mary must be lonely when the tumult of children and grandchildren weren't around. It seemed crazy that this ordinary, narrow-minded woman was standing between Caroline and her only spark of hope.

'Ah, love. You really want the truth?'

'Of course!' *You won't like it*, whispered a little voice in her head.

'It's not what you'll want to hear.'

'I . . . just tell me.' *Before I waste my life savings on a doomed court case.*

Mary got up and crossed the room, dislodging some of the framed pictures of the grandkids. Caroline's child would never be one of them, never join them jostling round Granny for biscuits, or chasing the puppies through the farmyard, tracking mud into the Good Front Room. Never play with their cousins or eat soup at the big farmhouse table. She had pictured it so many times it seemed like it had really happened. But that child did not exist and never would. She could see that in Mary's heavy tread as she made her way to the sideboard and took something out. A letter, on faded lined paper. 'Read that.'

'What is it?'

'Just read.'

It was from Anto. She could tell that immediately from the writing, the wild loops and swirls of it, the smudges from the fountain pen ink he liked to use, that leaked all over his shirts and never came out in the wash.

Mum, please do something for me. It's about the fertility clinic . . .

Caroline looked up at Mary. 'Why did he write this? And when?'

'It came in the post the next ... the week after he ... you know. He must have sent it just before.'

Caroline didn't understand. Had he written this letter that morning, along with the note for her? Gone out to post it, taken stamps from her desk where she kept them, organised as ever? He had been calm enough to do all that? Then go home and lock himself in the bathroom?

'Why?' she asked, simply.

'He was afraid. The way he was – the pain of it – he didn't want to pass that on. You know my daddy, he was the same.'

'Was he?' She'd never heard Anto talk about his grandfather, long dead.

'Oh aye. In those days, they wouldn't bury you in the grave-yard if you did it yourself. So we said it was an accident, the tractor running into a wall. But he'd never been happy. Anto was just the same as him – so alive, full of fun and jokes one minute, then the next his brain would go strange, and he'd want to ... switch himself off, like. And Anto didn't want a child of his to go through that. We've no proof it even works like that, and we tried to tell him, but – he was afraid, love.'

Caroline gaped at her. 'So ... why were we trying, then? Why all those tests?'

'At first he thought he could have a family, be like everyone else. But he realised it would never work. He didn't know how to tell you. You'd your heart set on it, and he knew it was his fault it wasn't happening – the tablets he was taking, the drink.' That was true. They'd never discussed the fact that Anto's low sperm count was likely caused by drinking, and by the heavy-duty medication he had to take, though she'd gently tried to nudge him away from booze, have a few sober nights a week. She didn't know what he did when she was out. She thought of that day at school, whiskey on his breath at 4 p.m. *Oh Anto. Did I ever know you at all?* 'He stopped taking them for a time, even,' said Mary, folding her hands on her lap. 'The tablets. To see if that made a difference.'

'Jesus. He did?' But that was so dangerous. Was that why Anto had spiralled again those last few months, fallen into a pit he couldn't climb out of? Just to give her what she wanted? 'I . . . didn't know he'd stopped.' How had she not known?

'Aye. He had to go back on them, since things were getting bad, but . . . ' Mary didn't say, *but maybe that's what killed him.* She didn't need to.

'So . . . you're saying all the time we went through this, all the tests and poking and prodding, coming off his meds – he didn't even *want* a baby?'

Mary shrugged. 'How could he tell you that, love? You'd have left him.'

'I wouldn't have!' But would she? She'd never have married a man who didn't want children, would she? Was it different if he changed his mind? If he had good reason? 'We don't know that it's passed on like that,' she tried. Arguing with someone who wasn't here. The most pointless thing.

'No. But sure he wasn't in his right mind. He believed it was, and the risk was too much for him.' Mary laid her hand on the letter, her son's anguished final demands, written in the midst of such pain. 'In here, he asks me to make sure his wishes are upheld if he . . . when he goes. The form.'

'You mean . . . ' The enormity of it hit Caroline. All these months she'd been saying Anto wasn't thinking clearly when he signed it, he was forgetful, he was careless. Yet, he'd taken as much care as he could to make sure he was understood. And she hadn't wanted to see it. 'He ticked the box on purpose.'

'Yes.' Mary could be gentle, something Caroline hadn't realised about her. 'He didn't want you to have his baby, love. Not because of you. Because of him. I'm sorry. But that's just how it is.'

'He ticked the box on *purpose.*' And she realised the truth, hitting her like a stack of bricks – this was it. She'd never have his child. Her association with this family was, effectively, at an end. Anto was dead and no part of him was coming back, not ever. He was truly gone. A noise came out of Caroline's mouth, a terrible howl, loud enough to disturb the animals outside on the farm, but she couldn't stop herself, and then she felt Mary rubbing her back, like when someone is vomiting. 'There you go, pet. Let it out. Let it out.'

'He left me. He left!'

'I know, love. He loved you so much, he fought so hard to stay with you, but he just couldn't in the end. We tried our best to keep him here, we're devastated he's gone, we always will be – but it wasn't up to us. Sure we did our best.' Then she said, in a strange clear voice, as if she really needed Caroline to know this: 'It wasn't your fault, OK, love? Nothing you could have done would have changed him. Nothing.'

Josh

Josh, too, had been sent reeling by Sylvia's request. She was giving up. She would die alone, and Niamh was dead too and still her family wouldn't be honest with him, would deny him this one tiny flash of sanity in a world turned on its head.

They'd rather he stumbled in the dark forever than tell him the truth.

He'd left the hospital and gone home, since Sylvia was asleep, but he'd barely done a thing, pacing to and fro in the flat. He should have been making plans. Telling Maggie he'd made his choice, telling the magazine he could start next week, not to mention packing, cleaning the flat ... But he couldn't. He still couldn't leave it. Because the fact was, Siobhan *had* lied to him, and he wanted to know why, and the only way he was going to find out the truth was by asking the one person who'd know: Christopher Stone. Who – Josh checked his car clock; it was half six – was now walking down the street towards him, in a smart tweed jacket the colour of heather.

'Christopher ... Mr Stone. I'm so sorry, you won't have the faintest idea who I am. My name's Josh, Josh Mkumbe.' Josh had opened the car door and accosted him on the street.

The man blinked, as well he might. 'Right ... '

Josh thought how to explain. The madness that had engulfed him. That he'd been in this man's house, accidentally spied on his wife and young child. The stalking. Where did you start with a story like that? 'Can I talk to you for just a second? I promise I'm not crazy, or selling anything. I'm – my wife was killed at the end of this road, a few months back. Hit by a car.'

He saw Stone nod, sympathy replace the wariness on his face. 'Oh yes. I'm sorry.'

'I just want to ask you something. Please?'

'All right,' Stone said cautiously. 'Here?'

'If you want you can ... ' Josh indicated the car, and after a moment's consideration, Stone nodded and climbed in. He looked nervous. Josh didn't blame him. It was so strange to see him close up, this man he'd been obsessing about for weeks. Just an ordinary man, after all. He was handsome, silver in his stubble and hair, a shirt from a shop Josh liked himself. Belfast accent.

'I heard about the accident. Terrible thing. I'm very sorry. But . . . ' *But what does that have to do with me,* his expression said.

'There was no reason for her to be in this area. It bothered me for ages – why was she here? Why hadn't she told me where she was going, or any of her colleagues or family? She told her family everything, literally everything. Drove me mad sometimes. So I started to look into it. And . . . ' Josh stopped. Because he had suddenly figured it out. Sitting here beside Christopher Stone, the man who'd taken up so much of his thoughts, watching him wrinkle up his nose as he tried to understand, he was hit by a powerful punch of memory. And Josh finally got it. This man had not been having an affair with his wife. Likely he didn't even know she existed.

'Yes?' Stone was waiting.

Josh said, 'Um, I just wanted to check if anyone saw anything. To explain why she was here, or why she ran out.'

'No. I'm sorry, I was at work when it happened. My wife was home with our daughter, but she didn't see anything. I remember she was so upset when she heard. I'm really sorry for your loss.'

'Thank you.' Josh was hearing his own voice as if from a long way away. 'I know I shouldn't hang about here, but I just . . . I needed to know, if anyone saw her.'

'I get it,' said Stone easily. He seemed like a nice man, someone Josh might have liked in other circumstances. 'Was that . . . ?'

'Oh, yeah. That was all. Thanks. Sorry to bother you.'

As Josh told his lie, he watched the man get out and walk away, and knew that he would never tell him what he'd figured out. It was the only kind way.

He shouldn't be driving when he was this angry. It pulsed inside him like a living being. He wondered if this was what it was like for his brother Sam, who'd always been trigger-happy, lashing out with fists. He knew he had to control it, try to calm down. But all the same, he was in the car and on his way to a place he'd only been once or twice, since they always went to Mammy's for get-togethers – Siobhan's house.

'How could you do it? Just stand there and lie to me – not once but twice?'

Siobhan's face was a mask as she sat on the edge of her expensive sofa. Unreadable. Her house was tidy, quiet. The kids had moved out, and Gerry was somewhere else, the golf club, maybe, or the gym. Josh had caught her doing yoga in front of the TV, in an exercise brand he knew cost a hundred quid per pair of leggings. 'What choice did I have?' Her voice was very quiet.

'You could have bloody told me the truth! Not let me run around Belfast, chasing my tail like a madman! Christ, I even broke into his house! His wife almost caught me!'

She seemed to wince slightly at the word *wife*. 'You shouldn't have done that, Josh. What if you'd got arrested?'

'Yeah, well. You do crazy things when you're grieving.'

A half-laugh, half-sob caught in Siobhan's throat. 'You think I'm not? Josh, Niamh was my *daughter*. My little girl. I gave birth to her, when I was only a wean myself, and I had to pretend she was my sister for all of her life. I had to lie everyone. To Gerry, to my other kids, tell them she was their auntie and not their sister. And then she died and I had to pretend I wasn't a grieving mother.'

He hadn't thought about that. In his rage, he'd not been able to imagine what it was like for her. 'You could have . . . '

'No. It was the eighties in Ireland. I'd have been cast out, disgraced. And I loved Christy, and I was never allowed to see him again. He didn't even know I was pregnant; he just thought I'd finished with him. I was told I was lucky to even keep Niamh nearby, that she wasn't adopted quietly away. Sent to America, even. My whole life's a lie, Josh.'

He was silent for a few moments. 'How did she find out?'

'God knows. I think it was when Mammy was sick. We were clearing out the house a bit, just for something to do, you know, stop us going mad, and she must have found the picture. This one.' Siobhan crossed the room to her Marc Jacobs handbag (a real one), and took out a picture – herself as a teenager, red-faced but beaming, holding a newborn baby in a hospital bed, clearly having just given birth. 'I found it in the room she'd been sleeping in back then, the week she died.'

'She never told you she knew?'

'No. But she was strange with me all those months. I should have guessed. Did she . . . did Christy know? You saw him?'

'I don't think so. He didn't seem to make the connection, and I didn't tell him I'd twigged.'

Donnelly – it was a common name. There was no reason for Christy to link the unfortunate woman hit by a car near his road with a girl he'd known thirty years ago.

For a moment Siobhan's impassive face was vulnerable. 'How was he?'

'He looked good. Married, with a kid. She's about six, I guess.'

She nodded sadly. 'I dropped out of school when it happened.

Liam wasn't allowed to talk to him any more, either. Those were the conditions. For keeping Niamh. Christy couldn't know a thing.'

Josh could hardly imagine it, this quiet tragedy at the heart of such a noisy family. The terrible bargain Siobhan had been forced into, by people as mild and inoffensive as Mammy and Daddy. 'Oh.'

'So she never met him?' said Siobhan. 'She didn't make contact?'

'No. I guess she went to his house, and then, I don't know, she saw something that upset her, and she ran.' In his mind's eye he could picture it. The neat terraced house, the child's shoes lined up by the door, the pink scooter in the front garden. Had that been it? She learned her father had another child, a life? That he didn't even know she'd been there in the same city all her life?

Siobhan wiped her face. 'I don't think we'll ever know. But at least you can be sure now, she loved you. This was nothing to do with you. It was my secret that she kept. Was it worth all this, Josh, to find out?'

'I don't know.'

'Will you tell them? Gerry, and weans?' Her voice was cool, but her hand shook as she put the picture back in her bag. He wondered why she hadn't got rid of it, something so dangerous. Maybe she couldn't bring herself to.

'Of course not. It's not my place.'

Her shoulders seemed to sag. 'Thank you.'

'But that's it for me. I'm done with your family, and your lies. I'm out.' And he left, out of the warm lighted house and back into the cold grey evening.

Caroline

Sometimes, it was a blessing when you didn't have time to fall apart. Josh was leaving so soon, packing up his flat, selling his car, that most of the work of getting Sylvia home fell to Caroline. They had to persuade the hospital someone would be with her all the time, find a night nurse who could administer pain meds, organise meals and shopping. She didn't begrudge it. It went some way to taking her mind off everything. The fact that she wasn't having a baby. That Anto was really gone, and Josh was going too, and she had to find a way to carve out a whole new life.

Sylvia wanted to walk over the threshold of her house herself, but it was painful to watch her totter out of Caroline's car when they brought her home. She met Josh's eyes – they both itched to take her arm. Josh was wearing designer trainers and a denim shirt. He looked like a cool dude, a Londoner, already gone from her. She nodded to him – *go on*. He moved forward.

'Syl, would you mind if I just grab your arm? Caroline, aka the sergeant major here, just washed the steps down and they're slippery.'

Sylvia let him. She was clinging to the handrail, letting out little grunts of effort. 'I can ... do it.'

'I know you can. It'd just make me feel better.'

Caroline followed, closing the door behind them. 'A real sergeant major would never put up with your nonsense, mate.'

Josh smiled back at her. Would she ever find someone who got her like this? Just a look or a gesture and you were understood? It was priceless, that.

Inside was clean and neat, the washed windows letting in the weak spring light. Sylvia stopped. 'Oh!'

'Hope you don't mind?' Caroline came beside her. 'We just wanted to . . . get it nice for you.'

Sylvia stood for a moment, clasping together her bird-like hands. 'Oh, my dears. You are . . . so very good to me.'

Caroline resorted to briskness to quell the tears in her throat. 'Not a bit of it. Sure didn't you give us your book, and help us through these last few months?'

Sylvia made her way, very slowly, to the mantelpiece, where Iris's picture stood. She straightened it gently. 'Hello, my darling. I'm home.'

This time Caroline couldn't bear to look at Josh. She knew she would cry if she did. Instead, she went for the stopgap of all Irish people at every moment awkward, quiet or difficult since time began. 'Right. I'll put the kettle on.'

Not long afterwards, Sylvia said she was going to bed. She had barely drunk any of her tea, and refused help to get up the stairs, so they had to listen to her clomp and gasp her way. Josh winced. 'We should have moved her bed down here.'

'I know. And she's only going to get worse.'

'When's the nurse coming?'

'Nine. I'll just wash up these cups and then we should go, I suppose.'

In the kitchen, they stood side by side, Caroline with her Marigolds on and Josh with a tea towel. 'So I solved the mystery of Niamh,' he said easily, putting a cup into the cupboard.

'Er, what?'

He told her. Caroline gaped. 'Wow. So he was Niamh's *dad*?'

'Yep.'

'And her sister was her mum. I mean, it used to happen all the time. The good old days. And he never got to meet her?'

'No. I think that's the worst part. It's far too late now.' Josh

272

stared into the cup he was drying. 'The family had split them up, Siobhan and Stone – they were just kids when she got pregnant. So he never knew Niamh existed. Never got the chance to meet her. He has a little girl now, six or so. Niamh's sister.' His voice was so bitter. Caroline wished she could claw the cobwebs off him, find the sweet, gentle Josh he used to be. 'So it was pointless. She died for nothing. I guess she was upset – maybe she saw his family and she ran. It wasn't his fault at all. If anything it was Siobhan's. She lied to me, all this time. They all did.'

'And . . . you're leaving.'

'Yes. Very soon.'

'For . . . for good?' Her voice quavered.

He shrugged. 'I don't see what would bring me back.'

Caroline absorbed that blow, and when she could speak again, said, 'I spoke to Mary, too, as it happens. Had it out with her.'

'Oh?'

'Yeah. Turned out I never would have won my case anyway. Anto told her what he wanted before he died. Wrote a letter, even. He wanted to make sure he never had a child. Too worried about passing on what he had. He really did mean to tick the box.'

Josh frowned. 'I'm so sorry. That's awful.'

'Ah well. At least I hadn't spent all my money on it before I found out.'

'Will you keep the house, then?'

'God, I don't know.' She sighed. 'There's some people interested. I guess, if they still want it, I might sell anyway. A new start.'

'So you're definitely dropping the case?'

'I have to. No baby for me.' She said it as lightly as she could, but all the same a bone-crippling loss ripped through her – never, she would never have Anto's baby, and maybe no baby at all now – and she gasped. Josh came up to her and threw his arms around her, clutching tight.

'I'm sorry,' he mumbled fiercely into her hair. 'I'm so sorry. For all of it.'

'Denial.' Caroline wiped a hand over her face. 'Magical thinking. It makes us do crazy things. Both of us. At least it's over now. Come on, let's get this finished.'

'I feel so bad leaving,' he said again, disengaging and going back to drying. 'I know it's not helpful to say that, but . . . I do.'

'You're right. It's not helpful.'

He flicked the tea towel at her. 'Stop guilt-tripping me. Seriously – will you be OK?'

She was silent for a moment, rinsing a cup. 'After you go . . . I think I'm going to stop doing the support group.'

'Really?'

'There's no point in it,' she said dully. 'Or anything. He's gone. He's really gone. I just have to accept that. Nothing's going to help – not the group, not Syl's book, nothing really.'

Josh didn't try to talk her out of it. 'Oh crap, Car. When does it get easier? Does it ever?'

'I don't know.' Caroline gave a sad laugh. 'It's bad, isn't it? When you finally accept it.'

Josh was very close beside her. His face was kind, and handsome, and that made her feel even more hopeless. Here he was, this lovely attractive man, her dear friend, and all the same she wished she'd never met him, because that would mean Anto might still be with her, and everything would be like it used to be.

'I know. Car, you know that stupid stages of grief thing they always push on you?'

'I hate that thing.' Sinead was big on it. *Caroline, this is classic denial.*

'I know. But I wonder . . . all of these plans we've had, helping Sylvia, me trying to find out about Niamh, you with your legal stuff – that's bargaining, I guess. We thought if we could make our plans work, it would bring them back somehow. But it won't. Then there's anger, when you realise you were wrong. I don't know about you, but I've been furious for weeks now. I gave Siobhan both barrels. You remember what comes after that?'

'Depression,' said Caroline, robotically. Like the kind when you can't get up off the sofa and you watch endless reruns of *Friends,* their fake plastic lives and fake laughs surrounding you in a bubble.

'Right. So actually it's a good thing. We're on our way to acceptance, maybe.'

Caroline peeled off the rubber gloves, her hands red underneath. Was that true? Was this creeping numbness, this sense that nothing would ever be all right again, the road to feeling normal? 'Maybe,' she said. 'But Christ, Josh. It's just so hard. When I was trying . . . when I had a plan, I guess I felt all right. Like there might be a solution.'

'I know what you mean. I had one, too. But I have to face facts. Niamh was keeping a huge secret from me. She wasn't who I thought she was. Her family lied to me, to my face, even when they saw how heartbroken I was. Niamh lied to me, too.'

'That's not fair,' said Caroline, a bit more animation creeping into her voice. 'She's not here to defend herself, so we can't judge her. That's the privilege of being dead. The benefit of the doubt, like.'

Josh brooded. 'But how could she? Shit, I loved her *so much.* How could she? Why couldn't she bloody look twice before crossing the road?' He slammed a fist onto the draining board, making the mugs rattle. 'Sorry. I guess a bit of anger is still lurking.'

'They do say it's not linear, the process.' Caroline sighed. 'What a pain. If I have to go through this, I want to at least come out the other side.'

Josh was massaging his fist. 'Look at the state of us, eh? We should be out partying, or having sex, living life. No ... stuck here trying to work out what dead people wanted.'

'Come here.' She pulled him into a hug again, trying not to notice how good he smelled, how warm his skin was. He breathed into her neck, his face a little damp. The hug went on. It still went on. *Why isn't he letting go?* But she wasn't letting go either. *I don't want to.*

She was aware of something. A feeling, where for weeks there had been none, creeping its way down from her chest, through her stomach and into her thighs. Warming her to the centre. Desire. She wanted him, from a deep hungry part of herself that didn't understand about grief and emotion and friendship and appropriate social behaviour, and just knew that she was a young woman, who hadn't been touched in months, and he was a sexy man, intense and kind and gentle and angry, and she wanted him. God, she wanted him.

They stayed like that for innumerable seconds, or maybe just five, and it was like the kitchen all over again and it felt so good to be in his arms, to feel him strong and warm and alive, that she was about to say something, although she didn't know what, when her phone went. *Goddammit.*

Josh pulled away first. 'You should get that.'

She didn't want to. It wouldn't be good news. The concept of good news no longer seemed to exist in her universe, while other people her age got engaged and had babies and went travelling and were promoted. All that happened to Caroline was people died. 'OK.'

She fished the phone out of her jeans and saw she had a message, a Facebook one. She hadn't been on in a day or two, what with getting Sylvia sorted – anyway it was nothing but a parade of other people's achievements, weddings, babies, happiness – and had forgotten about all the messages she'd sent out. This was from someone called Annabel Crosland.

Hello, I saw the message you sent my mum, Heather Smyth as was. My mum is a bit of a bigot I'm afraid, but I'm not. I'd love to meet my great-aunt.

She had finally found one of Sylvia's family. But now it might be too late.

Josh

Annabel, Sylvia's great-niece, was twenty, at Queen's studying Sociology. She had a line of piercings all the way up one ear and had shaved the underside of her head up one side.

Josh and Caroline were now standing awkwardly in the hallway outside Syl's bedroom. Annabel was in with Sylvia, talking to her intently. Fiercely, she'd explained that her mother was, in her words, 'An unreconstructed bigot. Still thinks Auntie Sylvia's a sinner, after all these years. I want to show her we're not all like that.' Annabel wore a REPEAL T-shirt over a long-sleeved top, and a printed ankle-length skirt. She was maybe the coolest person Josh had ever met.

'Do you think it's better?' said Josh suddenly, as they waited there, listening to the low murmur of voices.

Caroline frowned. 'What's better?'

'Dying like this. Slow, measured. Time to say goodbye. Or is it better to go like Niamh did? And your Anto. Quick, gone in an instant.'

Caroline winced. 'I don't know how quick it was for Anto. I don't like to think about it.'

'Sorry.'

'It's OK. I don't know, to answer your question. Can you ever say goodbye properly? Is there ever a moment where you feel, right, that's it, I can go now?'

'Sylvia's ready. Or she thinks she is. Maybe that's the same thing.'

'Maybe.'

He checked his watch. His flight to London was booked for early the next morning, his flat was mostly packed up and going back to the rental agent. His life here was almost tied up; he'd worked his last day at the *Chronicle* earlier, with a cake and speeches and a growing ache in his chest watching Maggie pretend she wasn't sad, at the demo CD Oisin gave him, at the bound collection of his articles that was his leaving gift. God, it was hard to let things go, even things you hadn't loved. No wonder he couldn't let Niamh go, when he had loved her so very much.

He sighed. 'God. I have to finish packing. Will you let me know how Syl is?'

Caroline looked stricken. 'She won't last the night, Josh, I don't think.'

'I can't stay. I'm sorry – the flight's booked. I'll miss my first day otherwise.'

He looked up, and saw Caroline's eyes on him. An expression there he'd never seen before. More open. Vulnerable. 'So you're definitely leaving. For real.'

'I – well, yes. It was this job offer, too good to turn down, really.'

'I never told you this, but I read what you wrote. The article about Niamh.' Caroline fiddled with a picture frame, straightening it. 'It was ... you're an amazing writer. Really.'

'Thanks. It was all those conversations with you, really. I'd already said it all – just needed to let it flow out.'

'I ... I hope you'll be happy in London. I suppose it makes more sense to be there. Your family, friends – all of that.'

'Thanks.' Josh wanted to say he would visit, but would he? What was there here but painful memories? It was very possible he'd never see Caroline again. Maybe they'd send the odd email, perhaps try to meet up if she came to London on a hen do or training course, not quite manage the dates. Let it drift. He didn't know why that thought made him feel so sad.

'The funeral?' she said, rubbing a hand over her tired face.

'I won't be able to get back so soon. It's always so fast here. I'm sorry. Car ... ' He was going to say something then, maybe, he didn't know what, but something. But he didn't. There was too much to lose, both of them just too far apart, on separate islands of grief. He hesitated for a moment, but something stopped them hugging, perhaps remembering the moment in the kitchen earlier. Then he moved off down the hallway, without saying anything else. No goodbye. No explanation. The same way Niamh had left him. It was time to get on with living, in a world that no longer contained her, and now not Caroline either. And that was the hardest thing of all.

Caroline

Caroline was only half-right in what she said to Josh. Sylvia lasted till nine the next morning, and Annabel stayed with her the whole time, talking, listening to Sylvia's failing voice, trying to pack a lifetime's worth of family history into one night. They talked about Iris, about Annabel's childhood, about her mother Heather and aunt Lynn, who'd moved to Australia, about Annabel's boyfriend Fintan, 'a real ally'. Caroline tiptoed around them, holding Sylvia's weak hands, bringing water and bites of dry toast, ferrying tea to and fro even though nobody wanted it, just for something to do. The lights of the house burned themselves out, and dawn came, and she was slipping away.

Around eight, Caroline was sitting in the living room, hollow-eyed with tiredness and grief. Josh's question played around her head – was it better this way? To die slowly, in your own bed, a candle burning and your loved one's presence all around? Or fast, snuffed out in an instant? She didn't even know how quickly Anto had died. It had happened in the time it had taken her to go round the shop, decide between crumpets and croissants, pay and come home. And he'd had to find paper and a pen – tearing some from one of the exercise books on the dining table, which she'd been intending to mark that day, had her husband not died – and write the note. Perhaps he'd also posted the letter to his mother, or maybe he'd done that the day before, planning ahead. She'd never know. His death must have been quick. But not as quick as Niamh's. He would have known what was happening to him, for at least five minutes or so. That seemed a long time to be dying, in pain. At least Sylvia was comfortable, drugged up to the eyeballs as she was.

Caroline. Please don't go in. Call police first. That was all he'd managed to say to her, after four years of love together. Eight words and one of them was her name, as if she maybe wouldn't know who the note was for. God, Anto. He'd left her with so little. Eight words. No explanation. Maybe there was none to give, when it came right down to it, no way that he could explain why he needed to go and leave her here.

That was when Annabel, pale but composed, opened the door. 'I think it's time,' she said, and inside the room, Sylvia was dying. It was happening.

Josh

Josh got the news on the Tube into London, exhausted from the early flight and journey from Heathrow. He read what Caroline had to say, but he knew it was too late to do anything to help, and with a heavy heart he put his phone away. He'd done it. He'd left, hopelessly disorganised, his things crammed into boxes and Ikea bags. Given the hurry, he'd decided to put things in storage in Niamh's mammy's garage, and then presumably he'd come back one day and pick them up. Or would he? He'd arrived in Belfast with two cases, the rest of his minimalist belongings at his mum's, and everything else had been bought with Niamh. The turquoise retro phone, the little bottle vases that only held one flower, hopelessly impractical, the neon wall sign saying COFFEE – all of it stamped over with her memory. Maybe it was best to leave it there, go back to the person he'd been in London, who didn't own or need much, just really good trainers and the best speakers, coffee machine, and bike he could afford. He hadn't been one for clutter, just big, great things. Like Niamh had been. But that was over now.

As Josh rubbed his eyes and tried to wake up, he told himself he was home. It shouldn't feel this sad to be back where he belonged. But it did.

Caroline

She told herself she had accepted the news about her case, about Sylvia dying, about Josh leaving, that she was zen and calm. *Give me the strength to change the things I can, accept the things I can't, and the wisdom to know the difference.* But student wall-poster sentiments were not helping, and after Josh had gone, in the days after Sylvia's death, Caroline found herself spiralling. She walked around her house, which soon would not be hers, picking things up and putting them down. Thought about drinking a lot, realised that would help nothing. What were you supposed to do when you were sensible, but also maybe having a breakdown? It was hard.

She'd thought life was bad when Anto died, that terrible day she came home and the house was silent and she just knew, in some deep part of herself. But at least she'd still had the hope of a baby, and Josh, and the group, which had come to mean more to her than she'd realised. What did she have now? No one, nothing. She was thirty-six and her life felt over. Even worse – she had run out of biscuits.

Caroline had been holed up in the house, the empty gap-filled house, for two days now, ever since Sylvia had closed her eyes for the last time. Nothing she had done, none of her crazy plans and schemes had made a difference. She was dimly aware that she hadn't washed her hair in a while, and that another support group meeting had been and gone, but somehow she couldn't bring herself to care. She was onto series six of *Friends* – objectively, the worst one – and couldn't bring herself to turn it off.

Denial, Josh had said. She'd known, of course, that it was to be expected. She had conscientiously read all the books about grief, as well as going to the support group. She'd thought she was dealing with bereavement really well, as people kept telling her. But it turned out, no, she was just in denial too, like Josh with his stupid investigation. She'd thought having Anto's baby would make up for losing him. But of course it wouldn't. And she wasn't going to have a baby at all now. She was a childless widow and she was thirty-six and had run out of time.

More tears slipped down Caroline's face. She had to start mentally Tipp-Exing Josh out of her head. She'd just rewind, reset to before the support group. Never meet him. They weren't real friends, anyway. Just fellow grief survivors, like people you bump into on a backpacking trip and they're your best mates for weeks and then you never speak to them again in your life. She had to go the rest of the way alone.

'You could use a donor,' Jenny had suggested, trying to be helpful, when she came over one night with Doritos and wine. 'They have some lovely ones. Big, strapping Danish lads. Blonde hunks.'

'You know I won't actually get to meet them?' Caroline had managed to get out. That was an option, maybe. But the idea of it – the lonely insemination all by herself, the baby with no father, even a dead one – made her feel even worse. Perhaps she'd be a fond auntie and godmother. Take up gardening and do charity work. Get a lot of cats.

Slumped on the sofa, Caroline started to cry again at the bleakness of her future. It was so unfair – she didn't even like cats. Why did men get so much more time? Josh would have years to meet some young thing and get her up the duff, if that's what he wanted. Caroline had maybe six years, at a push. To meet someone, get the point of being ready for a baby (marriage could go out of the window), then start trying. And it might take years again. Then IVF. Which could also take years. Was it worth it? Was it better to give up hope, because at least then you knew where you were, and could put your energies into growing really nice begonias? Caroline didn't even know what begonias were.

She was sitting dully in front of Netflix, thinking about biscuits but lacking the will to go to the shops. At the thought of organising Sylvia's funeral, her heart, already sodden with misery like a sponge, sagged even further. Of course Sylvia would have to die now. Her stupid book hadn't saved her from a life of loneliness, mourning her lost love, and it hadn't helped Caroline, either. Maybe nothing could help. Maybe you just had to endure. She wondered was that how Anto had felt. Like nothing was ever going to get better, that each day would be as bad as the one before. A pit of despair. Unbearable. She thought about it for a long time, her youth slipping away in front of rubbish telly, unable to get off the sofa. She didn't want to get up, but on the other hand she really did need some more biscuits. She dragged herself up, moving as slowly as a sloth, and pulled on an old hoody of Anto's that was hanging by the door. It smelled of him still, just, and she would have cried had her heart not been too heavy.

She went to the corner shop, because braving the supermarket was just out of the question, and the lady behind the counter, who knew her of old, looked at her pityingly. 'You all right, love?'

'Yeah.' She heaped Tunnock's tea cakes on the counter, added several packets of biscuits and a cheap bottle of rosé wine.

The lady tutted. 'Where's that fella of yours then, these days?'

She'd been fond of Anto – purveyors of alcohol had tended to be. She must not have heard what had happened.

'Gone.' She could only manage words of one syllable. How could she explain he had left her, died, closed the door behind him?

'Don't drink this all at once, will you, pet?' She reminded Caroline of her parents, who'd been calling, but she was ignoring them. She didn't want to admit they'd been right after all. It was a stupid plan, the court case. All it had done was hurt her more.

Outside on the pavement, she cracked open a packet of Jammie Dodgers and shoved two into her mouth, thick and sweet.

'Caroline?' She looked around at the sound of her name, confused, her mouth full of sugar.

'Ugghm?'

Someone had jogged past, in tight spandex, bouncing pony-tail, glowing skin. Cassie. Caroline almost didn't recognise her, she looked so much better. 'Are you OK?'

'I ...' Caroline swallowed, shrugged, indicating her thin plastic bag of booze and biccies, her unwashed hair, her dirty, oversized clothes. 'Well, no.'

'God love you.' Cassie sighed. 'I've been in this stage. The booze and binge-eating and crying in front of home-decoration shows. Will I come back home with you? You live near here, right? Come on.' She started to lead Caroline off, as if the other woman was a pensioner.

Caroline wanted to say she was all right, that she just needed some biscuits, that she was coping just fine. But instead other words came up.

'He left me.' A big sob gulped up in her throat. 'He left me! He's dead, Cassie. *Dead!*'

'Ah pet, I know. Come on now, come on. Let's get you home.'
And Caroline let herself be led, and taken care of, like they
had taken care of Sylvia when she was ill. How much kindness
counted for, when you were really at rock bottom. She'd have to
remember that, if she ever dragged herself off it again.

Josh

'You want tea? Food? Cereal? A sandwich?'

Josh's mum was in the kitchen, where she always seemed to
be, and he could see his life stretching ahead of him, night after
night in front of the TV with her, explaining the plots of shows
and eating too much, until he got chubby again like he had in
secondary school. 'I'm fine, Mum.'

'You don't seem fine.'

He scowled. His mum had always been able to see through
him. 'It's just . . . I feel I'm leaving her behind there. Niamh.'

She said nothing for a while, putting bread in the toaster
even though he'd said he didn't want anything. 'You had friends
there, too. A life. Two years, it's not nothing.'

He thought of Billy. Maggie, Oisin. The Donnellys and their
secrets, cutting him out. Sylvia, gone now, and he hadn't even
begun to process what that meant, another person lost for ever.
And Caroline. 'Some. Not really.'

'What about that woman you mentioned all the time?'

God, his mother had witchy powers. She was as bad as Sylvia.
'Who?' he said vaguely, looking round the kitchen for his keys.

'Caroline, was that it?'

'Just a friend.'

'Hmmm.' After a while, she said, ultra-casual: 'You know,

you're allowed to find happiness again, Joshy. One day. Niamh would want it.'

He wanted to shout back at her that she'd barely known Niamh, and anyway Niamh was hardly even dead and he hadn't just lost her, he'd lost his whole idea of her, and her happy family. '*You* didn't.'

His mother looked up sharply; they never discussed Josh's dad, who'd died when he was eleven. 'That's different.'

'How? She was my wife, he was your husband. Is it different if you have kids?'

'I was . . . older.'

'Not that much older, Mum.'

She frowned hard. 'Are you eating this toast or not?'

Instead Josh stomped out, already irritated by his family. 'I have to get ready. It's my first week, I can't be late.'

Caroline

'I can just picture it,' she said to Anto. They'd finally moved into the new house, after long delays when it had variously been diagnosed with dry rot, rising damp and death-watch beetle. Caroline had seen a lot of tradesmen shaking their heads over the last few months, but, like a patient on their deathbed who miraculously pulls through, the house was now theirs. She spun in a circle in the living room, boxes all around, imagining it. 'A piano there, a nice rug here. At Christmas, we'll have the tree over there, and when we have kids, they can put the star on top, like me and Paul used to do.' Her parents had kept the decorations in the attic, in an orange Pampers box, and seeing that box had always meant joy and excitement.

Anto followed her in, carrying a groaning crate of books. His mood had

dipped from the euphoria of first finding the place, through the hard slog of
buying it and fixing it up. 'You're so sure they'll come along, these kids.'

'Of course they will,' Caroline said firmly. 'Now come on. If we get this
done in two hours I've a bottle of champagne in the fridge.'

His face didn't change. 'Car . . . what if I can't? The baby thing, I mean.
The way that I am . . . you know. What if it just doesn't work?'

She waved it away. Refused to hear what he was trying to tell her.
'There's loads they can do nowadays. It'll be grand. Come on, get these
boxes done!'

'It's a lovely place,' said the woman, peering at the built-in bookshelves. This was their third viewing, and the next step would be
to confirm the sale. 'We're so relieved. Everything we've seen's
been some awful modern box, or ancient and falling down.'

Caroline smiled. 'You should have seen it when we got it. We
did a lot of work to it.'

And had it been worth it? Buying this beautiful place, ivy
curling round the windows, stained glass round the door, fixing
it up over the years, getting it just right, only to sell it now?

'Well, we do like it,' said the husband cautiously, coming in.

Caroline averted her eyes from the baby strapped to his chest,
only to find her gaze irresistibly drawn. Kicking frog legs, huge
eyes taking everything in. But it was always going to be like
this, wasn't it? She was always going to see babies, and that was
a good thing. Her friends would have kids. Her nieces would
grow up. Anto's lot would have more weans, and maybe she'd
get to see them someday. She'd already arranged to go and visit,
to watch Grainne's latest Irish-dancing show, now that she and
Mary had called a truce.

'I'd love to see a family in here,' she said, and she meant it. She
had pictured her and Anto's children playing out back, maybe

hanging a swing from the apple tree. That was never going to happen now, but least some other kids could enjoy it.

'So are you buying a bigger place yourself, or ...?' said the mother, fishing. Caroline bet they had speculated as to why she was selling, and for such a good price too.

'A smaller place, actually.'

Rented first, while she thought about her options. Maybe she'd go travelling again for a bit. Join some kind of saddo group for the over thirty-fives, take an organised tour of Machu Picchu.

'Oh?'

'Yes. My husband died, you see.'

The woman's face paled. 'I'm so sorry!'

She decided just to say it. 'It's OK. In fact, I should probably tell you in case this makes a difference – he died here. In the bathroom.'

The couple exchanged a quick look, the kind Anto and Caroline used to do. There was no one she had that with now. Except, maybe, Josh, but he was gone so it didn't count. 'Did he?'

'He took his own life. He was – he wasn't well, never had been, really. We did our best to keep him here, and well, we managed it that long.' She'd decided she liked Mary's way of phrasing it. And if it put people off buying the place, well, so be it. She didn't want Anto's death to be a shameful secret. There'd been too much of that in Ireland over the years.

The woman said, bravely, 'I suppose people have died in most old houses.'

'Right. And we were happy here, before that.' Caroline swallowed hard. 'The place was ... full of love. For a while, anyway. So you'd be getting that, too. The happiness, along with the sadness.'

Maybe the sale would fall through because she'd told them,

but if they wanted it enough, they'd understand. She was sure of that now.

Josh

'Dad?' It was late, maybe eleven o'clock, and Josh had school in the morn-
ing. Sam, aged five, was fast asleep in his twin bed upstairs. But Josh was
awake, and when he heard the front door open, he crept downstairs, the dark
house lit only by the street lights outside.

His dad was in the kitchen with only the light of the cooker on, stirring
a Pot Noodle. He glanced around. 'What are you doing up?'

Josh hadn't seen his dad all day – he'd been out working in the supermar-
ket where he collected trolleys, and now he was on his way to his night job, as
a bouncer in a club. 'I finished my World Cup sticker album. Want to see?'

His dad must have been pushed for time, and exhausted, but he just
looked quickly at the clock and said, 'Show me while I eat this.' And he sat
and leafed through it, as Josh explained how he'd got each sticker, swapping
them with boys at school, offering ten more common ones for a prized one.
'Great, that's great.' He got up, put his fork in the sink and the container
in the bin. 'Be a good boy tomorrow for your mum, OK?'

'OK, Dad.'

He put on his black bomber jacket and went out. Josh never saw him
again. They were woken up early the next morning by the police; his dad
had been punched in the face in a scuffle with a punter, had hit his head on
the concrete pavement, and was dead.

Josh lay awake, stewing with anger. Sam was out again, though the light-up numbers on Josh's clock read 3.23 a.m. Josh had work the next day, and was still trying to make a good first impression, navigate the rules of the office which were so different from the *Chronicle*. They seemed to include, be funny on Twitter, and always send out for lunch. He'd seen their bewildered looks as he rolled up each day with his mum's gigantic Tupperwares full of food.

Bloody Sam. He was selfish, irresponsible, lazy. He wasn't even working at the minute, so he slept all day and was out all night drinking in the rooftop bars of Peckham, matching with girls on Tinder and Bumble. And where was he getting the money for the drinks? From their mum most likely, who could hardly afford it.

Finally, gritting his teeth, Josh heard the key in the lock – missing it several times – then heavy steps on the stairs, splashing of water in the bathroom, loud spitting as teeth were brushed. When Sam finally came crashing in to the room, Josh hissed, 'Don't you have a job interview tomorrow?'

'S'cool, I'll be there.'

'Will you? Cos I'd have thought you needed a job, instead of living off Mum all the time. She can't afford it, Sam.'

Sam sat down heavily on the bed, pulled off his expensive trainers. 'And how would you know, man? You've been in another country.'

It was true. Josh did feel guilty about abandoning his mother, to cope with and support Sam by herself. 'I've been grieving for my wife. She died, did you know that? Cos you didn't come to the funeral, that's for sure.'

Had he gone too far? He saw his brother's head turn in the darkened room. 'Wondered when you were gonna bring that up.'

'Well, you didn't, did you? I mean, Christ, Sam. She was your sister-in-law.'

'The funeral was like the next day! You seen the price of flights? Why they have to have it so fast?'

Josh didn't really understand that either. 'I'd have sent you the money. I needed you there.' He'd felt so alone, Niamh's family's pressing, hysterical grief forcing him out. His mum too upset to say anything, exhausted from the 4 a.m. flight she'd taken to be in Belfast on time. 'You've not even mentioned her to me all this time, Sam.'

Suddenly his anger had evaporated, and he was just so sad. Was this it for him? Living with his thoughtless brother and busy mum, no one to talk to about Niamh? No one to confide in about his grief? No one, like, say, Caroline? He had to stop thinking about her.

'I'm sorry.'

He wasn't sure he'd heard right at first. Sam never apologised. 'Yeah, well. It's too late now.' He turned over, making the springs in the old bed groan. He was thirty-four, he'd been married. What was he doing in his childhood bed, still getting cross with his little brother?

'It reminded me too much of Dad.' Sam spoke in a really quiet voice. Josh didn't answer for a moment.

'Why?'

'Cos, man – they never let me go to his, did they?' Sam had been thought too young, both for the funeral and to know the truth. 'Nobody would even tell me what happened. I just – I couldn't see you like that, the way Mum was when Dad died. Destroyed, like.'

'I didn't know.' They rarely talked about their dad. Gone now for more than two-thirds of Josh's life.

'Yeah, well, it's hard for me too. I know you missed him more, you were older. I know you miss Niamh. But it's hard for me, too, being here with Mum, his picture still on the wall. She never even dates, you know? I feel like I have to stay here, not leave her on her own. There's a guy at her church always asks her to things, but she never goes. I think she feels, I dunno, it's betraying Dad. But he's been gone for years. Maybe if you talked to her, I dunno.'

Josh felt it weigh him down onto the half-wrecked bed. All this time he'd thought he had a monopoly on grief, and his mother was still living inside it, his brother too. Did it last for twenty years, the loss? How could he survive that? Or was there a life for him still to come? 'I'm sorry,' he stiffly. 'I'll talk to her.'

Sam said nothing for a while, and Josh thought he might have gone to sleep. Then: 'She seemed top, like. Niamh.'

'She was,' said Josh, his voice thickening. 'I wish you'd got to know her better.'

Caroline

Sylvia's funeral was held two weeks after she died – this was a very long delay for Ireland, but she'd wanted to be buried with Iris, which had created some delays. Caroline organised it, along with Annabel and Cassie, who had made such massive progress, crediting Sylvia's advice for getting her out of the hole of grief. She'd even contacted her parents, started playing netball again, and her face had animation and she almost never had wet hair. So that was something. Corners could be turned. Things could get better.

Sometimes Caroline felt that organising funerals was what she was born for. She was extremely capable, she knew when to be tolerant and when to be firm. Crying didn't work on her (a legacy of teaching kids for years), and she had an impeccable instinct for what was tasteful and what was too much. For how much cooked ham to order. For whether to offer booze or not. Plus, the person who was the centre of attention wasn't in a position to answer back, so it was much simpler than the hen dos or thirtieth birthdays or christenings she'd also organised. She'd done a lovely job on Anto's funeral, everyone said. For the first time she wondered if there was something a bit strange about that. If maybe she should have allowed herself to break, instead of handling everything herself.

She sighed, scanning her checklist. It looked as if Sensible Caroline was back. She'd told Paul to keep his money, spend it on the girls, but her house was still being sold, the nice couple having taken it after all, and she was surrounded by boxes of her things. She'd decided it was actually time to let it go. Living every day with Anto's ghost probably wasn't doing her much good.

Her hand hovered over the track pad of her laptop. Should she tell Josh when the funeral was or not? She'd not heard a word from him since he left, and a selfish part of her didn't want to be the one to make contact. He'd said he wasn't coming back for it. He'd have asked if he wanted to know, wouldn't he?'

One night she went over to Matt's again, having agreed to babysit so he could meet his friend for a drink. But when she got there he was on the sofa, glass of wine in hand, in jeans and a soft grey jumper. 'Oh – you're not ready?'

'John cancelled on me. He's torn his rotator cuff playing tennis, the eejit.'

'Should I just ...?' She was surprised how much she didn't want to go back to her empty house, which already felt like someone else's.

'No, no, stay and have a drink, will you not?'

He poured her out a glass, and she sat down, feeling odd. Another woman had probably chosen these glasses, this sofa. Patricia's photo was on the mantelpiece, a smiling bottle-blonde in a wedding dress, and another of her with Matt, Peadar and Maddie. She had died before they got a chance to take one with Ryan in, poor wean. Her heart ached for them. 'How are you, then?'

He made a see-saw motion with his hands. 'I think the kids help, you know. It makes it harder, the way they don't really understand – but they don't know to be sad all the time, either. Ryan has no idea, God love him. He still smiles at bubbles and rubber ducks and I can't help smiling too – sometimes, at least. He'll have no memory of her at all. Even for Peadar, it's fading.'

'How's Maddie?'

He sighed. 'I'm the most worried about her. She's so calm, somehow. Like a wee robot, almost. You teach kids, right? Should I take her see someone?'

'Can't hurt. I can send you some numbers, if you want. Charities who help, that sort of thing.'

'Thank you. God, you're so good, Caroline. Helping every-one. Me, Cassie, poor old Sylvia, God rest her . . . '

Caroline took a sip of wine. 'Ah no. Cassie's been helping me, if anything. I haven't been coping so well of late. I think . . . in some ways it finally hit me, you know? That this is it. For the rest of my life.'

'Yeah.' He stared at the blank TV screen, his eyes wide with tiredness and sadness. 'Does it ever get easier?'

'I've no idea. Sylvia seemed to have found a way.' But then she'd been so keen to let go, to re-join Iris. That didn't suggest she was happy with her life alone. As happened so often now,

Caroline was slapped by a wave of it, the utter futility, the slog of another forty years without Anto. Maybe with no children. Alone. 'Oh *God*.'

'Oh, come here, come here.' Matt set down his wine, worried, and rubbed her shoulder. 'Jesus, I didn't mean to upset you. You're young, Caroline, you've your whole life ahead of you.'

'I'm not that young,' she said, thickly, trying not to cry all over him.

'You look twenty-five.'

'I'm not, though. I'm thirty-six. What man's going to want that, when he could have some bright young thing?' She'd done some thorough internet stalking of Josh's new workmates, and at least half of them seemed to be beautiful, trendy young women in clear-rimmed glasses and elaborate hairdos.

'Ah come on now, Caroline, sure you're beautiful. You know that, don't you?'

She didn't know why it happened. She'd never even felt a flicker of attraction to Matt – how could you, when he was so broken? – but he was a good-looking man, and he was very close, his soft wool jumper and scratchy beard and the wine on his breath, and then his mouth was on hers.

For a moment she let it happen – but it was clumsy, wrong, full of pain – and she pulled away. 'Sorry.'

Matt gave a shaky laugh. 'Ah God, I'm so sorry. No idea what came over me there. You just looked so sad.'

'It's OK. My fault too.'

'I'm not ready to even think about any of that, not for ages yet, maybe ever.'

'I know. Let's just forget it.' They both drank their wine, and the moment passed. Caroline even gave a little tearful laugh. 'Eejits, the pair of us.'

Matt looked at Caroline from the corner of his eye. 'What about you and our wee friend Joshua?'

'What about him?'

'You two always seemed thick as thieves. And when you ate the head off him in the street that time, well. Sparks were flying, let's just say.'

Caroline thought about it. Now that Anto was truly gone, with no prospect of any part of him returning, her mind seemed empty. Cleared out. But what did Gilda, a devotee of Marie Kondo, say about that? If you clear things out, you leave space for new ones. 'He's hardly thinking about any of that. He's still in love with his wife, for a start.'

'She's gone. He'll have to realise that eventually. She's gone and we're still here and that's just the truth of it.'

'I know. But Jesus, we're the walking wounded. Also, hello, he literally just walked out to move to London.'

Matt thought about it. 'There are flights.'

'Sure they're a wild price these days,' said Caroline, in her mother's voice, and they laughed, and finished off the bottle.

Life has to go on. That's the annoying thing about it, and why the days after a death are so hard, because the big event has passed and now you have to figure out how to live without someone, in this new world, this bombed-out city that is your life. There was no word from Josh, a silence so complete it was as if he was dead too. And yet she was still here.

Gradually, she began to re-join the world. She went on a night out with Cassie and her netball team, and threw up in a bush while the goal attack supportively rubbed her back. She visited her parents, and let her mother lecture her about buying a more sensible house next time, 'a lovely wee newbuild' or something.

She let Jenny take her to a spin class, after which she almost threw up again. She ordered travel brochures and bought a guide book to South East Asia, researched group holidays. She made an appointment to get inoculations, and organised travel insurance. She completed on the sale of the house, set a date to move out. She went back to support group, and when Sinead wasn't looking handed out copies of Sylvia's book to Ruma, and Matt, and a new person who'd joined, with the shell-shocked look they'd all had at the start, a twenty-three-year-old guy called Shane whose girlfriend had died from an allergic reaction to a peanut while on holiday in Santa Ponsa. People were dying all the time, and yet life went on. Babies were born. The sun rose and set. Broken hearts healed over, at least a little. She lived without Anto, first one day, then the next, then another. It was the only way to do it, she had discovered. One day at a time.

Josh

'Josh, maaaate, how are you settling in?'

Josh looked up from his glass desk with the ultra-modern iMac perched on it, a half-written article about face serums on the screen. Not the kind of thing he'd expected to be writing in this job. He tried to spin the chair, but he still hadn't worked out its complicated ergonomics; apparently it had won design awards. 'Hi, Calvin. I'm fine, thanks.'

'Up for a quick one tonight?' Calvin made a drink-lifting motion.

Ever since he'd started, the team had been on at Josh to go for beers. Likely more than beers – Josh had noticed their glassy-eyed gaiety of a Friday afternoon, after long trips to the bathroom. He knew he should say yes. Apart from the boost to his career, he hardly knew anyone in London any more – it turned out they'd all got married and/or had kids while he'd been away, and moved to Zone Six where all they could talk about was allotments and the horrifying expense of child-care. But he just couldn't. His heart felt like a heavy sponge in his chest.

Likewise, he couldn't summon the enthusiasm to look for a flat, even though living with his mum and Sam was driving him slowly insane. Despite their heart-to-heart, his brother's phone still buzzed all night with texts, and sometimes he watched videos in bed at 2 a.m., sound up loud. Josh didn't know when he ever got sleep, and if he complained to his mum she just gave him a look like he was fifteen again, which was how he felt. For sure he needed to be away from the smell of Sam's trainers and the twenty-four-hour force-feeding he endured from his mother – he'd put on six pounds already – but the will just wasn't there. He remembered what London flats were like, a parade of black mould and suspicious smells, landlords who took inspiration from Victorian slum owners, and flatmates who appeared to be in witness protection after involvement in a dodgy murder or two. His lovely studio in Peckham now cost twice what it had when he sold it two years ago. If he wanted a place on his own, he'd be looking in the suburbs somewhere, an hour's commute each way. His heart sank at the memories of evenings in Belfast, home in twenty minutes and sometimes what Niamh called a 'spin' out to the countryside or the Lough, time for a walk and a bite to eat out if they felt like it. The way it didn't get dark till eleven in the summers.

'If you change your mind,' said Calvin, winking, 'I know that new hottie in accounts has her eye on you.'

That was the other thing that made Josh uncomfortable. Hadn't that sort of clammy sexism been left behind in the 1990s? Not to mention the fact they'd literally hired him because his wife had recently died.

'Thanks, mate, will do.'

As Calvin left, Josh heard the ping of an email. Perhaps one of the flats he'd half-heartedly asked to view. Sigh. Instead, he saw to his surprise it was the contact at City Hall, the assistant who'd left all those months ago who might have had information about the expenses scandal, the story he had so half-heartedly worked on then handed over to Bob. Davina was her name. *Sorry for the delay,* she said. *I went travelling, didn't have email. I could chat to you now if you want? I have loads of dirt!*

The word dirt was underlined heavily. Typical. All that time slogging away at the story and now when he'd left he had a breakthrough. He could have just ignored it, thanked her and let it go, but Josh was not very good at letting things go. It was what made him such a good journalist, and so bad at getting over bereavement. He picked up his phone and dialled Maggie's number. He imagined her peering over her glasses, stabbing away at the mobile like it was a corrupt politician.

She answered, her husky forty-a-day voice taking him back to another office, tea-stained and distinctly untrendy. 'City Boy. This is a surprise.'

He filled her in on Davina.

'All right, ta for that, we could do a follow-up piece. We'll get the bastards in the end, eh? You working on something good over there?'

'Eh ... kind of.' They seemed to have him on skincare and dating, rather than the hard-hitting investigations he was used to doing. 'How's everything there?' He'd been hit by a wave of missing the place, the Belfast rain on the reinforced windows, the scale-filled kettle that no one ever cleaned. Even Oisin's terrible demos and Maggie's smoker's cough.

'Ah, we're hirpalling along. I was going to send you something, now I think of it. How do I take a photo on this yoke?' There followed a lot of swearing and the beeping of buttons. 'There you go. Take care of yourself, City Boy. Don't be a stranger.'

Maggie's message had come through. 'JOSH,' it said, all in caps, of course, 'WASN'T THIS THE OLD DEAR YOU BEFRIENDED? THOUGHT YOU MIGHT NOT KNOW SHE KICKED BUCKET. HOPE THOSE TRENDY WANKERS ARE TREATING YOU RIGHT. LOVE, MAGS.'

He clicked on the photo she'd attached, a shot of the *Irish News* funeral announcements (these were even on the radio in Ireland). Sylvia's funeral was the next day – he'd assumed it would already have taken place by now, it being Ireland, and had half-thought Caroline might have let him know how it went, despite what he'd said to her when he left, which he was vaguely ashamed of. Her silence had been deafening, and made him feel even lonelier in this vast city he used to call home. But no. He hadn't missed the funeral. Not yet.

Josh began to think. He'd only been in this job for two weeks, he could hardly go gallivanting off to Ireland. On the other hand, Finn the layout manager had already worked from home three days in a row in order to 'collect parcels', so he didn't think they would mind too much.

301

12. SAY GOODBYE

Caroline

It turned out Sylvia and Iris had chosen the graveyard Anto was buried in. Caroline was conscious of it the whole time walking behind the funeral procession, collecting grass and mud on her sensible black court heels. He was just over there, under the rain-sodden trees (of course it had rained), his body, what was left of him. The bit of him stored in the fertility clinic had already been destroyed, as he'd wanted. And that was it.

She'd kept herself afloat with the funeral arrangements, picking the hymns along with a reluctant Annabel, who didn't believe in religion at all. Caroline had been surprised a church funeral was what Syl wanted, after being rejected so comprehensively by her family and faith, but she'd clearly stated it in the will she'd left behind with her lawyer, outlining all her wishes. Caroline could have wept – such beautiful organisation. If only Anto had thought to do the same – *PS pls don't use the sperm in the freezer after all, kthx bye.* On the other hand, it meant there was nothing for her to do except book it all – the funeral home, the church, the tea at a nearby hotel, the choice of sandwiches (two meat, one vegetarian). She'd decided against drink. Undignified, sloppy, drunk crying and maudlin singing, that was really more of a Catholic thing.

Sinead was at the church when she arrived, sitting up very straight in a pew, in a smart black coat and hat with veil, like a professional mourner. She narrowed her eyes at Caroline. 'Will you be at group this week? You missed quite a few there.'

Caroline bit her lip. 'I'm sorry, I will come from now on. I just . . . things got a bit too real for a moment there.'

Sinead nodded. 'That's how it works, you know, grief. It's not a *line*. It's more like . . . swiggles and swirls. A roller coaster.'

'I'm realising that,' said Caroline drily. 'Thank you for coming, Sinead.'

'Part of the job.' Her mouth was a pinched line, and Caroline wondered if grief had done that to her. If even twenty years could not heal you entirely. 'Josh is away back to London, I hear.'

'Yeah.' Would it ever not hurt?

'You two were very *close*.'

'I suppose.'

'I see it all the time, you know. You wouldn't believe the number of flings we've had in my support groups.'

Caroline's mouth fell open. 'It wasn't a fling!'

'It's OK, you know. You're allowed to move on. That's the *point* of the support group.'

Caroline gaped at her. 'But your Terry . . . '

'My Terry was a good man, God rest him. Not perfect, but I loved him. Doesn't mean I didn't move on.'

Caroline gaped some more. What?

Sinead sighed. 'My partner, Craig, he's always on at me to get married again. I couldn't even think about it, for *ages*. Maybe I wasn't totally over Terry. But I have to admit, Sylvia, her book . . . '

'You read her book?'

'Of course I did. There was a lot of sense in it.' Caroline's mind was boggling. The world was upside down. 'Though really I feel she was a *wee* bit harsh on essential oils. I mean, I think they have a lot of uses.'

'Right . . . '

'Anyway, I've said yes to Craig. The wedding will be in the summer. I'm thinking Lake Como.' Sinead leaned over and squeezed Caroline's arm with her bony hand. 'You're doing all right, you know. If you've let yourself break, that's the first step.'

'Thank you,' said Caroline, frankly stunned. 'And thank you ... thank you for all you did. I don't think I could have coped in the first months after it happened, without the group.'

Sinead looked slightly mollified, nodded. Then her mouth tightened again. 'There will be tea after, won't there? I *really* don't hold with these modern funerals where you don't even get a cup of tea.'

Caroline bridled slightly. 'Well, I organised it, so of course there'll be ... ' She forced a smile. 'Of course. Do join us after. We'd love to see you.'

Annabel was in the front row, as befitted family, and had brought her boyfriend Fintan, who had white dreads and a huge hole in his earlobe. They both wore rainbow Pride T-shirts, which Caroline thought Sylvia might have liked. As well as Sinead, Cassie and Ruma were there, and Matt had brought Maddie, in a little grey frock. She hadn't been to her mother's funeral, and Caroline had suggested this might help her process it. She smiled at Matt as she passed him, spotting dried egg on his tie. He was a good lad, Matt, even if she knew there'd never be anything between them. Jenny had come, too, which Caroline was overwhelmed by, since she hadn't even known Syl. 'You'll get your reward in heaven,' she muttered, passing her friend in a further-back pew.

Jenny flushed with pleasure. 'Ah no, sure you know I love a good funeral. Better than weddings for gossip.'

The service was starting, and the only person missing was

307

Josh. It was OK – this was how he'd wanted it, a clean break, no looking back. All the same, as the vicar began to speak, Caroline felt her chest grow even heavier. He wasn't coming back. Not ever again. She was on her own.

Caroline found it all surprisingly moving. She shouldn't feel so sad, she knew. Syl had been ready to go, sure that she would see Iris again. And maybe she would. Who knew? No, Caroline was mostly crying, somewhat selfishly, for herself. Josh had gone, and she missed him, not because she loved him (she told herself), but because she'd lost a friend. Because the two of them had been something, a life raft in the stormy sea of grief, and it was over now.

The service was short, glossing over the fact that Syl was predeceased by her 'greatest friend, Iris'. Annabel snorted audibly at this. Afterwards, she moved about the church shaking hands. Ruma was there, headscarf shrouding her from the rain, and with her was a young girl of about twelve, who had glossy dark hair and a Taylor Swift T-shirt. She marched over to Caroline in the aisle. 'Hiya.' She had a strong Belfast accent.

'Hello,' said Caroline, who was generally firmly kind to children. 'Is this your mum? Hi, Ruma.'

Ruma smiled, pressed her hands to her chest in a gesture they recognised.

'Yeah, I'm Callie. Mum wanted me to come to translate today.' She spoke to Ruma rapidly in what Caroline thought must be Bengali. 'The thing is, Mum doesn't speak English all that well, but she can understand it OK.'

'Oh?' Caroline had never been sure, and her attempts to find out had only been met with silent smiles.

'Yeah. That's why she kept coming to the group. I know you

thought maybe she couldn't understand but – she did. Some of it. Enough.'

'Right,' said Caroline cautiously. 'Sorry about that, Ruma. We didn't know.'

Ruma waved it away. She said something else to her daughter, who rolled her eyes in a teenage way. 'Yeah yeah, I'm getting to it. She says, like, she listened to you all. She watched what was going on, with you and the handsome boy. Who's that?'

'Josh,' said Caroline, embarrassed. 'She must mean Josh.'

'Yeah, him. She says . . . it's very sad you lost your man. She lost my dad last year but he was like, old. Much older than her. She says you're young. Plenty of time.' Ruma said something else, then gently touched Caroline's stomach. Callie rolled her eyes again. 'Um, personal space, Mum? She says there's still time for you to have babies. If you want.'

'Oh . . . ' Caroline seemed frozen. 'Thank you? I think.'

'That's her general message, I guess. You have time. And the handsome boy, too. Is he here?' Callie sounded hopeful.

'He's not coming,' said Caroline, hearing the heaviness in her own voice.

'Shame. Am I done now, Mum? No more wise words you want to share with them?'

Caroline stopped her. 'Callie, wait . . . can you ask your mum, does it get better? Being a widow? Do you move on?'

Callie asked this. Or Caroline assumed she did – she could have been saying anything.

'She says you don't move on exactly. But you can move another way instead.'

'Right.' Caroline wondered what that meant. That the lives they had hoped for, her and Josh, had expected, with all the confidence of healthy young people in an affluent country, who never think the worst will happen to them, those lives were gone, and they had to find new ones? That there were lots of other lives open to them instead, a million doors open instead of just one closed one?

'Thank you,' said Caroline, trying to sound firm but coming out wobbly. 'Tell your mum ... that means a lot.'

'She'll understand. Her English is getting better. She's OK in writing too – your accents just like, really mess her up. You talk too fast, she says.'

That was probably true. 'I'm really sorry. See you soon, Ruma. Next time at group, I promise I'll try to speak slower.'

Caroline reached out to squeeze her hand, and Ruma smiled, and said, 'You will be fine. You will.' It was the first time Caroline had ever heard her voice.

Then they processed out into the rain, like a weird version of a wedding. As she passed the back of the church Caroline froze, then slowly moved forward again, barely glancing at the man she had spotted in the back pew. It was Josh, damp and moody, in a dark suit and discreetly toting an overnight bag. Josh. She stumbled past without meeting his eyes, her heart beating a crazy tattoo. Why was he here? Why hadn't he texted if he was coming? And how did he know it was happening?

Outside the ground was marshy underfoot, and the vicar said a hasty few words before the coffin was lowered by the funeral home pall bearers. Aside from Annabel's boyfriend, who had a trapped nerve from skateboarding, there was only really Josh who could have done it, and they hadn't known he was coming. Why had he, she wondered? Caroline deliberately didn't look at him, and wondered even more. Was there hope still? Was that what Ruma had been trying to tell her?

Josh

He'd barely made the funeral in the end, a panicky dash to the one bus every twenty minutes from the airport, rain pebbling the windows as it seemed to do every bloody day in Belfast. He'd taken a taxi to the church, but the driver was affable and unhurried, and Josh had sat on his hands, wishing he could ask him to go faster, knowing you didn't do that here. He'd slipped in just as it started, catching a glimpse of Caroline up the front, in a smart black dress. During the service he'd tried to think about Sylvia, the short time he'd known her. How pretty she'd made her house, even when she could barely see. The life she'd carved out with her Iris, even when the world left them only scraps. How much they'd given up for each other, how brave that had been. Then the things she'd done for them, the binder of advice she'd left them, a road map through the maze of grief. Had it helped? He didn't feel any better than he had when he'd started it. In fact he felt worse, because at least then he'd had his friend. He'd had Caroline.

He didn't know what to call her. His best friend, for a time. The only person who really understood him, where he was at. The last two weeks he'd felt the lack of her practical kindness, which stopped just short of bossiness. Her warm efficiency towards children and old people alike. Her self-deprecating humour, making fun of her own madness in launching the court case. She was thirty-six, he knew. She wanted kids. That meant, brutal as it was, she didn't have much time. She deserved to meet a nice guy, a grown-up who'd realise time was of the essence, who'd do his best to give her that baby she longed for. But who? Were there decent men around of that age? Caroline was lovely, the way her fair hair skimmed her face. The way she flushed

311

when she had a sip of wine, the way her laugh slid down to dirty so quickly. The kind, exasperated honesty in her eyes. The way she ate a pizza slice, rolling it up like a wrap.

Er, hello? Niamh's voice spoke in his head, and Josh realised with a lurch he hadn't heard it for a while. That he'd been thinking in a way he hadn't for years. The way you thought when you met a new person, someone you found interesting in a very specific way. But this was Caroline. He knew her. He'd never had these thoughts about her before.

Oh really? What about all those awkward hugs, then?

She turned to smile at someone near the front, a sad funeral smile, and he wished she was smiling at him. Maybe she never would again, after the way he'd behaved, running off and leaving her to cope with Sylvia's death, plan the funeral by herself.

What's that you're up to, Joshy boy?

Nothing. I'm sorry.

Why are you sorry? I'm gone, babe. I'm not coming back. It's OK to be interested in other people.

And Josh found that he was crying, and the old woman next to him passed him a tissue, and he couldn't help but think that Caroline would be like this when she was older – organised, kind, always with tissues, and that Niamh would never get older, and that just made him cry even more. Damn funerals.

He hung back at the interment, not knowing what to say to Caroline, lost in thoughts of death and suffering, of Niamh's grave in the cemetery out near her family. He hadn't heard a word from them since he left. Maybe he should reach out, try to forgive. They'd been doing their best, after all, and they had loved her, kept her among them.

'What are you doing here?' He jumped. Caroline had come

up to his elbow without him noticing, and was wiping grass off her high heels.

'Oh. Someone sent me the funeral announcement from the paper, so I thought I'd come.'

'You're truly Irish now, you know. The English have no clue about the power of the newspaper death announcements.' She shook some rain from her umbrella. Of course she had remembered to bring an umbrella.

'You organised this, I take it?'

'Most of it, aye.'

'It was lovely. Well done.'

She gave an ironic curtsey. 'We all have our skills, and mine just happens to be funeral planning. Maybe I should go into business.' She paused. 'How is it, over in trendy London?'

'Oh you know. Trendy. Expensive. How are you?'

'Grand. Sort of grand. I still have nowhere to live once the house is sold.'

'Neither do I. Sharing with my brother is like being fifteen again, only with back pain and fading eyesight.' The conversation faded as the rain on her umbrella increased to a thunder. 'Is there something after this?' he asked, raising his voice over the noise of the downpour.

'Of course. Sandwiches and tea at a hotel; you don't think I'd organise a funeral with no tea?'

'Of course. Stupid of me.'

'How long are you home for?' *Home*, she'd said. Was this home?

'Um ... I was going to head back tonight. Work tomorrow.' Even as he said it he felt how wrong it was. He didn't belong in London, crammed into his mum's house and writing reviews of face creams. He belonged here, with the people he'd found, people who cared for him. If they still did.

'I've got my car,' said Caroline after a moment. 'Come with me, it's tipping it down.'

They began to move off over the wet grass, and then, suddenly, Caroline paused. She was staring at something.

'What is it?'

'Oh. That's so weird. I knew it was here, but I just . . . for a second I forgot where it was.'

Josh looked at the grave they were standing in front of, sodden green turf and a slate headstone. Tasteful, unlike some of the hideous marble monstrosities topped with little stones. He'd bet Caroline had been responsible for this, her impeccable taste kicking in again. The headstone read *Antony John Carville, 1980–2019. Beloved son and husband.* 'Oh. It's him.'

'Yeah.' Caroline heaved a sigh. 'Where is Niamh, by the way? I never asked.'

'Out near her folks. They have a family plot.' Josh hadn't thought of it before, but if he stayed in London he wouldn't be buried with her. Did that matter, if you didn't believe in an afterlife? If you believed that after death we were simply gone, decaying bones and flesh? He didn't know. And what if he met someone else, got married again? His life stretched in front of him, long and unknowable. 'I wish you'd known her,' he blurted out. 'You would have liked each other. She wasn't sensible like you, but she admired it in other people.' Caroline could have been Niamh's organised friend, the one who had painkillers and plasters and made the holiday bookings.

'That's me,' she said. 'Doomed to be the sensible friend. I wonder what you'd have made of Anto. He wasn't like you at all. Very loud, very passionate, emotions all over the place. Up and down like a roller coaster. Drank too much, probably.'

An odd choice for someone like her, so even and calm. He

caught himself wondering if that was the type of man she'd want again, one like Anto. A man nothing like him. *Josh, what are you doing?*

After another moment, Caroline shivered. 'Come on. No sense standing here getting soaked. Anto's not here, is he? He's nowhere. It's just . . . a place to go.'

'Yeah.'

They made their way to the car. The other mourners had dispersed already. They spotted Cassie in the car park, shivering but radiant, a pretty blonde woman by her side.

Cassie was smiling. 'Um . . . you guys, this is Mary. We met at an ice hockey game, so we did. '

Josh and Caroline exchanged one of their swift looks, and it made him ache, to think how much he would miss this. Why couldn't you hold on to everyone you met in life, everyone who mattered? Why did they have to get swept away? 'Hi, Mary. Good of you to come.' Caroline shook Mary's hand, hugged Cassie. She turned to Josh. 'This one here saved my life the last few weeks. She caught me having a breakdown over some Jammie Dodgers.'

Caroline having a breakdown? Was she coping worse than he thought?

'Ah, you were fine. We should go,' said Cassie, blinking up at the rain. 'I'll see you at the hotel. Listen, you guys . . . I'm just going to say something. Because if funerals show you anything it's that there won't always be time to say things. You know? You guys . . . you need to say the things you have to say to each other. And do it now. OK? Just . . . before it's too late. I think Sylvia would want it.'

Caroline opened her mouth as if to correct Cassie's garbled syntax, then closed it. 'We'll see you there.'

She unlocked her car – clean, with a blanket on the back seat, and the oil no doubt always kept topped up. 'What did she mean?' he asked, as he buckled his seatbelt.

Caroline adjusted her mirror. 'Hm?'

'You and me. What do we have to say to each other?' He'd heard once that couples had more arguments in the car, because they didn't look into each other's eyes and feel empathy. He remembered that trip to Galway with Niamh, getting lost on the country roads and her trying to open the door and get out of the moving car after he'd snapped at her about her terrible map reading. People always thought of the good times when they mourned a loved one. But he missed the bad times too, the rows, her untidiness, the boring evenings in. Maybe he would never stop. But that was OK. Missing someone, it just meant there'd been something good in your life, something to mourn in the first place.

'I don't know,' said Caroline vaguely. He knew she was pretending, because Caroline didn't do vague. It would be up to Josh to bridge the gap between them, and fair enough – he was the one who'd left, after all.

'Since I've been away, I've realised how much you came to mean to me . . .' he began.

'Do you know where this hotel is? Can you get it up on your phone?'

'Caroline! I'm trying to say something here.'

She sighed. 'Do you have to? I've had my fill of big dramatic conversations this year, to be honest.'

'Well, me too, and my fill of them is exactly none, but . . . Cassie's right, you know? Aren't there things you would say to Anto if you could?'

'Don't kill yourself, for a start.' She sighed again. 'Sorry. All right. Remember I'm Irish and very uncomfortable with genuine emotion. I can sing you a sad song and drink ten pints, but feelings ... not so much.'

'I'm English! Surely we win at that.'

'Yes, OK. Call it a draw.'

The windscreen wipers scraped rain from the glass.

'I don't even know what I'm going to say,' he said. 'I've just missed you. A lot. I wish we'd never fought that time.'

'I missed you too,' she said, quietly, eyes on the road. 'I had to eat a whole pizza by myself last Friday. I've put on five pounds.'

He thought what to say next. Why was it so hard? Surely once your wife had died nothing else could be hard. But it was. Life still went on, regardless. 'I don't want to miss you, Caroline. I want you around. Like, a lot.'

'You moved to London,' she said crisply.

'I was upset. Angry. Not at you, just at ... the world, I guess. You push people away, don't you, when you're hurting like that.' A terrible urge to take the worst and make it even harder.

Her tone was casual as she changed gear. 'You're saying you might come back?'

Was he saying that? Quit *Dude* magazine after two weeks? Give up his flat search? He'd nowhere to live here, either, but at least it was cheaper. Would Maggie have him back at the *Chronicle*? 'I'm ... thinking about it.'

'What would it take for you to do that?' Caroline's voice was still oh-so-casual.

'I ... I don't know. Maybe if I was ... with someone.' Josh couldn't believe he was saying this. It had hardly occurred to him before, and yet now he realised he'd thought of little else the whole time in London. Everything funny or interesting or annoying, he wanted to text Caroline about it. He picked up his phone a hundred times a day to message her, put it back down again, afraid to reach out.

'That's what Cassie meant about you and me, you're saying.' Again, she was so calm.

'I think that's what she meant, yeah.'

'Matt said the same to me once. That you and I ... had feelings for each other.' Caroline signalled, made a left turn. Emotionally significant conversations would not stop her from driving with due care and attention. Josh suddenly could see it, their life together. Ordered, supportive. Comforting. Loving. Never being lonely, because they had each other.

'And what did you say?'

'I'd never thought about it, I guess, until we fought that time. You know, when I lost my rag in the street and screamed at you – don't know if you remember?'

He looked at her but her eyes, so clear and blue, never left the road. He looked at her hands on the wheel in the correct position, her shapely legs pressing down the pedals, the way her hair curved against her cheek. *Caroline.* 'That means you do have feelings?'

She sighed. 'God, I don't know. I'm a widow. I'm deranged, didn't you know?'

'Me too. All I know is ... I don't want to be in London, missing you, and you be here ... '

'Missing you too,' she said quietly, and his heart leapt. She stopped the car.

'Why have you stopped?'

'Because we're here.'

'Oh.'

She switched off the engine, and seemed to think about it for a long time before giving herself a little shake. 'Josh. When

Anto died, a bit of me died too. I don't know if I'll ever get over it, not really. Or ever stop loving him, at least a bit. I think you feel the same about Niamh.'

'Yeah.' So it was a no. The answer to the question he hadn't even known he was going to ask was a no, of course it was a no. It was ridiculous, anyway, so why did he feel so crap?

'But . . . ' His heart lifted. The clouds parted (only metaphorically, since they were still in Belfast). 'I mean, we're alive, aren't we? They aren't. We can't feel guilty towards them, because they aren't the same any more. They're just . . . ' She pressed a hand to her chest. 'In there somewhere. And you're . . . ' She reached out her other hand to him, tentatively, put it on his wrist, pale and cool against his skin. 'You're here.'

Josh took her hand, and there they were, sitting in Caroline's Corolla, holding hands, in the rain, at a funeral. So very Irish, as Niamh would have said. What would she say if she knew he was even thinking about another woman? About loving again? *I'd say be happy,* she told him in his head, except he knew it wasn't her, it was just his memory of her. Something precious, but in the past. Someone he would never forget, never get over, never stop mourning. But all the same, Caroline was right. Niamh and Anto were gone, and never coming back, as terrible and crushing and life-destroying as that was. And he and Caroline, they had to get on with living, or just give up and die too. He was alive. Niamh was dead. And he might have fifty years ahead of him, a hundred other lives to live without her. With Caroline, maybe. Just maybe.

'That's right,' he said, and he was holding her hand as the rain fell, and she was smiling at him, turning to face him at last, her lovely kind face that he had missed so much. 'I'm here.'

ACKNOWLEDGEMENTS

Thank you to everyone who helps me get a book out of my head and onto the page.

To everyone at Sphere – Thalia, Darcy, and especially Maddie, who suggested doing a book set in Belfast.

To Diana, superstar agent, who always has my back.

To Angela, who worked out what was actually going on with Niamh.

To Nat, for daily pep texts.

To all my other wonderful friends, family, and readers – thank you!

If you've enjoyed this book, I'd love to hear from you on Instagram, @evawoodsakaclairemcgowan Twitter (@inkstainsclaire) or via my website, www.ink-stains.co.uk

Now read on for Eva Woods' heartwarming beginning to

How to Be Happy

Day One: Make a new friend

'Excuse me?'

No answer. The receptionist carried on clacking the computer keys.

Annie tried again. '*Excuse* me.'

That was a level-two 'excuse me' – above the one she'd give to tourists blocking the escalator and below the one reserved for someone with their bag on a train seat. Nothing.

'*Sorry*,' she said, taking it to level three (stealing your parking spot; bashing you with an umbrella, etc). 'Could you help me, please? I've been standing here for five minutes.'

The woman kept typing. 'What?'

'I need to change the address on a patient file. I've already been sent to four different departments.'

The receptionist extended one hand, without looking up. Annie gave her the form. 'This you?'

'Well, no.' *Obviously.*

'The patient has to change it for themselves.'

'Um, well, they can't, actually.' Which would be clear if anyone in the hospital ever bothered to read the files.

The form dropped onto the counter. 'Can't let another person change it. Data protection, see.'

'But—' Annie felt, suddenly and horribly, like she might cry

'—I need to change it so letters come to my address! She can't read them herself any more! That's why I'm here. Please! I – I just need it changed. I don't understand how this can possibly be so difficult.'

'Sorry.' The reception sniffed, picked something off one of her nails.

Annie snatched the paper up. 'Look, I've been in this hospital for hours now. I've been sent around from office to office. Patient Records. Neurology. Outpatients. Reception. Back to Neurology. And no one seems to have the slightest idea how to do this very simple task! I haven't eaten. I haven't showered. And I can't go home unless you just open up your computer and type in a few lines. That's all you have to do.'

The receptionist still wasn't even looking at her. Clack, clack, clack. Annie felt it swell up in her, the anger, the pain, the frustration. 'Will you LISTEN to me?' She reached over and wrenched the computer around.

The woman's eyebrows disappeared into her bouffant hair. 'Madam, I'm going to have to call security if you don't—'

'I just want you to look at me when I'm speaking. I just need you to *help* me. *Please*.' And then it was too late and she was definitely crying, her mouth suddenly filling with bitter salt. 'I'm sorry. I'm sorry. I just – I – really need to change the address.'

'Listen, madam ...' The receptionist was swelling, her mouth opening, no doubt to tell Annie where to go. Then something odd happened. Instead, her face creased into a smile. 'Hiya, P.'

'He-ey, everything OK here?'

Annie turned to see who was interrupting. In the doorway of the dingy hospital office was a tall woman in all shades of the rainbow. Red shoes. Purple tights. A yellow dress, the colour of Sicilian lemons. A green beanie hat. Her amber jewellery glowed orange, and her eyes were a vivid blue. That array of colour shouldn't have worked, but somehow it did. She leaned towards

Annie, touching her arm; Annie flinched. 'So sorry, I don't mean to jump in front of you. Just need to very, very quickly make an appointment.'

The receptionist was back clacking, this time with a jaunty beat. 'Next week do ya?'

'Thanks, you're a star. Sorry, I've totally queue-jumped!' The rainbow beamed at Annie again. 'Is this lovely lady all sorted, Denise?'

No one had called Annie a lovely lady for a long time. She blinked the tears from her eyes, trying to sound firm. 'Well, no, because apparently it's too hard to just change a patient record. I've been to four different offices now.'

'Oh, Denise can do that for you; she has all the secrets of this hospital at her fabulous fingertips.' The woman mimed typing. There was a large bruise on the back of one hand, partly covered by taped-on cotton wool.

Denise was actually nodding, grudgingly. 'Alright then. Give it here.'

Annie passed the form over. 'Can you send care of me, please? Annie Hebden.' Denise typed, and within ten seconds, the thing Annie had waited for all day was done. 'Um – thanks.'

'You're welcome, madam,' said Denise, and Annie could feel her judgement. She'd been rude. She knew she'd been rude. It was just so frustrating, so difficult.

'Brill. Bye, missus.' The rainbow woman waved at Denise, then grabbed Annie's arm again. 'Listen. I'm sorry you're having a bad day.'

'I – what?'

'You seem like you're having a really bad day.'

Annie was temporarily speechless. 'I'm in the bloody hospital. Do you think anyone here's having a good day?'

The woman looked round at the waiting room behind them – half the people on crutches, some with shaved heads and pale faces, a shrunken woman hunched in a wheelchair in a hospital gown, bored kids upending the contents of their mums' bags while the mums mindlessly stabbed at phones. 'No reason why not.'

Annie stepped back, angry. 'Listen, thank you for your help – though I shouldn't have needed it, this hospital is a disgrace – but you've no idea why I'm in here.'

'True.'

'So, I'm going now.'

'Do you like cake?' the woman asked.

'What? Of course I . . . what?'

'Wait a sec.' She dashed away. Annie looked at Denise, who'd gone back to her blank-eyed keyboard stare.

She counted to ten – annoyed at herself for even doing that – then shook her head and went out down the corridor, with its palette of despair-blue and bile-green. Sounds of wheeling beds, flapping doors, distant crying. An old man lay on a trolley, tiny and grey. Thank God she was finally done. She needed to go home, lose herself in the TV, hide under the duvet . . .

'Wait! Annie Hebden!'

Annie turned. The annoying woman was running down the corridor – well, more sort of shuffling, out of breath. She held a cupcake aloft, iced with wavy chocolate frosting. 'For you,' she panted, thrusting it into Annie's hand. Each of her nails was painted a different colour.

Annie was speechless for the second time in five minutes. 'Why?'

'Because. Cupcakes make everything a little better. Except for type II diabetes, I guess.'

'Uh . . . ' Annie looked at the cake in her hand. Slightly squished. 'Thank you?'

'That's OK.' The woman licked some rogue frosting off her hand. 'Ick, I hope I don't get MRSA. Not that it would make much difference. I'm Polly, by the way. And you're Annie.'

'Er. Yeah.'

'Have a good day, Annie Hebden. Or at least a slightly better one. Remember, if you want the rainbow, you have to put up with the rain.' And she waved, and skipped – was it the first time anyone had ever skipped down the Corridor of Doom? – out of sight.

Annie waited for the bus in the rain, that grey soupy rain that Lewisham seemed to specialise in. She thought what a stupid thing it was that the woman had said. Rain didn't always lead to rainbows. Usually it just led to soaked socks and your hair in rat-tails. But at least she had somewhere to go. A homeless man sat beneath the bus shelter, water dripping off his head and forming a puddle around his dirty trousers. Annie felt wretched for him, but what could she do? She couldn't help him. She couldn't even help herself.

When the bus came it was rammed, and she stood squeezed up between a buggy and a mound of shopping bags, buffeted by every turn. An elderly lady got on, wobbling up the steps with her shopping trolley. As she shuffled down the bus, nobody looked up from their phones to offer her a seat. Annie finally snapped. What was wrong with people? Was there not a shred of decency left in this city?

'For God's sake!' she barked. 'Could someone let this lady sit down, *please*?' A young man with huge headphones slouched out of his seat, embarrassed.

'No need to take the Lord's name in vain,' said the old lady, tutting disapprovingly at Annie as she sat down.

Annie stared at her feet, which had left grimy marks on the wet floor of the bus, until she got to her stop.

How had her life come to this, she wondered? Losing it in public over a change of address? Weeping in front of strangers? Once it would have been her raising her eyebrows as someone else had a meltdown. Offering tissues, and a soothing pat on the arm. She didn't understand what had happened to that person. The one she used to be.

Sometimes it felt to Annie like her life had changed in the blink of an eye.

Eyes shut – she was back in the bedroom of her lovely house on that last sunny morning, and everything was good. She was filled with excitement, and hope, and slightly exhausted joy. *Perfect*.

Eyes open – she was here, trudging back to her horrible flat, catching the bus in the rain, lying awake full of dread and misery.

One blink, perfect. Two blinks, ruined. But no matter how many times she closed her eyes, it never went back to how it used to be.